PASSPORT CONTROL

Gila Green

S & H Publishing, Inc.
Purcellville, Virginia

S & H Publishing, Inc.
P. O. Box 456
Purcellville, VA 20134
www.sandhpublishing.com

Publisher's Note: This is a work of fiction. Names, characters, places, and incidents are a product of the author's imagination. Locales and public names are sometimes used for atmospheric purposes. Any resemblance to actual people, living or dead, or to businesses, companies, events, institutions, or locales is completely coincidental.

Ordering Information:
Quantity discounts are available. For details, contact the "Special Sales Department" at the address above or email sales@sandhpublishing.com.

Passport Control/Gila Green
ISBN 978-1-63320-054-8 Print Edition

ISBN 978-1-63320-060-9 Ebook Edition

And the few dust swirls rising above

all the shot bits of relatives

lost in the falling of the dice.

Excerpt from "Jerusalem" by Atar Hadari

Chapter One

Ottawa, Canada, March 1992

BY THE TIME I STAND, gasping, out of breath at the central university bus stop, it's too late. As the packed bus tears off campus, I'm heaving in the exhaust left behind. My heart pounds from running so hard with my heavy backpack, and I can feel the sweat trickling down the back of my neck and pooling in my armpits.

I'd allowed myself to be distracted by a novel in the library. Albert Camus's *L'Étranger* caught my eye, and I lingered over it too long. That was a whole hour of studying flushed down the tubes, time I need if I want to ace the semester and keep my grants.

Forty-five minutes later I sprint up the steps, past the first-floor garage, to the apartment I share with my father.

"Miriam. You're late."

"I missed the bus, Abba."

My father grunts and motions for me to sit with a tilt of his head. He remains standing, his arms at his sides and I sense trouble. I knew it the minute I heard the television switch off as I ran in the door. The last time my father switched off the television, my adolescent world ended. That was five years ago, the

1

day my mother was killed in a car crash. The TV's been on ever since.

My father clears his throat and I stifle my impatience, fussing with the laces of my Skechers. He has no concept of how much schoolwork I have waiting for me to plow through in my bulging backpack and how desperately I need to dive into it.

"I've taken care of you the best I can since your mother died."

I sit straighter, as though a heel is in the small of my back and a fire begins to heat in the pit of my stomach. My father never speaks about my mother. And he's full of it. He hasn't changed one bit since my mother died. He was hands-off then, and he's hands-off now.

"Still, kids can't run your life."

Run his life?

"That's what Jacquie says, that I let you run my life. She says you're grown up now, that we deserve something, too."

My father's facial expression remains stony. The fire in my stomach turns up a degree.

"I want to get to the point. We had a big discussion last night and we think it's better if she moves in," he says. "We'll save money on that lousy apartment of hers. Her landlord is a cheat anyway. Aren't they all in Ottawa? At least we own this place."

"There's not enough room here for me and your girlfriend," I answer. "It won't work. It's nice of you to try to save her money."

2

I smile at my father again, more of a grin and abandon the couch, my mind already turning to my homework. There is no need to panic. It's just Jacquie's financial problems he's worried about. How romantic. Well, maybe she'll start winning at bingo on her breaks instead of looking to my father to bail her out.

"Miri, you're not listening. You said it straight. It's too small for the three of us. You're hardly home anyway."

I freeze with my eyes on my backpack. Slowly, I turn and look at my father. I really see him. He doesn't avert his eyes. He never has.

"You're asking me to leave?" I can hardly get the words out.

"You're a big girl, Miri. It's strange with you and Jackie around. When I was your age," his voice trails off, as it always does when the past seeps into his present.

3

Chapter Two

I LIE AWAKE ALL NIGHT, but my epiphany only comes toward morning. I peer out through the blinds in my bedroom onto an Ottawa spring day, the light blue sky dabbed with white clouds thin enough for the sun to shine through and it comes to me. I'll show my father transfer; he can forget it if he thinks I'd apply to some university in Toronto or Vancouver, or any other Canadian city.

As a student with a local address I'll never receive dormitory priority if I stay in Ottawa, and the cost of an off-campus apartment is out of the question.

I'll call the one place he doesn't want me to call and write a letter to the one person he doesn't want me to contact. If my own father's throwing me out of his house, I'll make it so painful that he'll regret it and I'll prove to myself that I lost one parent and don't need the other.

I wait for my father to leave the house for his regular early morning jog before I slip out of my bedroom, shower, brush my teeth, and make myself a cup of instant coffee.

In the old days he'd have been back in thirty minutes. That was pre-Jacquie. Now he meets her for breakfast at the local McDonald's every morning. Not that my father would do more than drink a black coffee in a fast food restaurant. Still, I have to work quickly.

It is easy enough to get the address from my father's worn address book in the top drawer of the kitchen. Not really a book of any kind, but decades old lists of numbers and names he adds to every once in a while, in his square slant in English alongside his beautiful Hebrew script.

As he grows older, he tapes the ones he considers important on the tiles around the phone that's hung on the kitchen wall, so the tiles around the telephone resemble a bulletin board. I'll write a letter to my father's estranged brother Moshe Damari in Israel and ask him if I can come for a visit.

My hands shake as I open my uncle's response when it finally comes, after weeks of opening the mailbox, almost without breathing. I know I'm not brave enough to fly across the world entirely alone on the other side. I am used to aloneness, but in a language I understand.

My uncle Moshe has scrawled his phone number at the top of a lined, white sheet of paper. He's invited me to his kibbutz in Israel for any weekend I am free. That's it. Two lines. But the semester doesn't start until October. Could I trust this note not to expire before then?

When I turn the paper over I notice another few lines scrawled on the back, an afterthought quickly added on before the envelope and stamp.

P.S. I live only an hour's bus ride from the Haifa University dormitories.

After my father sat down in his favorite oversized chair, he asked me for a grilled cheese sandwich. It was too hot to cook but I agreed. I brought him a cool glass of water and the sandwich he'd requested. Then I show my father his brother's response. His mouth tightened into a thin line. He hasn't said a word to me about moving out since that first conversation as the light dimmed on an otherwise perfect spring afternoon.

This case-closed attitude is typical of my father. He declares or states something, anything really, and expects me to comply. I always have. I must be taking care of his new demands because he never asks twice. I'm sure that was the end of this thread in his thoughts.

Jacquie must have explained to him over one of those black McDonald's coffees or in the short drive home from the bingo hall that students normally transfer in September for the beginning of a new semester, and they'd have to wait out the summer before they could have the place to themselves.

I'd stopped communicating with him, unless it was absolutely necessary, and then I spoke in short sentences loaded with resentment, but he either didn't notice my verbal bullets or pretended not to.

"Israel. I thought you didn't like Israel. Not high class like Canada."

"How would I know if I liked it or not?"

"Are you talking back to your father?" I lower my eyes and count to ten under my breath. "Besides, you'll never have the money, Miri. How are you going to study there? The government's giving you money to study here. Not there. You're not throwing your three years of study away. Nice dream."

He rises out of his chair, his now empty plate in one hand, the half-filled glass balanced on top, and leaves me alone in the living room. I have a few months to earn enough money for the flight, rent, and food, and I still have time to work. It's no dream, but I'm not letting my father in on that. I've already received a full scholarship to study at Haifa University in Israel's north. Whether he wants to believe it or not, I've opened a door for myself.

I fly out of Ottawa at 5 p.m. Today. I'll catch a connecting plane in Toronto at 7 p.m., and then it's a direct twelve-hour flight to Tel Aviv.

I stand, bent over in the hallway labeling my two suitcases. I'm wearing jeans folded at the bottoms and a white T-shirt with a tight black leather jacket for the flight. My boyfriend calls it my Winona Ryder look. It's warm weather for the jacket, but I prefer it to an undersized, scratchy airline blanket.

My bedroom already looks ditched. It smells of the Lysol I use to clean the garbage bin, dispersing any trace of my own perfumes and body lotions.

It has been a spare room only for a quarter of an hour, but with the floral cotton sheets my mother preferred now crammed into the laundry hamper, it's official. I imagine within a day or two my mattress will be covered with satin, silver or night-blue sheets, similar to those Jacquie had put on my father's bed. The thought makes me never want to give that woman a chance.

For once my father's girlfriend isn't here for lunch and I wonder if it's deliberate, but I don't dare ask. I don't know what answer I want to hear.

Noon is prime television time for my father. All of his favorite shows are on. He's addicted to talk shows, people displaying their problems like hawkers at a market. *Maury* must be coming on any minute or *Jenny Jones*. If he is really lucky there'll be something super sticky on *Jerry Springer,* the ultimate tabloid talk show.

There's no need for him to miss out to say goodbye to me. Still, he jumps up, tearing his eyes from the screen whenever I enter the kitchen to search for a granola bar, fill my water bottle for my handbag, or dig for a pen in a drawer. *Maury* blares in the background.

"Israel is hot, Miri. Desert. There's no air over there like Ottawa or Toronto."

"Mmmhmm."

Does he think he'll deter me at the last minute because of the weather? I have the upper hand now that my suitcases, which I'd taken time to polish to perfection, gleam by the front door. I don't know why he doesn't want me to go to Israel, but I am determined to find out. I'll seek out this long-lost brother of his, maybe he'll be relieved to talk.

Of course, I'm unsure about these private calculations. Moshe's letter had been as close-mouthed as my father's might have been, and it's not as though I'd heard from him in almost two decades, not even when I lost my mother. I don't recall a card or a phone call, but who knows if there wasn't a letter of condolence stuffed away somewhere in a space I'd never seen. My father's the type who thinks he has the right to filter out things.

I glance at him and he's looking all stoic and it bothers me that my heart reaches out to him a little. I roll my shoulders back; I won't retreat.

In the few minutes before my ride to the airport, my father reluctantly slips a piece of torn notebook paper in my hand with his brother's phone number scrawled in blue ink and watches me with unmoving eyes as I cram it into the outside pocket of my carry-on.

"In case you lose your copy."

There is a honk outside.

"Your taxi," my father says. He's switched to Hebrew, and I am suddenly aware that he will no longer have anyone to share his native tongue with in his home. There's nothing remotely Jewish about Jacquie.

He picks up my heavy suitcase without even an extra intake of breath and heads outside, face stonily forward. He doesn't stop until the suitcase is in the trunk and he's exchanged a few words with his friend, the driver.

9

"My friend will give you a good discount. I've fixed this taxi for him in a jam more than once. No point in me wasting the gas," he says, circling around to the passenger side. He opens the back door for me, but I don't move.

"No point, no." I whisper, and I don't know if he hears me or not.

"Where's that dummy boyfriend? Not here to say goodbye even?"

"No."

"*Goyishe kop.* He's lucky you ever looked at him." My father attended an Ashkenazi school growing up in Jerusalem and still uses many Yiddish phrases. "Don't worry about yourself in Israel. You have the Israeli army to protect you."

Would I need an army?

"Thanks."

This is the point when I want to rewind my steps back to the safety and control of matching the blue inky polish to the leather of the suitcases or press fast forward to the even temperature of an airplane.

In a moment, my father will recognize that his only daughter is leaving him, and he'll react in that slice of time as a father.

A breath ago my heart was dancing in half jumps celebrating my departure, my triumph really, but now I can't handle the intensity. I'd earned the money, made all of the arrangements, but goodbye was part of the package and the unknown was waiting for me on the other side. I brace myself for a hug I can't avoid.

"Take care about yourself." He puts one bare arm on my shoulder and kisses the top of my head. The movement is swift, and it's over before I have time to react. "You look like your mother when I met her. God should watch over you, Miri."

My mouth has glued shut. I feel angry, sad, afraid, and excited at the same time. It takes another honk from the taxi to get me moving again, and I fall into the back seat.

I swallow my immediate thought: If my father was tired of watching over me, why would God be any different?

Still, I enjoyed that moment of affection from my father as much as I was filled with anger toward him. It is just like him to do this to me at the last minute, overwhelm me by saying something I longed to hear, a gift I both wanted to keep and spit back in his black eyes, his perfect teeth, and dark, smooth skin.

Although I am taxiing alone, I crowd into the corner next to the window, as though my rage and resentment toward my father is so large and so heavy there isn't enough space for me as well.

In spite of myself, before I know it, I'm in the back seat waving frantically to someone who has long gone inside and closed the door behind him.

At the airport, I wait patiently in the El Al line for passport control after I've gone through the airline's security check.

"Where is your Israeli passport?" the tall, slender woman behind the counter asks. She should be a model, not an airline employee. I have to inch my neck upward to look at her.

"I don't have one."

"Why not?" I peer at her name tag: Galit.

"Why would I have one? I was born here in Ottawa. I've never even been to Israel."

"You have an Israeli last name. Is your father Israeli?"

"Yes."

"Your father is Israeli, you are Israeli; you should carry the passport."

"Have they stopped letting Canadians in?" I smile, but my stomach churns. I've never flown alone overseas before.

"That is not the point. You will be fine with the Canadian passport getting in, but Miss Gil, I hope you don't have any problems getting out. I see you have an open ticket, so you have time to sort through things. Your luggage is processed. Have a nice flight."

Problems getting out? That seems far-fetched. I want to ask her to explain, but already the couple behind me had eased me out of the way, and a stern looking security guard was motioning for me to make space for them.

I busy myself with my carry-on, fussing with my items so that anything I think I'll really use on the flight is perched on the top, minimizing the need to dig to the bottom of my bag. At home all of my clothes hang in my closet on identical black plastic hangers, and they all face the same way.

Home. I don't have a home anymore. I blink hard and force myself to concentrate on whether I'll need hand moisturizer, toothpaste, gloss, or a novel to flip through and in what order. I don't know what's waiting for me, but I plan to be prepared. I can't screw up because in my heart I know this ticket might be one-way.

Chapter Three

Haifa, Israel, October 1992

WHEN I ARRIVE at my Haifa University dormitory apartment, I see a student who looks about twenty-five eating a diced tomato, cucumber, and onion salad on a plate. She scoops the salad into her pita, which immediately reminds me of my father. I don't know what else she's eating. Maybe hummus, maybe that thin white cheese spread my father's always running out of.

Behind her is a large window that looks all the way down to Haifa Bay, and her chair is so centered at the table, she appears framed by the view.

She has long, not quite black hair that reaches her waist; brown eyes; pale, pock-marked skin, and is plain looking. She's wearing a long-sleeved eggplant-colored tunic.

She smiles at me, and I smile back and close the door behind me, lugging my suitcase with one hand and my carry-on with the other. She says hello, barely pausing between bites. I recognize the sour aroma of goat cheese and zaatar from my own kitchen at home, but I try not to stare at her plate. Anything besides coffee and plain toast in the morning sinks my stomach into my legs.

"I'm Farzeen," she says.

"Miriam."

"Where are you from?" she asks.

14

"Canada."

"That's good news. I knew it would be a good day. A Canadian. Now someone who sees clearly will be living here from the outside world."

I wonder what that means. Someone who hasn't done the army? Who hasn't been trained like Ben Gurion Airport security to raise her internal antennas at the sound of an Arabic accent like hers?

"I've never actually met a Canadian before," she continues. "Have you ever met a Palestinian?"

"My father has many Arab friends. Egyptian, Lebanese."

"Really?"

"He spoke Arabic growing up in Jerusalem."

Farzeen moves her salad around her plate, drops her fork, and brings her long fingers together.

"But you don't speak Arabic?"

"No. In Canada we learn French and Hebrew at school."

"French? Of course," she says. "Would you like to eat with me? Please, you just got off the plane. Sit."

Salad at dawn. Exactly like my father's intolerable idea of breakfast. I'll never get it down, but I don't want to seem unfriendly.

She points to the chair across from her, and I sit. I leave my case and carry-on by the door.

"I ate on the plane, but I'd love a drink."

For the first time her smile reaches her eyes. "Please, juice." She points to a full glass of orange juice on the table, and I take a small sip.

15

Farzeen excuses herself for a moment, and I become absorbed by the view of the expanse of the city leading down to Haifa Bay out the window, grateful for a distraction from my growing anxiety.

I was so preoccupied with leaving Canada, getting out once my father had made it clear that there was no space for me and his new girlfriend in his life. Only an hour ago, I was whizzing north in a packed mini-bus without even a thought as to who would be waiting for me once I arrived. Now the idea that I hadn't considered my roommates, the women I'd be sharing an apartment with for nine months splashes over me like ice cold water.

After all of the sacrifices I'd made to come here — dumping my boyfriend, allowing Jacquie to slowly take over my home with her stacks of primary-colored eye shadow, her fake tan cream, and free sample anti-wrinkle tubes cluttering up the sink; and adding up my pennies nightly with an eye on the finish line as I worked two jobs to pay for the expenses of a year abroad, I hadn't considered the day-to-day, as in who am I traveling across the world to live with.

So what if she's Palestinian? I can't believe I'm even thinking about this.

"Sorry to have left you," she says. She eats the rest of her salad. "I have an exam already, and I keep running to my room to review my notes. I always learn in three phases, a memory trick I used in my first degree. Now I've done phase two. It works better at night, but I've run out of time."

"Exams in the first two weeks?" I ask stupidly. For locals the semester began two weeks ago. As a foreign student, I only start tomorrow. I twist my only bracelet around my wrist and keep my eyes on the table.

She picks up her pita and takes a small bite from the corner. Because she was eating, I never extended my hand and I'm convinced she's offended. Do they even shake hands here? At my home university women made a point of shaking hands.

I've only ever seen Israelis hug and kiss, but that was just in airports. I'd watched them as though observing wild animals in the wait-to-board area in Toronto and again at Ben Gurion in Tel Aviv. All of their gestures seemed to me louder, wider, inhabiting more space than was reasonable to expect.

Farzeen nods, dabs her mouth with a hand towel that looks more like a rag, jumps up to flick the switch on the kettle, and sits back down. The rectangular-shaped kitchen is two steps away, standing room only, white cupboards top and bottom, black countertops with a smell of bleach that reaches me at the table.

I notice a lone plate in the white dish rack, a few coffee mugs, and scattered cutlery. Everything is white.

I place my small suitcase at the side of the table that seats four and leads off the kitchen. Now it's wedged in the small space between the table and the door as if I don't want anyone else to be able to get in.

Of course, it's just the opposite. I'd never admit it, but sitting alone with a Palestinian is making me nervous. I long for someone to enter and save me, link

Jewish arms with me and tell me we're off to unpack in our new bedroom.

"What did you come to study? Would you like tea?" Farzeen asks.

"Middle Eastern studies. Tea would be nice."

She takes the two steps into the kitchen in one long stride and pulls two mugs off the rack, drops in two tea bags she picks out of a large rectangular blue box. For the first time I notice sugar is already on the table.

"Why would you want to study that?" She shoots me a look I don't understand.

Is she genuinely puzzled or is it just hard for me to catch the tone in her voice with the kettle rumbling more like a lawn mower, showing its age?

"It's the only option on the overseas program," I answer.

"To come from Canada for that." She sets our tea in front of us. It's loose-leaf. There are green leaves in her hot brown water. Mint? Chamomile? I wrap my fingers around the warm mug, but I really don't crave tea, no point wasting the sugar.

"I'll tell you something about the place." She leans forward and I can smell Turkish coffee and peach-scented shampoo. "I was born in Nazareth."

"Isn't that a Christian town?"

"There are plenty of us Muslims," she says. "I'm studying for an MA in international affairs. I'm a citizen, but they'll never let me work at an Israeli embassy. You would get hired before me."

Farzeen throws me off balance. I have no idea if what she's saying is true. Emboldened by my silence or perhaps she doesn't notice, Farzeen continues. "I can tell you because you are not from here. The others, those two who live there," she points with her chin toward the closest room and then her own. "They'd never listen. Where you're from, they will."

I stare at her dumbly, while she places the tea on the table.

She eyes me. Waiting.

"Well, you cannot be the only Palestinian studying international affairs or political science and at an MA level. Are you telling me they are all meant to be secretaries?"

"Clerks, or low level administrators, maybe the ones who fill out passport forms. There are always the Arab municipalities where we could work, but a diplomat who lives abroad? An Arab-Israeli ambassador from here? Have you heard of such a thing? Might as well ask a pig to sing."

My back straightens at the word pig. I am used to French Canadians complaining against discrimination in the workplace, in the government, in the media, but somehow Farzeen disarms me with her accusations against a state I'd lived in only for two hours in a taxi, except, of course, I have that vein that connects me with my Jerusalem-born, Arabic-speaking father, but I'm cutting him out of my life. Still, as jet lagged and disoriented as I am, that vein begins to pulse.

"I really don't know much about it. I mean, that's why I came here to study it, isn't it? But there are Arab parties in the Israeli government. International affairs and politics mix. And you're still a student. Maybe you'll be the first!" I add, clutching at anything that might help me rise to the occasion, defend the people who had offered me a full scholarship to study here, a door out of a life I couldn't breathe in any longer.

"There might be peace by the time you graduate. Who knows what you could do in the future with the education you're getting now." I try but fail to smile, and I'm already regretting this quick turn in our conversation. I'm in it now. "Besides, I think the first Israeli-Arab consul general was appointed in 1987. To Atlanta, I think."

I don't have a clue if any additional Arab-Israeli diplomats have been appointed since then or are up and coming. I just have a good memory for anything I read. Really, I don't travel in Jewish circles, and as far as I'm concerned, politicians are opportunists, populists whose pockets are never deep enough. I take a breath, and the air feels thick.

"Hah! One token, so what? What you are really saying is that I should give up my nationalism?" Farzeen rises in her chair. "Why don't Jews give up theirs? Why not a state for anyone, everyone born here? That's a state I could represent."

"Do Arabs need another state? It doesn't seem so unreasonable that Jews want one." I force myself to look directly at her now. She's seething.

"Except it's not theirs. They are not from here. We are. They are Europeans."

Europeans? I thought of my grandmother, born in Jaffa-Tel Aviv when it was nothing more than an anthill, my great-grandfather forced into the Ottoman army. I want to spit all of this at Farzeen, but something holds me back. This is too much. Farzeen is fed, well read, and well rested. I am not on equal footing. Maybe I had two or three hours of sleep on the plane. I relax my shoulder muscles. I have to live with this woman. Impossible.

I remember a line of advice a friend who had done the Tel Aviv overseas program told me before I left: "Make sure you hang out with Americans if you want to have fun; all Israelis only talk politics."

It is impossible for me to avoid politics if my only option on my program is Middle Eastern studies.

My eyes drift to the bedroom doors. Farzeen had already indicated that two other women occupy the first room or did she mean one in each room? Either way, I can't ask her if she's my roommate. Surely the administration wouldn't have gone that far. I could pinch myself now thinking back on my politely written request, the one I'd typed after-hours on a borrowed university computer, and then printed alone at school in the small hours of the night, feeling as though I'd thought of everything.

Dear Admissions,

I understand you group the foreign students program participants together in shared dormitory apartments, but I'm looking for an authentic Israeli experience. I kindly request to live with the students in the regular Israeli program.

Had I no sense of nuance? Did I think Israelis were homogenous like the jocks and the preppies in the university dormitories back home? But I always had to go one step beyond everyone else so that I could pat

21

myself on the back later, at how forward thinking I am, how detail-oriented I am, how stupid am I?

I want to repeat that my father is Israeli, but I bite my tongue. I don't want to speak about him.

To give me something to do, I take my cold teacup to the sink and turn it over, watch the cold liquid swirl down the drain. I should care if she finds this insulting, but I don't. For all I know her family is filthy rich and thriving in Israel. On the other hand, they may be poor enough that she's here studying on a full scholarship, too, perhaps, as a graduate student, her second degree.

"Well, have you nothing to say?" Her brown eyes dance now.

"There are many Jewish Israelis who have been here for generations."

"Hah! Let's get to the bottom line already: Do Israelis look anything like Middle Eastern people? Tel Aviv is filled with blue-eyed blondes. Like I said: Europeans."

My own hair is as black as Farzeen's and my skin at least two shades darker than hers, which is merely sallow; mine is somewhere between toffee in the winter and bronze in the summer.

"All those Jewish blondes? The Germans said how *not* Aryan they look, how foreign, and by that they meant dark, didn't they?"

Farzeen snorts and kicks the leg of the chair. Or does she just slip? Lose some of her balance with rage? There's no doubt her eyes are angry, and her lips have disappeared into one line.

The kettle clicks off and I'm grateful for a diversion. I fish around for the packet of coffee I'd slipped into my pocket on the plane. In my carry-on I still had the roll and pocket-sized butter and strawberry jam condiments. In a minute, my coffee is ready. I need it. The one I had on the plane in that half-sized mug has worn off.

I put one hand to my forehead. She knows how to push my buttons, and I let her. My Canadianness has surely fallen tens of stories down her mental well of disappointment, gurgled into disgust.

I use the teacup as a focal point to collect myself while the steam evaporates until there is none left. Fatigue washes over. I no longer know what to do with myself. Sit down and face Farzeen or put out my hand in a truce? Not for the first time, I'm unprepared.

"I thought Canadians stood in solidarity with the Palestinians." Farzeen clicks her tongue. "That you accept refugees in your country."

"I don't know what you mean. Canada has usually sided against Israel, but the government's not the people."

"You don't know what I mean? We suffer here and we're going to fight back, that's what I mean. You know why I'm studying so hard? To fight the occupation better. I'm going to change things for my people."

"And who's paying for it?" I don't recognize my own voice. It sounds borrowed.

"I deserve this university grant. I was born here." Farzeen stamps her foot. "Besides, it's all paid for with blood money, isn't it? All those dead Jews turned to ashes. My grant is the reward for so much world sympathy." She seems breathless now.

No one has ever spoken to me like this before. An acid forms in my stomach. "Israel's making money off its own dead? Is that what you said?"

She lowers her chin closer to her chest, but is otherwise still.

I pick up the mug of coffee and lunge forward in one movement. My elbow juts out and straightens with full force. The coffee splashes onto Farzeen's chest and shoulders, spilling onto the chair and floor. She gasps. I stand frozen, the empty mug dangling between my thumb and forefinger. I've never thrown a drink at anyone.

Back at the sink, I pour myself a glass of water from the tap and drink noisily, slamming the glass onto the counter.

"Don't you ever say that to me again," I say slowly. There must be bravado in the air here. That's how Israelis live through the wars and bomb scares.

Farzeen centers herself in her chair, her tunic a deep purple, almost black, where it's wet, and resumes the pose she had when I first entered.

I look down and see the mug on the floor where it slipped out of my hand, miraculously undamaged. I need to pick it up, but I can't place it on the table between us like a smoking gun.

I pray for her to leave. I want to clean up the mess on the floor when she's gone.

With steady, deliberate bites she finishes the last of her pita. Once the last bite disappears from her plate she takes a couple of deep breaths, her eyes on her hands.

She has to study I remind myself. She isn't here to waste time.

Farzeen rises, rinses her cup, plate, fork, knife, and spoon with water and a drop of the green dish soap on the edge of the sink.

After placing them in the rack to dry, she wipes her wet hands on a stained kitchen towel, nods toward me with that same expression on her face, the one she had on when I entered that I thought was a smile but now recognize as a grimace, and walks past me, her leg just brushing mine, before entering the second bedroom door on the right.

The door closes, I hear the click of the lock, and she is gone.

Chapter Four

A KNOCK AT THE DOOR wakes me.

"Come in." I glance at my travel clock. I'd slept away the whole afternoon.

The door opens and a woman enters. She looks older than me, maybe twenty-three or twenty-four.

"I'm Dalit."

She holds out her hand and I shake it. My body is warm from my nap. Dalit smiles like someone who is used to making good impressions or at least strong ones. Her earrings jangle while she examines the room. I notice her red lipstick matches her nail polish.

"I live in the first room. I study social work."

Dalit gives over this information almost as though I'd expected an official report and, before I can respond, she is busy opening and closing all of the toiletry items I'd recently lined up on the one shelf over the desk on my side of the room. She makes small and varied exclamations as she turns caps, twists, and sniffs.

"You don't mind, Miri?" Dalit says, using the name only my father uses for me. I bristle. "I like things from America."

"Canada."

"Canada. America. What is the difference? America with a lot of snow, no?"

I smile. Sure. In less than a day, I have regressed to a fifteen-year-old girl lamenting that someone has first insulted me and then touched my things. I am certain she could smell this on me through my almost Calvin Klein perfumes and no-name ocean body spray.

"I heard you arrived. I have connections in the administration."

Dalit talks through her smile. Perhaps they share the same makeup, Dalit and her administration connections. I nod, feeling the fatigue of the flight at the back of my neck pitter-pattering lower, into my spine.

"What are you studying?"

"Middle Eastern studies."

"Yech. So boring. Who cares? The Palestinians and the Palestinians. I just finished two years giving up my life in the army, and I don't want to hear about it anymore. I'm so sick of it. I would be happy to never think about it for my whole life."

"Mmm."

"You want to eat with me? I just came from the *makolet*."

"No. Thank you. I had tea with Farzeen before my nap." Another lie, but she'd woken me up, and now I needed some time to myself.

"Farzeen? You should have waited for me. I am kosher, I bring my own plates. They are in my room. Leave those dishes for the Arabs."

"Kosher?"

It did not occur to me that anyone who kept kosher would live in the dormitory. I remember reading that the university does not provide kosher facilities. Besides, my previous images of Jews who kept kosher were not ex-soldiers with ruby lips and blue eyelashes, but girls whose connection to an army didn't extend beyond a movie screen and who sported long skirts, minimal natural shade makeup and long-sleeved blouses.

So far none of my reference points work in Israel. The ones my father had drilled into my head for so long must belong to a time that no longer exists.

"I can see you are still tired. I will eat and study and see you later. By the way, your roommate is coming back only tomorrow. She sleeps here two nights a week. You have a room practically to yourself. Lucky."

Crash! My perfume bottle, just purchased at the duty free, hits the floor.

"Oh. I am sorry. Look, not broken. Smells so good. Sorry, sorry. You have so many good things in America."

Dalit doesn't blush, but puts the bottle back where she found it. It's fine. Believe me I don't own anything worth any money. Even the money I do have seems less valuable than other people's.

"It's okay."

"I'd better go before I really break something," she says. "You sleep."

The door closes behind Dalit, and I search for my clothes. There is another knock at the door, and Dalit sticks her head in. The ends of her henna-rinsed hair catch on her thick lipstick.

"By the way, I need you to agree to complain about Farzeen. I'm working on a letter for everyone to sign — including you."

"Farzeen?"

"Jews are supposed to live with Jews and the Arab with the Arab, but the numbers were not even this year, so they gave us two Arabs. This is what my connection explained to me. I only want to live with other Jews—except the Druze girl, she is the best—but the whole apartment needs to put in a request, otherwise she stays."

"I don't know."

"What do you mean you don't know?"

Her neck seems unnaturally long now, her head is so far into my room or I'm just so jet-lagged.

"I can't complain about someone who hasn't done anything to me, who I don't even know."

"Ah hah. I see. You just got here, but you will see. We give up two years of our lives defending the country, so in case something happens to you overseas, you have a safe place to go, but you know better?"

I can feel the color rising in my face. I lick my lips. "I didn't say that," I answer.

"It's obvious she doesn't like us. She should live with other Arab girls like her. Everyone will be happier."

I am too exhausted to argue. It would be like arguing with someone about the existence of God or karma or the soul. Either you believed or you didn't, and I didn't believe in this automatic hatred of Farzeen. Besides, my mind was breaking down her words: She gave up two years of her life to ensure a refuge for me?

Dalit is staring at me now, but I don't meet her eyes. Her lines have cast me under a pile of mismatched socks. I smell the Comet cleanser from the bathroom where my father cleans on Sunday mornings while I sort the laundry, including matching our socks. His broad hairy back spans the tub while he reaches the hard-to-get places. *Who do you think I fought for? Drove that tank hot as hell.* Dalit's eyes scan mine.

"Fine. I will leave you now, but you will see."
Dalit lets herself out for the second time, but softly, the way someone closes a door for a baby to nap.

Chapter Five

THE NEXT MORNING IS MONDAY, the second day of the work week in Israel. The flood of demands for the shower I'd anticipated among a group of women sharing one bathroom isn't even a trickle. I am the only one wrapped in a towel while I brush my teeth. I can hear the scrape of three simultaneous vegetable peelers, the chopping and cutting as I step out of the shower, still anticipating a bang on the door that didn't come.

When I finally emerge, dressed in jeans and a T-shirt, there are three women at the breakfast table eating three salads, squeezing three lemons, sharing one saltshaker and two bottles of olive oil. My roommate had yet to arrive, but Farzeen's roommate is there.

"*Boker tov*, Miri. Good morning. This is Arslan," Dalit says, her voice sounding like a broken doorbell to my ears at 7 a.m. I smile at my new roommate, who beams back at me.

"Good morning," Arslan says.

I understand from her Arabic-accented Hebrew that this must be the Druze student Dalit mentioned yesterday. With her long, loose black hair and her equally long, flowing flowered dress, Arslan is the modern image of a Biblical shepherdess, but with plenty of red lipstick and even more dark kohl around her eyes.

I return Arslan's wide smile.

31

"How old are you?" she asks me in Hebrew.

"I'll be twenty-one in December."

"I'm eighteen. This is my first time out of my village," she says. "I am from Karmiel, in the north."

"I'd love to see it sometime," I answer.

"Good idea," Arslan says.

"If you would shower the night before, you'd have time for a real breakfast, not just junk," Dalit says.

I couldn't argue with that. Unaccustomed to early morning conversation, I shrug my shoulders. Besides, Dalit's confidence nails mine to the wall. I wonder how they'll feel if I light a cigarette, but I don't want to make another bad first impression. I open my mouth to say good morning to Farzeen, offer a smile, but one look at Dalit's hard eyes and I clam up.

I leave the three of them at the table and head to the kitchen to retrieve my cornflakes. I eat them dry in a bowl. There's no toaster in the kitchen, so cereal it is. Morning is not my favorite time of day, but classes are at eight. I suppose the administration feels they've given the foreign students enough of a break, allowing us one Sunday off, something unheard of in Israel.

Farzeen is already finished with her breakfast, nodding in my direction and making a place for me, which I see as another slight to my low character. I threw coffee at her and here she's made a place for me to eat at the table, a kind gesture, and I hadn't even said good morning and still I sit silently under the weight of Dalit's frosty gaze.

Maybe this cold shoulder is the beginning of the price I will pay for not signing their complaint letter. If I say something nice to Farzeen, it will be a reinforcement of last night's rejection of Dalit. I'm not complaining about a thing.

My two fumbling encounters have trapped me and I squirm. This is not at all what I was looking for when I chose to spend a year in Israel. I glance at Arslan for help, but if she can fill in the blanks and lighten up the atmosphere, she chooses not to.

No one speaks as Farzeen rinses her dishes, grabs her black briefcase, that makes her look more like a lawyer going off to work than a student, and leaves. We hear the clacking of her high heels echoing down the corridor. We are on the first floor, so it is only a short flight of stairs to the exit. I thought that would make our apartment noisy, but so far, it's quiet.

When the door closes after Farzeen and her footsteps fade, Arslan bursts out laughing.

"I'm so happy she is gone. She's been torturing me all night."

Dalit does not slow down or stop at this announcement. She continues spicing her salad to the last bite, chewing, adding more salt and pepper, a drop more of lemon on the smallest square of cucumber, as though Arslan has merely hummed about the yellowness of the sun shining on our breakfast table.

"My father is a career officer in the Israeli army and Farzeen says he is a traitor, fighting for the Zionists. She says, more like spits."

Dalit clicks her tongue sympathetically and wags her head. As Arslan speaks, they share one teaspoon between two coffees, but Arslan doesn't miss a beat.

"She kept repeating *traitor*, and she knows you cannot understand her Arabic. She knows even if someone hears, even if I open the doors and windows you won't understand."

My heart sinks as Arslan narrates what must have happened last night on the other side of my bedroom wall as I slept. My second-chance theory crumbles like badly baked bread.

"If you live in this country, you should be willing to defend it," Arslan bangs her fist on the table. I admire her apple red nail polish, her velvety scent, which makes me think of cashmere.

"Does she think Saddam Hussein could control his missiles from the sky to avoid killing us Arabs? That Israel doesn't need an army?"

"Don't worry. I'll watch over you, Arslan," Dalit says. She shoots me a loaded look. "I worked with Arslan's father in the army and when I finish my degree I will work with him again in a bigger position." Dalit directs this last line to me. There's no other possibility because she says it in English.

Arslan, her mug tipped to her mouth, nods, and some of her coffee spills over the sides.

"Oh, look what I've done." She wipes at the sides of her mug with a kitchen towel. It is obvious Farzeen has rattled her.

Dalit puts a hand on Arslan's shoulder. "It will be *beseder*, okay? No one gives me problems. I'm like a tank. Vroom."

I force myself not to react. Still, a pang of envy sits in my throat. Just once I'd like to have the confidence to imagine myself as a vehicle with natural armor. Instead, I am hardly convinced my skin covers my nerve endings.

"My *protectzia* in administration will help. She got me my own room, didn't she?" Dalit glances sharply at me, and I shrink and look away.

When Dalit catches my eye again, she takes a different tack, pointing at a soft yogurty cheese on the table I'd picked up and sniffed to see if it smells the same as the one my father buys at home. My stomach lurches. It does.

"That's *labane*. You want?"

I shake my head and force a smile. She shrugs only one shoulder and resumes chewing.

I want to think about what it might be like to be Farzeen. But it is too early in the morning and I am feeling conspicuous enough chewing on dry flakes of corn and sugar and who knows what chemicals and preservatives, while the others eat fresh vegetables, including raw onion; olives from jars; and fresh soft cheese.

I have to remind myself that I haven't been in Israel for twenty-four hours. Who cares about my opinions on their lives? It is apparent I'm in way over my head, and this is only my first morning.

There is a lull in the conversation while my two roommates watch me in a single gaze. I don't know if this is some kind of test. I suspect they're watching me to see if I'll stick up for Farzeen or declare my intention to sign their complaint letter.

I pour milk into my coffee, the cheapest local brand, and grimace at the lumps of coffee grinds that float to the top. I couldn't afford the imported brand. In another minute, Dalit resumes her nonstop chatter in too-fast Hebrew with Arslan. They gather their dishes, wash them, snatch their backpacks and leave. I can't help but wonder if they'd purposely hesitated over their meal, so they wouldn't have to leave together with Farzeen.

I am left to finish the yellow crumbs in my bowl and finally I can smoke, but I don't want to be late. Israeli class schedules are heavier than the foreign students program, but I want to make the right move this time, on my first full day. Any right move would be welcome about now.

Foreign students have a week to try out classes and make their final decisions about registration. Curiosity about the other participants in the program is a tingle on the tip of my tongue I hold back.

The view of Haifa Bay on my way to the administration building distracts me, and I perch on a bench to admire it. It's so blue it looks dyed. I have a few minutes before the first class. My mouth gapes open like any tourist, the culture shock all but labeled on my forehead.

On the sunny campus I hear Arabic, Russian, and Hebrew. Everyone is talking at once and there is a flurry of movement under the swell of blue sky.

Gazing at the male students makes me think of Neil, and my shoulders sink. The responsibility of the relationship rests with me. I left him. He wasn't at all gracious about it, but I like having a boyfriend; especially now so cut off from my father, a warm letter with a Canadian stamp would have been a comfort. He'll forgive me once he's had enough time to miss me. He's crazy about me. He thinks I'm special. I cock my head to one side, trying to tune in to this internal voice. But Neil hasn't spoken to me since I told him I received a scholarship to Haifa University. It is already far away.

"*Slichah*, got a light?" An American accent. I look up to see a girl as wide as a doorway, who looks my age, in faded blue jeans, a V-necked flowered T-shirt, and sneakers. Her bangs are straight and sit on her eyebrows, and her thin hair is feathered on the sides. She's waving an unlit cigarette around in the air between us.

"Sure."

I fumble in my back pocket for a lighter. She offers her open pack.

"Thanks. I got my own."

We smoke for a few minutes on Carmel Mountain, watching students rush by, observers to a morning traffic jam; my previous inclination to be on time vanishes into the scenery.

"I'm Valerie Rubin." The American girl holds out her hand.

"Miriam Gil."

"Where you from?"

"Ottawa."

"Where?

"Canada."

Valerie drags deeply. "Los Angeles" comes out with the smoke. "Nice to meet you. I met a Canadian once, I think. You must be on the overseas program, too." Then she laughs this outrageous laugh like ones you hear on TV sound tracks.

"That's so funny. I thought you were Israeli when I approached you. You look it."

"My father's Israeli."

"Mine, too."

She pauses. "Actually, my father was Israeli. He's dead."

"I'm sorry."

"That's okay. I hated him." Valerie drops her cigarette on the ground and dabs at it with the toe of her shoe. "You with someone?" she asks, saving me the need to respond to the comment about her father.

"I don't know a soul."

"Good. Let's go check out the classes. I bet most of them are going to make me puke."

Valerie saunters away before I can finish my cigarette. I follow her with the now burnt-out filter between my fingers.

I wait until I pass a garbage can before tossing it and have to speed up to catch Valerie, who has disappeared through a classroom door, saving me a trip to the administration building for directions.

The map they gave me yesterday had vanished along with some of my naiveté about Israelis. I'd absorbed so many of my impressions from my favor, it was work to ignore them, and create my own.

I slide into the empty seat next to Valerie, rummage around my backpack, and pull out my notebook. Welcome to Intergroup Relations: The Psychology of Conflict & Conflict Reconciliation.

The class of twenty-three students, all Americans as far as I can tell, would hardly allow the lecturer to finish a sentence. They appear to me to have come as a tight-knit group, to be keyed up from their flights, from the strength of the Mediterranean sun in October, from the promise of possibility that saturates all beginnings. They did the two-week pre-program together. My grant money didn't cover that.

The young American instructor flares his nostrils after the first thirty minutes, and I draw a line through the course on my sheet. This is an elective year. Exasperation is something to avoid.

Valerie tags along with me as we sample another five classes and hand in identical forms at the end of the school day.

"Want to do potluck with me for dinner?" Valerie asks. My eyes brighten. Anything to avoid my own apartment sounds good.

"I only have peanut butter and cornflakes to contribute. I may have swiped a pack of Pop Tarts on my way out of Canada."

There is that laugh again.

"Take a chill pill. The *makolet*'s open."

She grabs my elbow and steers me to the campus corner store. Twenty minutes later we emerge with eggplant, zucchini, tomatoes, and onions in clear plastic bags.

"This will be awesome ratatouille. My mom's a great cook and she taught me everything she knows."

Back in Valerie's room, Valerie takes over as head chef and I nod at all of her instructions. Her mother may be a great chef; mine was great at buying instant dinners. I am the only person I know who can describe Swanson

TV dinners in intimate detail: the apple cobbler dessert in the first row center; the mixed peas, corn, and carrots in the triangle on the right; the pureed potatoes on the left; and the main meat dish in the bottom center—three pieces of chicken on the bone or a Salisbury steak. It all comes in a foil tray the same size as any airplane meal, minus the plastic cutlery and tiny bags of salt and pepper.

Our conversation stays on the surface and centers on our immediate concern: dinner. We both smoked instead of eating lunch.

"Will you wash the tomatoes, pass me the long spoon, do you have garlic in your room or basil?" *Yes, okay, I'll run down and check.*

But it's nice to eat with someone in your own language, and she is like me, not sharing an apartment with any other overseas students, except all of her roommates are Jewish. I don't ask her if she wrote a letter to the Haifa administration requesting an authentic Israeli experience, too.

Her eyes widen when I mention I live with one Druze and one Palestinian, Muslim student, but she doesn't respond with more than "I didn't think they'd do that here." I skip the part where I threw a cup of coffee at Farzeen. I'm already revising it. Maybe I didn't hurl it. Maybe it slipped out of my hand.

Jet lag settles in not long after my plate is empty and I am embarrassed to ask for more than the side dish Valerie put out for me. She'd already told me she's on scholarship, too, and I noticed her worn looking overalls and the empty shelves and cupboard on her side of the

40

bedroom. We both ignored the other overseas students when they headed for the cafeteria for lunch. Still, I don't rise to leave. The later I return to my room, the better my chances the others will be in bed.

"So, Miriam, why did you come here?"

Valerie drags deeply. I'd quit smoking the entire summer to save money for my year abroad and only bought a pack at the airport on my way out. I could see hanging out with Valerie would make it impossible to stay off cigarettes.

"I can tell you I couldn't wait to get away for a while, even to a war zone," she says.

"You really think it's a war zone?" I ask. She sounds serious.

We are sitting together on her bed, an ashtray between us. Valerie lights a cigarette for me off the end of hers. Outside her open window I can hear the hum of student chatter. The sky is peach, pink, mango with patches of blue.

"Of course it is. That's why every second person is armed and everyone has to do the army." She looks at me as though I've been living under a thick blanket for a year.

I shrug. Israel is not the only country with compulsory military service and not the only westernized country with conscription either. I'm not sure if the presence of so many soldiers is enough to call it a war zone, but I don't want to poke Valerie into clamming up. I want company. I look at her eagerly, prodding her into continuing.

"I have these two older brothers. My oldest one is a real hardcore creep. And my mom just works round the clock, you know."

I didn't know, of course.

When I don't answer, Valerie tries to catch my eye.

"What about you?"

"I live with my dad. My mom died almost six years ago."

"When you were fifteen? Me, too."

I look at her open-faced.

"My dad worked in a diner. He was shot in a robbery when I was fifteen."

"My mom was killed in a car accident. They think she fell asleep at the wheel."

The silence grows too long.

"That sucks," I blurt.

"He was a bastard."

The sun has set, and there is a long shadow over one side of Valerie's face. The door is locked, but I can hear Valerie's roommates at the kitchen table. Voices rise and fall, and there is laughter and the clattering of dishes hitting the sink.

"He used to pull all kinds of shit with me. Killed me long before anyone ever killed him. I came to get a break from them all. Meet someone new."

Valerie puts out her cigarette and reaches for a paper bag on her desk. Her hand disappears inside the bag and pulls out three chocolate pastries.

"*Rugelach*," she says, stuffing two at a time into her mouth. "Take."

I'd love one, but shake my head.

42

"You were saying," she says, her nose in the bag now. "About your mom." I take a deep breath before I speak.

"It turned out my mother had a lot of debts my father didn't know about. A year after her death we had to move into a little place on top of a garage."

I've already said more than I'd have liked, and I'm skimming around the hard parts, but Valerie's story about her dad put me at ease, or at least more at ease than usual.

I didn't sound like such a freak next to her narrative. I stopped short of asking her what she meant about her dad, that he killed her. It felt too much like treading on territory I had no right to be on, trespassing on someone else's sorrow.

When the pastry bag is empty, Valerie crumples it up and tosses it into the garbage bin.

"What does your old man do now?"

I pictured my father sipping a black tea in the living room as the house darkens; he is scrupulous about saving electricity and will live out the rest of the evening by the light of the television set. Monday nights Jacquie works late and baby-sits her grandson in Vanier. I've heard her invite my father there on the phone, but he always refuses. He prefers his own territory.

The room itself is choking on television sets sweet-talked away from senior citizens. He spends half his weeknights repairing their old TVs for resale. He is peering out the window between sips.

The garage looms over an elongated driveway crammed with second-hand cars he picks up from

43

heaven- knows- where that he refurbishes when TV sales are slow.

I don't know if he sees his childhood in British Occupied Jerusalem, his lost wife or just the minus symbols on his bank account when he seems disoriented, moon faced, looking out the window. I have never felt confident in my ability to pick up the threads of his imaginings, follow them to their roots.

"He can fix anything, TVs, stereos, car engines. That and lifting weights, but he'll always be kind of broken I guess." My mouth had run dry. "He's got a new girlfriend now, Jacquie, and it's Jacquie says this and Jacquie says that all day."

"Ooh, Jacquie. Do tell," Valerie says, moving closer to me on the bed. I can feel Valerie's appraising gaze on my face.

"She's the real reason why I'm here. They wanted space to be together." My hands have balled into fists.

"Ouch!" Valerie's eyes crinkle with laughter.

"One night she latched the top lock, and I couldn't get in. Can you believe I was locked out of my own house? I practically banged down the door, and when she finally let me in, she stuck her chest out at me like a mother hen and asked me about my wild hours. Yeah, wild hours at the library."

"Does she think she's your mother?"

I snort. "More like my father's keeper. Like he needs protection from me! She told me that I was aggressive and immature."

"Ouch!" Valerie furrows her brow.

"I did threaten to phone the cops." A giggle escapes me.

"You didn't?"

"I did. I was fuming. I told her to get out, and she laughed in my face. She was right, of course. What would I say to a cop? 'My dad's girlfriend refuses to leave'? I wanted to trip her in those hot pink jellybean sandals to tell you the truth."

"Where was your dad this whole time?"

"Out fixing some guy's car stuck on the Queensway. I didn't even notice his car was gone before I practically busted through the front door."

"Sounds as though you needed out of that city, out of the whole damn country."

"Yeah." We're silent now, and I bite my lip. All at once I long to change the subject. "I miss my boyfriend. You got one?" I stand up, stretch my arms over my head, push the window open wider, and inhale the fresh air. Valerie shakes her head and pats the space beside her. I sit. She looks at me expectantly, a smudge of chocolate around her lower lip.

"Mine freaked out before I left," I add. "I thought he'd miss me and get over it, but you know when it's obvious you're lying to yourself?"

"Guys aren't worth having a cow over." She laughs, slaps her big hand on my knee, and kisses me wetly on the cheek. I swipe at my face where I imagine there's chocolate now. I stop myself from inching away. I'd seen Israeli girls walking to classes with their arms around each other, and the boys kissing each other on both

45

cheeks at the airport. Maybe Americans are like that, too. I'd have to get used to it.

"Oy, such a long face you've got on now. Pretty girl, there are so many fish in the sea. It's like you never heard the song. Cheesy doesn't suit you. He should have been happy for you that you had a chance to get away from that permanent house of mourning. I can relate. It strangles you."

She shoves another *rugelach* into her mouth. Where did a second bag come from? She reaches under her bed and pulls out a bottle of Coke, fills two glasses that had been sitting empty on the desk.

"Well, we had been dating for two years."

"Then he really should have known how much you need a break. How selfish can you get? Don't get offended, but he sounds like a dipstick. Besides, have you looked around at Israelis? Wake up. They're gorgeous."

There is a bang on the door and then another.

"Valerie, *motek*. Open! I need to come in. Why do you eat in the bedroom and not with us? You're missing the party."

"My roommate, Maayan," Valerie says.

Valerie pointed Maayan out to me on our way back from classes. Maayan is six feet tall in flip-flops. She had piled her black hair on top of her head, adding another three centimeters to her height.

Maayan opens the door.

"I have a key after all," she says, waving it in the air. She tumbles over and kisses Valerie on both cheeks. "You have dinner with your new friend and not us, Val. Did you like the *rugelach* I bought for you? Save one for me or did she finish them?"

Maayan glances down at me, and I'm certain there's tomato sauce on my face and splotches of red on my shirt.

"They were delicious, Maayan. Buy those often," Valerie says. She brushes the bangs out of her eyes and laughs that deep laugh I'd first heard this morning. Maayan takes Valerie's hand and leads her to the kitchen, babbling non-stop about the party she's missing. I look around for my backpack and follow a few steps behind them, not bothering to close their bedroom door.

I can see the coffee's being passed around and everyone seems to be sharing urgent news in fruity voices, some accents more guttural than others. A pack of cards appears and then a backgammon board. I'm not invited to play. I say goodnight to Valerie, who waves, but otherwise hardly notices me around the excited buzz of her five roommates.

Chapter Six

BACK AT THE ENTRANCE TO MY APARTMENT, I turn the handle and it opens. There's no need for a noisy key. I practically run past the kitchen on my toes, down the hall and into my own bedroom, without breathing. It worked. I saw lights under the other bedroom doors and in the bathroom, but no one was in the common areas. I don't know how I'd handle another confrontation with anyone, and the odds are against me.

I toss my backpack in a corner and change into a pair of sweatpants and an undershirt. Slipping under the covers, I grab one of those practical Israeli aerogrammes. I lean against the wall adjacent to my bed, and write faithfully to Neil. The lined aerogrammes are pale blue and I have to be careful not to write over the margins because the paper doubles as an envelope, and those bits will have to be glued to the sides when I'm done.

As I write about the pull of the bay just outside my window, I hear Neil's disembodied voice:

"I once went with a girl who cooked like you, out of a can."

"Lovely."

"What she did." His lips thinned. "Some girlfriend."

I sighed. It was as though he was just waiting for me to cross the line and here I am.

There is a tap, and my door opens before I can respond. A redhead wearing large glasses enters. On anyone else, her baby doll dress paired with cowboy boots would have looked outlandish, but she makes the pairing chic. Unlike my other roommates with their bulging backpacks, she has a leather student book bag draped over one slim shoulder.

"So, you are here. I'm Simona."

Simona hugs me, pulls back, and shakes my hands together in both of hers. Her fingers feel soft and cool. I am perpetually sweating, reapplying deodorant and panting in the heat, next to these refreshed, perfumed natives.

"Where are you from?"

"Canada."

"Canada. Paradise. No wars. Lucky."

"And you?"

"I'm from Herzliyah. You know it?"

I shake my head.

"Nice, but still Israel." Simona sighs and sinks onto her bed.

"What's wrong?"

"I miss my boyfriend already. He got into Tel Aviv University, but not me. That's why I put all of my classes into three days. I want to go back to him as much as I can."

I nod with sympathy toward this new roommate who misses her boyfriend.

"Sharing a room means we might get along or not. Still, I'm sorry to leave anyone, especially a tourist, here with the dummy most of the week. I hope you don't think that's how Israelis are."

I would have to adjust to Simona's direct, penetrating speech if I'm going to share a room with her.

"Dummy?"

"Dummy Dalit, the Moroccan in the first room. Arrogant, out of date. You'll see. She's from a small town in the North, not like the big cities in the center."

My head clouds. Maybe I'm flattering myself thinking I'll ever understand the local culture. The last time I'd responded to a provocation things hadn't gone well. It's better to pretend to be easygoing.

"Tell me something, Simona." I fish out a smile. "What is a Druze?"

"A Druze? You met the girl in the middle room? Sweet, young Arslan. They're Arabs with a secret religion and loyal to Israel or whatever country they're in, Syria, Lebanon, whatever."

"Ah. I thought I read something like that."

"You want some chocolate?"

Simona holds out a chocolate-covered almond bar that she's removed from the side pocket of her chic bag and breaks it in half.

"How's my English? I'll practice it with you, okay?" She sighs deeply, approaching a groan. "Did I tell you how much I miss my boyfriend?" She pulls out a photograph of a dark-skinned boy with black eyes, who could be a university student anywhere.

"He is Yemenite. We can't wait to finish school and travel the world together, anywhere with no wars." Simona licks the chocolate off of her fingers. Mine's half melted in my sweaty hand.

"I thought you just said you didn't like Moroccans."

I assumed Simona's dislike of Moroccans extended to all non-European Jews.

"What does that have to do with anything?" she asks. Her voice is patient and she keeps it down. She has only a trace of an Israeli accent, but nothing she says is familiar to me.

"My father's Yemenite." I hand her back the photo, but our fingers don't touch in the exchange.

"You? You're so white. So you do know what I'm talking about."

I don't bother to correct her. My father's family hasn't been in Yemen since the 1880s. I recognize myself less and less since I got off the plane, and I already doubt my ability to read others in this foreign place.

I imagine this self-doubt filled my father years ago when he first landed at Montreal's Mirabel Airport, and again, before he ever met my mother, a girl from Ottawa who had never been past New York.

"You want to have dinner with me? I brought so much food from Tel Aviv. Come. Fresh pitas, hummus from the shuk. And coffee. Come." She repeats. Then, "How's my English?"

"*Metsuyan*," I answer. "I want to ask you one more thing."

51

Simona is busy now arranging her bags of cucumbers and tomatoes. The smell of fresh fruits and vegetables fills the room, and I'm still hungry from my mini dinner with Valerie, hungrier than I was before I ate.

"Look. Flowers." Simona produces a small bouquet of luxurious looking orchids, four fuchsia and four white. She pops them into a large water bottle that's had the top cut off. I hadn't noticed it on the ledge before. She removes her thermos, opens the lid, and pours water into the makeshift vase. The juxtaposition between such expensive flowers sitting in a recycled vase strikes me as quaint.

"They're really nice."

"The best," she says, leaning toward them and inhaling deeply. "It's good for your psychology."

I nod.

"I want to ask you." I stumble here, sensing dangerous waters.

"Yes."

"Dalit asked me if I'd complain about Farzeen and sign a letter to have her moved out of here. They said there are plenty of apartments with Arab students and there's no reason—"

"See. I told you. Backward. I hope you don't think that's what Israelis are like."

"She said after her army service—"

"What did she do in the army? Take people around the zoo? I did the army, too, and I don't care." She groans and pushes her sleek hair off of her face. "*Primitivim.* Let's eat."

52

Simona won't let me help her with the grocery bags she bustles out the door. She clomps down the hallway in her cowboy boots equally weighted down on both sides. Before I can wash my hands and join her in the kitchen, she is already deep in concentration preparing a salad. Chop, chop, chop. The fine vegetable salad is half complete in less than five minutes.

Simona adds lemon, fresh parsley, fresh cilantro, olive oil, salt and pepper. Each item appears out of her shopping bags reeking with fresh vegetable scent, as though we are on the set of a cooking show — or that might just be my perception as someone who normally eats Chef Boyardee when I tire of Swanson dinners.

"You just set the table. For two," Simona adds.

"It's very nice of you to share your food with me. I'll stock up tomorrow."

"Nonsense. It's nothing. You think I can eat all of this myself?"

I set the table with the plates and cutlery that had come with the kitchen. Simona places the food between us and sits across from me with her back to the bedrooms.

"You're thinking about something," Simona says between chews.

"Someone."

"You miss your parents?" I flinch at the word *parents*, but she doesn't seem to notice.

"No. I miss my boyfriend."

"I know all about that." She squeezes my hand on the table between us. "If you miss him so much why did you leave him for a year to study here? Why didn't you wait until you both graduated and travel together?"

She doesn't add "like I'm doing with my boyfriend," but her eyes say it.

"I got a full scholarship, and I didn't want to lose it. It's not really a year. It's two semesters."

"Mmmhmm."

I couldn't convince someone I'd known for a quarter of an hour.

"Hey! Simona, you take my blow dryer again?"

It's Dalit's razor-sharp voice.

"What? You talking to me?"

"Yes. I'm talking to you." She stomps over to us. Her hands are on her hips, and the shoulders of her shirt are wet from her freshly washed hair. "My blow dryer is missing, and last time I found it in your room. I would just go in and take it back, but now that Miriam is here, I don't want her to think Israelis have no manners. You want to find your own and give mine back now?"

Simona stands. Her white skin under her freckles approaches the red color of her hair.

"You accuse me of taking something from you? I wouldn't touch your things."

She wrinkles her nose, as though the idea of approaching an object of Dalit's is as appealing as rooting through a bin of moldy vegetables.

54

"Are you done acting? I have much studying to do. Just give it back, and you can go to your dinner. Bon appetite." Dalit directs this last comment at me.

"Do you mind? Some of us adults are here to study." Farzeen has emerged from her bedroom, where she spends all of her time as far as I can tell, unless she's eating brief meals at the kitchen table. "You're both always talking so loudly, I can't concentrate."

I catch most of the Hebrew, even with the Arabic overtones.

"I'm sorry to disturb you, Farzeen. Some people don't know when or how to shut up," Simona says.

"Come, Dalit. Take my blow dryer," Arslan calls from her bedroom. Then she appears, her hair wet down her back.

"Take." Arslan wraps the cord around the end of the blow dryer and puts it on the kitchen table. Now that their door is open, I can hear the Arabic DJ talking on the radio in Arslan and Farzeen's room. I shouldn't try to peer inside, but I turn my head at what I hope is an unnoticeable angle and glide my chair back an inch.

"This is so sweet, Arslan, but not the point. This *snobeet* only comes two nights a week, so why should she hurt herself schlepping a blow dryer back and forth to her boyfriend? Instead, she comes into our room when we are not here and takes ours, without asking. *Kelba!*"

"Hah! Chutzpah! You dare! I've never been in your room. When did you see me? When?" Simona's voice is too high, and the red color has seeped from her face into her neck.

"I said be quiet." Farzeen's voice is one note under a yell. "Little girls don't understand the value of study and time, my time." She spins around and returns to her room, closes her door. The handle turns several times.

"You blame me because you bumble around, can't find your things. I've never been so insulted. Who do you think you are?" Simona whispers now.

Simona picks up her plate of half-eaten food and stomps down the hallway. Midway to our room she yells, "I apologize for their behavior, Miriam, but I cannot digest my food with that backward dinosaur near me."

Dalit grabs Arslan's blow dryer, flings a "thank-you" at her, mutters to herself about rich, white Jews and slams her bedroom door.

Chapter Seven

IN A MINUTE the whirring of the blow dryer fills the small eating area. I swallow my last two bites of the pita Simona brought from the Tel Aviv shuk.

Arslan laughs through her nose.

"*Snobeet*. She thinks she's better than all of us because she's white. She's the foreigner here, the European. Dalit is from Morocco and you, too, you're like us. We belong here."

She puts her hand on my knee. This time I'm determined not to react to petty politics that I hate more now than I ever have. I replay Farzeen's words in my head. She's definitely the oldest one living here. I glue my belly button to my spine and count to ten in my head.

"Have you ever had coffee with *hal*?" she asks. "It's okay to laugh. I'm laughing. Do you have homework?"

"Very little." I exhale, thrilled to change the subject. "I don't think they want the overseas students to work too hard."

Unlike my other roommates, Arslan doesn't speak a word of English and she tells me she's not as good at Hebrew as she should be. I need to concentrate on my Hebrew and reference my pocket dictionary to communicate with her. It's obvious she translates from

57

Arabic before speaking. I want to ask her what a secret religion is but don't want to offend her, too.

"Good. Farzeen will go to tutor in a few minutes. Then we can have Druze coffee in my room with chocolate. You know Druze coffee? You didn't answer me about the *hal*?"

"No, I've never tasted it."

"Now you will. My friends brought me chocolate from my village. I love coffee and chocolate together."

Arslan's warmth distracts me from my own internal fumbling and my inability to grasp the context behind the tensions in the apartment. We wait without speaking, until Farzeen exits her room, nods toward both of us, and leaves for her tutoring job.

I flip through the dictionary until I get to H. Scan the rows of words until I find *hal*. This is how I discover Arslan is offering me cardamom in our coffee with square pieces of rich dark chocolate and a homemade dessert her mother sent called *osh-al-saria*, a mixture of cream, honey, rose and orange blossom water with the consistency of Jell-O, topped with ground pistachio nuts.

Arslan chats to me about her first impressions of life outside of the village, her drop-down disappointment to discover on a hunt through the foreign students program in the overseas building that real Americans look nothing like the glamorous, leggy blonde models and suntanned, broad, muscular males she sees on cable television. She laments their real life baggy track-suits, mousy brown hair, and big glasses.

I laugh out loud at her descriptions. She has as many misconceptions about Americans as I have about

Israelis. She spoons a second helping on my plate, but I am finally full.

I am on the edge of my seat the whole time thinking any minute she'll ask me to help her get rid of Farzeen, but she doesn't say any more about her.

"Why don't we make a deal?" she asks. Her voice is soft, shy. "We both need to improve our Hebrew. We will study together once a day, find a half hour, expand our vocabularies." She looks up at me, "And also eat my mother's desserts. But no cheating. It must be five days a week. I need to improve my grades. I want to be a teacher, graduate at the top. In high school I finished first, also."

"That sounds like a deal." I smile back at her. I admire her ambition and feel the desire to succeed pulsing through her.

"Good. We start tomorrow. Ten p.m. I will decide which book we'll use, and you keep the vocabulary lists."

I tell Arslan I'm looking forward to our first study session and say goodnight, treading lightly down the hallway. Back in my room, I discover my half-written letter to Neil face-up on my pillow. Simona greets me briefly, as she slips on her lacy nightshirt and matching robe.

I can't recall exactly how I left the letter. It might have fallen to the floor, and Simon might have been kind enough to pick it up. I don't ask her if she read it, not after she'd already been publicly accused of stealing Dalit's blow dryer, but I tuck the thin sheet into my top drawer, just in case.

I'd promised to write him every night and it's already too late to tiptoe down the hallway, search the maze of buildings for a campus mailbox.

I want to savor the taste of the sweet dessert Arslan had shared with me a little longer, so I ignore my toothbrush and change out of my clothes into a sweatshirt and shorts. Under the covers, I struggle to sleep with the weight of a broken promise on my chest. I flip onto my side and stare in the darkness at my own naiveté casting its own long shadows on the wall, along with the moonlight seeping in through the half-open blinds.

I had plunged myself into political tensions I couldn't navigate, while Valerie had landed in the bosom of an instant family, even if she envied my privacy most nights of the week. A person could really expand in her own space given half a chance, maybe the solitude is worth it. Families come and go.

There's a soft knock at the door. I sit up and glance over at Simona. She doesn't move, and I can hear her breath rising and falling. Sliding out from under the covers, I tiptoe to the door barefoot and open it a crack, but my internal alarm is ringing. I should have put the blanket over my ears until the knocking stopped. A voice in my head screams: *Don't open it*. It's Arslan with a piece of paper in her hand. My heart sinks.

"Sorry, sorry," says Arslan, her bathrobe belted tightly around her waist and her red lipstick still on perfectly. "But the letter is ready now. Dalit just typed it up. Please."

In her right hand is a piece of paper I don't want to read.

"You want me to read it to you? You just have to sign and I'll give it back to Dalit. She will give it to her connection, you know. Dalit knows how to take care of things."

In Arslan's other hand is a pen. I don't want to get involved in this. I don't want to lose our opportunity to be friends either. I don't realize I'm shaking my head without speaking until a minute has passed.

"You're saying no to me? You can't leave me all year living with someone who curses me every night."

I concentrate on keeping my head still, but I don't know what to say. I resist the temptation to close the door in her face. She'll still be there in the morning.

"This isn't something I want to do. How can I make you understand?" I whisper. My hands are cold in the airy hallway. Someone's left the large window open in the common eating area.

Arslan's eyes narrow and a line forms on her forehead. She waves the paper in front of my face. It rattles. "Don't you think you're being unkind? Selfish. Where's your loyalty? And Simona's hardly here. You have a world of privacy. Farzeen studies in the room nonstop." Her face looks pinched. Anything I say now will sound like bullshit, and I know it.

"She only goes out to tutor and then she's up late with her papers, the light on. It's been three weeks of her cursing me, Miriam, not just me, my father, my entire family, my village."

Gila Green

Arslan's voice is moving from angry to desperate. I open my mouth, but nothing comes out.

"You're turning me down?" She pouts.

Inside I squirm. Arslan leans in closer to me, her shoulder brushing my own.

"What did Farzeen do for you? Last I heard you two speak it wasn't so nice. I need help. It's only autumn, what will be all year? And you think they reassign new roommates every year? For you it's a holiday, it's three years for us real Israelis."

There's a silence between us as I struggle for a response. At home my father has many Arab friends. He speaks fluent Arabic and I heard the language growing up all of my life.

This isn't working out. I never once stopped to consider what I might be running toward. I was too busy thinking about what I was running away from. Now I am in this unimaginable situation of an Israeli-Arab student begging me to throw out another Israeli-Arab student. I look at the floor, but I don't see any answers there. I hear footsteps. Arslan jerks her head to the side and her eyes widen.

"Farzeen's coming. Take it. Give it to me tomorrow. I know you will do the right thing, my friend." Arslan thrusts the paper and pen in my hand and hurries back into her bedroom just as Farzeen clip-clops down the hallway, her black briefcase bulging at her side.

I ease my door closed, lock it and climb back into my bed. I couldn't help but notice in the semi-darkness before I closed the door that Simona's signature was already on the sheet. No doubt Simona concluded immediately that Farzeen is better off away from these losers.

The only signature missing is mine.

Chapter Eight

AFTER ONE WEEKEND ALONE in the dormitories I resolve to phone my uncle. I hated the solitude from Friday evening until sundown on Saturday with nothing but a radio for company. I'd stalled on calling him all week.

On Wednesday morning I read every flyer taped on the bulletin board while waiting in line for a pay phone. I tear off a note from a student seeking a Hebrew to English translator and fold it neatly into my backpack. My comprehension of Hebrew is much stronger than my ability to speak it, and strong comprehension is all I need for translation. All the years of listening to my father without responding might pay off here.

Valerie is my only friend in the daytime, but she latches on to her Israeli roommates in the evenings. She has an open invitation to Maayan's home every weekend, and she loves living in a regular house for a night, sleeping on a real bed and eating real food. She didn't mention me, and I'm not keen to be a third wheel. I can't expect her to baby-sit me. She's mumbled something about feeling safer with bona fide Israelis. I think she watches too much news. My father survived three wars in Israel; I see nothing to fear.

When my turn comes my pace slows, but I feel dozens of eyes on me, waiting to snatch the receiver out of my hand. I dial the six-digit number and wait. I'm not sure if I should speak Hebrew or English to my only uncle. He picks up on the second ring.

"Allo?"

"Shalom. I'm looking for Moshe Damari."

"Yes. Who is looking?"

"This is Miriam Gil, Hanan's daughter."

"Hanan? Miriam?"

"Yes. Is this Moshe?"

"You are my brother's daughter calling me?"

"I'm in Haifa at the university."

"Hold on one moment, Miriam."

The crowd has already hemmed closer. After sixty seconds of privacy the line for the phone moves forward a hand's breadth and then another. I babble in my mix of Hebrew and English, practicing my plea to the wall. I'm worried he'll hang up or say he's busy.

Valerie appears and signals to me that she's heading to class, holding up three fingers above her head to let me know I have three minutes left, and holding out two fingers scissor fashion, as though she has a cigarette in-between them, to show me she's returned my cigarette to her box. There's no time to smoke. Just as well. That girl is turning me into a smokestack.

Maybe my uncle will let the line go dead. I'll be alone here every weekend. The idea fills me with dread. Everyone in my program has resurrected some long-lost aunt or cousin in Israel to visit on weekends and holidays. The Israeli university representative in Montreal told me the place is deserted from noon on Fridays until Sunday mornings, and he was right.

"I apologize, Miriam. A knock at the door. I'm back."

"I called because I want to visit you this weekend."

"Haven't I already invited you in my letter? Yes, you must come. Did you bring something? Maybe a letter from my big brother?"

"No, not exactly, but he gave me your number and told me I had to call."

I try to force this semi-truth through the telephone receiver, wish it down the line. My father had given me the number. At first, I thought it must be wrong because it had only six digits, but it was the same one Moshe had written at the bottom of his response to my note. Either my father had phoned Israeli information for me or Moshe's number hasn't changed in two decades.

"Come for *Shabbat*. I have place. Too much place. You know how to get here?"

"Not yet," I answer. My uncle's voice is soothing.

"Go to the central bus station, ask for the bus to Kibbutz Galim, and ask for me when you step down. Anyone will tell you where I am. You have a friend? She also is welcome. Shalom, Miriam."

Chapter Nine

VALERIE AND I ARE ON A DIET or that's what we tell ourselves. Really, we can only afford to eat vegetables from the shuk, white pitas with hummus and kilos of white rice. We make the vegetables into stir-fry on rice, chunky soups, salads, and snacks. It's so common to see students on diets that the only comment from her roommates is "Bravo!"

We drink only tap water or cheap instant coffee with low-fat milk, sometimes Turkish coffee. I can't afford what I eat. My rent is two-thirds of my budget, leaving me $50 a month for food, toiletries, school supplies, entertainment, cigarettes, phone, and transportation. The washers and dryers in the dormitories are blessedly free and the two of us have agreed to split detergent. I am convinced we will be best friends.

I've never been overweight, but no one had ever called me thin and the idea that they might in the future had an appeal all of its own. We work out to old Jane Fonda tapes in the one-meter of space between Valerie and Maayan's beds.

For some reason we exercise in Valerie's room, even though mine is empty half the week. I think Farzeen and Arslan make Valerie uncomfortable. I'm afraid to mention the letter still sitting on my desk in my room to Valerie. I don't know my own position. I cannot explain it to anyone else without sounding like a fool, a racist, or a traitor. Tonight I'll slip it back unsigned under Dalit's door.

It's a typical evening with dozens of students lined up for hours in the foyer to use the payphones with Bezeq cards or phone tokens. An overseas call inhales your tokens into the telephone's starving stomach, so international contact for me is almost non-existent outside of aerogrammes.

I called my father once to let him know I arrived and left a message on his answering machine or more accurately took a chance that the machine still records. Since my mother died he'd never used it, but maybe now that he's finally alone for a while he might notice a flashing message signal and consider it might be me. Her buttery voice is still on the recording. It's one thing he will never attempt to fix.

Hearing it in Israel sent shivers up my spine, but I didn't cry. The tape's so worn, it's not really her talking anymore, but a stranger's voice that may have come from the same town as my mother, used the same inflections in her speech. In my message I asked him to write me, though I don't expect any letters or phone calls from him. If he writes, I'll think of it as a gift. I don't have to admit that to anyone else.

I promise myself I'll phone Neil the minute I receive a letter from him, no matter how many phone tokens it costs. He knows how to find me.

When I find Valerie, who is easy to spot in the small crowd around the exit, Maayan is talking her ear off on her other side. She nods at me and the three of us walk together until Maayan turns to her own night class.

There is no time to talk. We slide into our seats. There is a slideshow to watch in our Modern History of Israel class. Beside me Valerie writes out our menu and exercise plan for the next week. Every once in a while, she tilts her notebook so I can read it and nod or shake my head.

My placement in the regular dormitories has separated me from my own program, yet I am hesitant about speaking to the administration. I'd already bungled things with my clever note, asking for a true Israeli experience. I'm the one who had asked not to be placed with the other overseas students. I am reluctant to provide additional interference that might land me in more discomfort.

I admire the professor, an Egyptian Jewish woman named Shulamit Malkah, who speaks with authority. Her black hair is gray at the roots and semi-clipped off of her face, the rest of it left to dangle to her shoulders. She wears a navy-blue suit over a white blouse, low-heeled pumps, and beige pantyhose, and her accent is deep.

She laughs easily, which makes me move my seat to the front row when Valerie takes a bathroom break. I am so uncomfortable about the tension in my apartment that I want some of her laughter to rub off on me.

"The British withdrew from Haifa on April 21, 1948, but kept control of the port facilities," Professor Malkah says.

"We're going on a field trip! Woohoo!" a tall guy with a baseball cap on yells.

The other students clap and cheer.

"I'm happy you read the hand-out, Richard," the professor says, but her eyes say she wants quiet.

"Two days later, the city was captured by the Haganah. Who is familiar with the Haganah??"

"The Jewish army before the IDF," Richard answers.

"Good, but hand up next time," the professor says. "Most of the Muslims who lived here at that time ran away, escaping through the British-controlled port."

I hear the low hum of an overhead projector. There is a guy beside me peeling an orange and slurping on each piece. I shoot sharp glances his way as he sucks and licks his fingers. There is a neat pile of peels on his desk next to a separate pile of pips. I can see he has a bag of chips sticking out of his backpack, and I sense that will be his next noisy snack, but I force myself to sit straight and listen.

"Are we allowed to eat in class, Sender?" the professor asks.

"I never ate dinner, ma'am," Sender responds in a strong Southern accent. "At home we don't have night classes."

"Yeah, they go to bed early in Texas," Richard, clearly a New Yorker, calls out. Everybody laughs.

"There's no eating in my class," she says. She glares at Richard.

"Yes, ma'am," Sender says.

Twenty pairs of eyes stare at Sender, and I sink lower into my chair because I'm beside him. I would have to sit beside the student everyone ends up staring at. He shoves his chips into his backpack and gives the thumbs up.

The professor clears her throat. "Look at the photocopies I passed around," she says in a singsong voice, directing her chin to two chatty students in the back row. "Do you know how many Christians and Muslims were left in Haifa after that?" She taps her desk with her ruler and points the ruler to the front of the class where a screen has been pulled down. She takes a seat near the back of the class after she dims the lights.

"There were still two thousand Christians and possibly as many as thirteen hundred Muslims left by June 1948 in the city," she says. "Today they are about ten percent of the city."

"This happened in Jerusalem, too," I call out. "The Arabs running away I mean. " Immediately my hand covers my mouth.

"Excellent, Miriam," Professor Malkah says. "You've been reading your assignments."

"It's something I used to hear my father say," I answer. Oh my God. All eyes are on *me* now. I force myself to straighten my shoulders.

"Your father?" the professor says.

"He was twelve in 1948 in Jerusalem," I answer. I can't believe I'm announcing this to the whole class.

"Really? He was here?" Richard asks.

The teacher doesn't glare at Richard this time.

"Yes. His family came under the Ottomans. He fought in the '56 war when he was twenty. Really, he hasn't told me that much," I say. "Hardly anything."

"That's so cool," Sender says. "So he's Israeli?"

71

"Yes, but he's in Canada. It's my first time here," I answer. "Sometimes he mentions things." *That's it*, a voice in my head screams. *No more public statements. Shut up.*

Professor Malkah walks toward me and puts her hand on my shoulder. My voice must be more emotional than I realized.

"Not a surprise," she says looking at me as though we're the only two in the room. "War alienates soldiers from their own societies; adding a new society on top of that would be a tall order for most of us."

My mouth opens, but nothing comes out. It's the first time I've ever seen my father as someone like Professor Malkah might. There's a lump in my throat and I swallow. The professor squeezes my shoulder and returns to the back of the class.

The slideshow stops abruptly, and the professor stands and points to the student nearest the light switch. She smiles and ten years roll off of her.

"You all deserve a break after our dawn hike to the nature reserve. When you come back, I'll show you the last slides of Haifa's three main wadis. Take ten."

I don't move from my seat, not even to join Valerie who already has a phone token in her hand. I'm a university student with no real knowledge of my background.

This is a new world for me here in Haifa and it is hard for me to internalize that I am connected to it. Maybe connecting to this place will help me with the disconnection from my father. Maybe something more than relatives had been robbed from me. Maybe actual pieces of me have been waiting across the ocean for me to retrieve them all this time.

Chapter Ten

AFTER CLASS I'M STARVING and Valerie is nowhere to be seen. I remember she'd mumbled something about a research paper, but it's not clear to me what she was talking about. I'm too shy to ask anyone else in my program if they want to join me for a late dinner, and I'm avoiding my roommates — the complaint letter burning a hole in my brain.

I head to the cafeteria on my own. Today I'm happy that my uncle has invited me for the weekend and to celebrate I'm splurging on a dinner.

The cafeteria closest to the dormitory is packed and noisy. Most of the students wear jeans as they do at home, but I notice how much older Israeli students are, how many are pregnant or walking around with babies as well as backpacks slung over their shoulders. I remind myself that most are here after two or three years of military service and another year or two of travel and work, even after marriage.

Every woman I see who isn't sporting a baby is wearing full-make up and my face feels naked in comparison. It had never occurred to me to put on lipstick for a university class let alone eye shadow, liner, and mascara. One of the lights in the corner flickers on and off, and I look away. It buzzes as it dies out, but it's so noisy in here, it's impossible for me to isolate the sound.

I stand at the end of the line, considering the menu. It takes me a minute to realize that the woman with the long hair standing in front of me is Farzeen. Before I can stop myself, my fingers are on her shoulder. She turns to look at me.

"Want to eat together?"

Farzeen tosses her long hair with one hand and turns back around. I shrug. Her hair is so close to me I can smell her floral scented hairspray. I inch back. I tried. I keep my eyes on the sticky floor. There are so many languages being spoken so rapidly around me my head swims. The smell of fried food is the strongest smell in the room, but I can't identify it beyond that. Falafel? French fries?

Finally, it is my turn to pay. I'd already chosen the largest Danish I could find in the row of desserts and received it heated up along with my hot chocolate. The change clinks on my tray.

I turn left and right, weaving between people, seeking an empty table, and finally find a two-seater in a far corner next to the only row of windows that are pulled open as far as they can go. Outside I can see the base of the Eshkol Tower, the highest building on campus, lit up in the night.

Bang! A tray loaded with a large salad, large sandwich, large Coke, and a healthy slice of chocolate cake lands on the table. I raise my eyes, and Farzeen is arranging the strap of her briefcase around the back of the chair opposite me.

75

"There were no other seats," she says. I can't read her face and it's rude to stare too long. I force myself to look away from her.

"It's nice to eat with you," I answer. I sound too formal. I clear my throat.

Farzeen settles herself in her chair and immediately tends to her food. She pours a clear dressing all over her green salad and mixes it with her knife and fork. With her first bite a cherry tomato lands on her lap. She blushes and fumbles for a napkin on her tray, but there isn't one.

"No big deal," I say. I hand her a napkin. She wipes her pants.

"Thank you, Miriam," she says.

It's a good thing I grabbed such a large pile. She lets the tomato fall to the floor, and fails to pick it up, allowing it to roll toward the next table. I watch it come to a rest under her chair, but don't say anything. She's still red and concentrates hard on the rest of her salad.

"I'm sorry about the other day," I begin. There's a stone in my throat as the image of Dalit's letter comes to my mind and I hear Arslan: *Please. I can't live like this all year. She hates me.* There's a dull burning in my stomach. I tell myself I chose an old pastry.

Farzeen shrugs. She looks at me and offers a small smile.

"Are there only Jews in your classes?"

I hadn't thought about this. I am unused to organizing the people around me according to religion.

"I didn't ask."

"Can't you tell?"

"No. Not really. I didn't think of it."

"You should pay more attention to who you're with. This is the Middle East."

"I guess so." I drum my fingers on the table.

"Do you like the professors?"

"Yes, I find them very professional and warm."

"You sound surprised."

"I didn't know what to expect."

"I understand. I wouldn't know what to expect if I studied in another country either." She smiles at me, and I smile back.

"Of course, I'd be prepared," she adds.

"I asked around but couldn't find anyone who'd been to Haifa and I spent most of the summer working two jobs to pay for the trip."

She nods.

"I worked all summer, too. Teaching Arabic to children with special needs, you know? Learning problems."

"That sounds way more interesting than seating customers in a restaurant or putting gym towels in a laundry basket."

We are both quiet for a few minutes, while we eat. My Danish is finished in a few bites, and I sip my hot chocolate. Farzeen still has half a salad in front of her. She hasn't even begun the sandwich or the cake.

"You see that table over there?" Farzeen points with her chin, her fork full of cucumber in mid-air. "First years. I tutor all of them in Arabic in the evenings. Most of them came to me from their older sisters who I also tutored. I don't take money."

"It's great you have the time." I try to catch her eye, but she's examining the contents of her sandwich, adding more pepper to the bread from a take-away packet. "I wish I could help other students for free, but I need to find translation work for the money."

"You don't have to apologize," she says.

"I was just saying," I answer.

"Right," she says.

I shred my empty hot chocolate cup. This line of tension is becoming too familiar between us. I'm already regretting my invitation to eat together.

Out of the corner of my eye, I see a man coming toward us. He is wearing a plaid shirt and jeans, not unlike many of the other students, and his face is screwed up. He notices that I've seen him and picks up speed. In ten seconds both of his palms are flat on our table. Farzeen jerks her chair backward.

His mouth is open, but his voice is low. He speaks without a pause in-between, but I don't understand Arabic. For a moment he is silent, eyeing me menacingly and then looks hard at Farzeen. He speaks again, even lower this time, and I resist the temptation to lean in, and Farzeen herself is leaning farther back, not closer, but her eyes don't move from his lips. His spit lands on the edge of Farzeen's chocolate cake. I don't know if she notices.

When he finally pauses for breath, Farzeen puts her hands on her hips and yells unapologetically. No one in the cafeteria so much as raises a head. It is so crowded and noisy, the yelling blends into the orchestra of high and low-pitched voices in Hebrew, Russian, English, French and Arabic. I rest my chin in my hands, my elbows propped up on the table, only inches from this stranger's big, dark hands—the same color as my father's.

Now the man, angrier than ever, flails his hands around in the air, but Farzeen continues screaming in a stream of guttural tones. She doesn't flinch, though he is easily twice her size. They are speaking at the same time, in an odd sort of competition because she drowns him out hands down.

Finally, he glares at me, spins on his Nikes, and stomps away, muttering to himself and shaking his head. The heavy smell of tobacco mixed with cloves is left behind for a moment after he is gone.

Farzeen begins to chuckle and then to laugh. The clunky silver necklace she wears rocks on her chest as her shoulders shake and her black mascara runs onto the backs of her hands, as she wipes her eyes. She brings her hands together in front of her.

"Do you know what he said?"

"No. What did he say? Who is he?"

"He's one of the new student teachers in my history class. He could use a good pinch." Farzeen stops speaking, and I imagine her standing up and squeezing the angry man's skin between her fingers. I inch my chair backward. She picks up her Coke with both hands, drains the cup. I am afraid she'll get distracted and stop explaining. "He said we are traitors, show-offs. He said who do we think we are?" She dabs at the corners of her eyes with a napkin and tosses the crumpled napkin over the chocolate cake. "He accuses me of being influenced living with Jews in the dorms."

79

"I don't get it."

"He said no one is fooled by us sitting here pretending to be Jews, speaking in Hebrew." She throws her head back and laughs again.

My mouth drops, but then I smile, too.

"Called me a show off, a liar, and an embarrassment to my people. Oh well. We must have deserved an admonition. Would you like half of my sandwich? I'm out of time."

She picks up half of the sandwich with two hands and takes a bite. It looks as though she's eating some sort of white cheese with cucumbers and black olives on whole wheat pita.

"Here, you know what? I'll have them wrap it. Put it in the fridge for tomorrow."

Before I can answer she is off to the cashier with the sandwich. In a minute she returns with the food wrapped in a paper bag, which she puts between us on the small table.

"That was really funny, no?"

I smile. At least we've shared a joke of some kind.

"I guess people make a lot of assumptions around here."

Farzeen looks at me. I can't read her eyes — again. At least she doesn't disagree out loud. She's finished half of the sandwich. She takes out her purse from her briefcase, unzips it, and digs around inside. She reapplies her red lipstick and mascara with a small mirror and returns her cosmetics to her purse.

"Have to run."

She scoops up both of our trays, nods at me, dumps the remains in the bin and the empty trays on top of the garbage can. In a minute the crowd swallows her up. Out of the corner of my eye, I can still see the angry man. He waves a finger at me and clicks his tongue.

I imagine that man following me back to my dormitory and I really want to leave, but I have nowhere to go. I decide to go for a run. I could use some exercise. I stand up and exit the cafeteria taking the longest route because it is the farthest from him. It is only after I open the heavy cafeteria door and walk into the fresh air that I realize I've forgotten the other half of the sandwich on the table.

Chapter Eleven

ON FRIDAY MORNING there are no university classes. I consider the argument I had with Simona last night when I returned all sweaty from my run. I replay it over in my mind, trying to unearth all of the smart things I should have said, but didn't.

She'd asked me to look over an essay she'd written in English, and before I'd finished she'd sat down beside me, her weight tipping me toward her on the thin mattress.

The truth is I was never entirely sure with Simona, the ground always seemed unsteady around me when we were together. It is obvious she considers me defective in some way, and I can't say that I disagree.

On the other hand, she offers to help me navigate university bureaucracy and find translation work and she has already promised she's visiting me in Canada with her boyfriend. She was insulted when I turned down her weekend invitation to Herzliyah.

I would love to see Herzliyah, but not as a third wheel to a couple, and she's made it clear what a great time the *three* of us would have. We're just not on the same wavelength.

"So, what are you going to do?" she asked. Simona is taller than me and I had to look up to respond.

"I'm editing your essay." I pretended not to notice her hostile body language and crossed my legs at the ankles. I took a comb out of my back pocket and ran it through my hair.

"The way you let Dalit intimidate you. You think I'm not here enough to notice how jumpy you are, like a frightened rabbit? I bet you're always hiding behind that fat girl."

Simona didn't pause between words. Her lines came out in a continuous stream. "And don't get me started on why you conceal yourself behind a fat girl all day long. One issue at a time. Did you come all the way across the ocean to let some girl frighten you? I'm a psychology graduate and you're a textbook case. Stand up to Dalit next time. You stood up to your boyfriend and your father and his girlfriend, and don't deny it."

The color rose in my cheeks, and my nostrils flared. Confrontation has always terrified me, and now I could see it like a live grenade sitting between us on the mattress. Simona had just admitted she reads everything of mine she can get her hands on, even my diary.

"Sign her paper gun, and she'll back off. Step two is to quit the guilt notes to your mannequin boyfriend, and then we'll deal with your large friend."

"Sign what?" I croaked. I did sound like a twitching rabbit looking for a hole to dive into. Calling my friend a fat girl, I'd already swallowed.

Simona tsked sympathetically, as though I was in even worse shape than she'd imagined.

"I could be the best thing that's ever happened to you. Like a mentor. I wish you'd let me," she said.

I stood up, stepped over to my side of the room and sat back down on my own bed. I needed space between us.

"Maybe I don't have the right to interfere. Maybe you just want to win points with Arslan to show how liberal you are." Simona's facial expression was so smug, I slipped and blurted, "Arslan called you a snob."

The minute the words were out I knew I'd lost.

"Now you're being childish. Well, children do scare easily." Simona clicked her tongue, her hands on her small hips. She wore jeans that hugged them perfectly and showed off her beaded anklet. "Look at you, wiggling around?"

I was bankrupt now and I knew it. My emotions had gotten the better of me—again. I wanted to hide. "I won't bother answering. I'm going to the bathroom."

I slammed her essay down on my bed, which was less than dramatic given that it was only a few pages and didn't make a sound as it hit the mattress. I stomped off to the bathroom. When I returned, drained of confidence, I was grateful that Simona was gone to spend the weekend with her boyfriend.

Now, sitting on the packed bus to the central station, I force myself to blot out yesterday, not to mention the bleating and blaring of the bus driver's radio, which is giving me a headache. I have to focus on the problem at hand, not dormitory politics. I need to make a good impression on my uncle. That is more important than this mess of a situation in my dorm room. My mind drifts again to Simona, and my stomach muscles tighten. She has a point about Dalit. I could sign her paper and get her off my back. But the idea of putting my name down on a paper that states I could not live with an Arab student disgusts me. Enough.

I watch all of the other buses on their routes to the center of town, making their way as I imagine they always do in the morning past Abba Khoushy Street. I stare through the bus windows at the dozens of men with their prayer shawls over their shoulders or in specially designed see-through bags tucked under their arms, heading back home after morning prayers or climbing into their cars on their way to half a day's work. Others are doing their pre-Sabbath errands before the shops close for twenty-five hours. Religious Jews are a minority in the city, where two-thirds of the Jewish population is secular, but for me religious Jews stand out like the female IDF soldiers with machine guns slung over their backs and the kosher McDonald's.

On our school hike to the nature reserve, I had stood off to the side on my own, attempting to distinguish the beauty around me. I inhaled deeply. It felt as though I was in a different body outside of the urban atmosphere, when in reality we were so close to Haifa's sloping streets and a bay you feel you can touch from anywhere. Haifa's nature reserve is filled with pine, cypress, eucalyptus, oak, bay, and olive trees, and almost seven hundred types of wildflowers. I'd never seen so many shades of green from myrtle to viridian at one time.

The bus jerks to a halt, and I get off at the crowded central bus station and tune into the usual morning street sounds, only sped up on a Friday when even I can see that time moves faster in Israel. One of my professors explained to me that time races on Fridays here until mid-day and then reverses, slowing down until it stops at sunset when traffic comes to a standstill.

At my bus stop at the Haifa University there were thirty or so students waiting with me, but here I am overwhelmed by the hundreds of people of every background and color around me, breathing down my neck, everyone's eyes peeled for what seems like hundreds of buses. Waiting passengers sit on any inch of open space; there are teenagers along the spines of the three benches at my stop, on top of the people crammed six to a bench built for four, whose belongings are spread out in front of the benches, underneath them and on their laps. Others are draped in every position along the railings meant to separate lines of travelers or are propped up on dirty, narrow ledges. There are even backpackers sitting on their backpacks on the stained floors littered with cigarette butts.

I glance at the beggars sitting or lying directly on the pavement along the far dirty tiled walls and force myself to look at my watch. Guilt runs through me. I am angry at the smoker who could have stuck his cigarette in my eye without even noticing, at the lateness of the bus, at my predictable uncertainty, while people who look and smell as though they haven't showered in days beg from the floor with their charity boxes waving in the air.

The bus to the kibbutz rumbles into the central station. There's no time for thinking on a battleground. I need to ready my elbows to board as the people around me immediately begin jostling for space. I hold my breath against the smells of sweat and rich, flowery smelling shampoos and force myself to put one foot in front of the other amid dozens of other equally determined feet. There are other people's belongings digging into my back and sides, but I press on, trying to make myself as small as possible, feeling as though I'm on the edge of an avalanche.

I thrust a bill at the driver and sit in the nearest available seat. In a few minutes the throng settles down, and I arrange my backpack comfortably at my feet without a glance at my companion. Conversation is the last thing I want to start. I need time to recover.

The disorder remains in my head the entire hour to the kibbutz bus stop, where I find myself alone on the end of a two-lane highway, my bus roaring off into the distance. I double-check the signpost. I see only one dirt side road. There's nowhere else to go, so I begin what turns out to be a 3-kilometer hike to the kibbutz entrance.

My bag grows increasingly heavy with each step forward, and I desperately need the bathroom, but the unpaved road is entirely bare. There is no tree or bush to hide behind.

Up ahead I see a couple of other backpackers trudging forward, but they are too far away for me to speak to them, and I watch as a minivan pulls up and they get in. I want to scream, "Wait for me!" but it's no use. I'm not built for causing a spectacle, and I watch as the minivan pulls away.

In another minute a car pulls up beside me, but I have no idea what the man on the passenger side is saying in Arabic, though he smiles broadly, and although I realize he's offering me a ride, I'm too scared to get into a car with an Arab driver. I shake my head and move on.

The sun beats down on my head, and the water bottle I'd slipped into the side of my backpack this morning is mysteriously missing. It must have been a casualty of my battle to board the bus. I dig into my jeans pocket, but there isn't even a stick of gum there to relieve my mouth of its dryness.

After forty-five minutes of trudging on a road that creeps upward, I am at the entrance to the kibbutz. I notice rows of deep green cypress trees and a security guard in a booth in front of a boom. Although there is also a twenty-four-hour security guard at the dormitory, at all university entrances, and around Haifa's central bus station, I am still unused to the appearance of widespread armed security guards. No one else on the bus glanced at the soldiers and security guards. I am the only one staring at them and they are everywhere: at the bus stations, in the strip malls, on the streets. I'd never seen a gun up close in Ottawa.

I edge around the boom, and the security guard does not look up from his newspaper. I don't know why I don't ask him if he can direct me to my uncle's home. Instead I press on until I arrive at a traffic circle adjacent to a large parking lot.

I might have felt refreshed waving goodbye to Arslan this morning, promising her I'd review the list of vocabulary words she'd passed me across the breakfast table, her cashmere scent detectable on the paper, but now I am sweaty and exhausted. My dormitory feels light years away.

"Excuse me. Could you tell me where Moshe Damari lives?" I ask the first person I see after I drop my backpack on the sidewalk and rub my shoulder. I have stopped a teenager riding an undersized bike, the old-fashioned kind with a basket on the handlebars. A small dog follows at his side.

He gives me directions in such heavily-accented Hebrew I can't understand him and pedals on, but he'd used his hands enough, waved them this way and that way, so that I am able to head in the right direction.

I've never seen a kibbutz before, and I am drawn back to many of the same colors I saw yesterday at the nature reserve, a canvas of tans and greens, except here there is a view of the Mediterranean, so close I feel as though I can refresh my hot neck, lose my arms up to my neck in its banks. This thought is so tempting I can taste it.

I see rows and rows of identical one-story homes, the only differences between them being white or rust-colored roofs. There is an overwhelming number of green lawns, trees and flowers with bike paths flowing in between and off to the side I see a basketball court.

I do not recognize all of the greenery, but I spot tall palm trees, pine trees, almond, and olive trees. Beside the parking lot is a large three-floor building. The walls of the middle floor are all windows, and through them I can see a cafeteria. I open the entrance, and to my relief I immediately see a sign for a bathroom on my left.

My uncle's home is less than ten minutes from the parking lot, and at least now I have splashed water on my face and neck. My legs grow heavy with each step forward. I read the small sign on his front door: *Family Damari. Blessed are those who enter.* I take a deep breath and knock.

The door opens and a small woman stands behind a screen door. Her face is narrow, and her dark brown hair is neatly pinned at the sides.

"Shalom," she says, throwing both arms around me and squeezing me to her chest. She takes a step back and just as I'm catching my breath, she hugs me again. "You are Miriam. How wonderful you've come."

She continues to look at me through approving eyes. I shift my weight from one foot to the other and smile back. She takes me by the hand and leads me into her living room. I notice she has a limp in her left leg.

"How was the bus?"

"I survived," I answer.

She laughs. Her skin is the same color as mine in winter. She wears a nude-colored T-shirt and matching shorts, both spotless, nothing like the sweat stains I imagine must be showing through my T-shirt, a hand-me-down of Simona's.

"How is the university? Moshe, where are you? Please sit down," she says, gesturing toward the couch. I sit, and the smell of boiled cabbage and meat washes over me.

"Moshe," the woman calls, craning her neck backward. "She's here."

"Coming."

I study the small one-floor house as Leah fusses around me, filling a glass on the coffee table with water, putting out an assortment of fruits and cookies. The

90

house has an open-plan kitchen, living room, and dining room. Sunlight pours in from all sides, although it is dimming now as sunset approaches. The shelves on the walls are plastered in a variety of seashells, some are so tiny they could sit on the end of a finger; others are fist-size.

"The dormitories are okay," I answer.

"It must be so hard without family. I hope you'll consider us your family while you're here. We're thrilled to have you. Please eat something."

"Thank you," I answer. I pick up a chocolate chip cookie.

"Forgive me," a man says. I look up and see my father's brother, my uncle, for the first time. "I do the crossword puzzle every Friday, a bet I have with an old friend. It's not worth explaining. So, you are Miriam," he says before I can answer about the crossword. He puts his arm, so much thinner but the same dark date color as my father's, on my shoulder and squeezes lightly. "Let me take your bag and show you your room."

"She just sat down," Leah says.

"After a week in a dormitory, I bet she's dying for a real bed," he answers.

He lifts my bag with no effort as my father had done a week ago with my suitcase. I ignore the family shadow I see in him, the same bowleggedness. It's too unnerving.

On the walk down the short passage I notice many photographs crowding the walls on both sides. All of them are of a girl with white-blonde hair. In some shots she is on her own, and in other shots she is with Moshe and Leah or just one of her parents.

In the standing shots the girl towers over Leah, who leans to one side, and in a few photographs Leah has a thin black cane. There are the usual ones representing babyhood and then adolescence and finally, in chronological order, a blonde teenager, her eyes squinting in the sun at a high school graduation.

It did not occur to me that I would have a blonde cousin, but I still sting from my first encounter with Farzeen, which has become a permanent reminder that I am an outsider here, so I don't ask about the bland looking teen girl, who appears at ease with herself in front of the camera.

"You look like your mother," Moshe says. "Hanan, a little maybe, but not so much." He cocks his head to one side. "No, not at all. He's black like me. You're white like your mother, maybe your soul is Yemenite since you are here in Israel. A Canadian with a Yemenite soul." He laughs lightly, but I am caught straight-faced on his mention of my mother. I don't know what Moshe's heard about her or what is expected for me to reveal. I'm not used to family, are they privileged to more information than others? There's no one to ask. There hasn't been for a long time.

"This is your bed, and I prepared this plate of fruit and cookies myself. I will be upset if you don't finish the whole thing. And here," he says, holding up a glass jar of candies, "is a bowl of sweets. Toffees and lemon drops."

He unwraps one of each, pops the soft pink toffee into his mouth, chases it with a lemon drop, and sits on the edge of the made-up bed. Sweets are a craving he differs on with his older brother. My father is religious about flossing and turns from sweet, sticky foods the way some vegetarians flee from barbecues.

"Thank you. It's nice of you to have me."

"You are my only niece. Who should I have? Rest now and use the shower right outside your door," he says, pointing to two folded towels on the end of the bed. "And Miriam." He pauses and lowers his voice. "Leah has been missing a daughter in her life. You've come at the perfect time. I hope you don't find her too overwhelming. She's never gotten over our daughter Yakira's running away or whatever she's calling it now — absence."

"You have a daughter?"

"Even this your father never told you?" There's a hint of astonishment in his voice, but I don't know him well enough. His heavy Hebrew and Arabic sounding intonations are familiar to me. It might be disappointment, confirmation that he doesn't register enough on his only brother's radar screen to warrant a mention.

I shake my head.

"You are a little older. She is a lovely girl, *motek*, smart, lots of friends, the light of our lives. But then in high school she became anti everything, especially the army, you know?"

Tears well up in my uncle's eyes and he lets them fall.

"Why would you know? They wanted to imitate some high school kids from 1970 called the *shministim* who complained about the occupation. You weren't even born then."

93

I press my back hard against the open bedroom door and stare out the bedroom window. I have a cousin out there somewhere. It's a lot to digest. She's not dead. That means she might return. We might meet. Stranger things have happened.

"I still have hope," he says, as though reading my thoughts. He wipes his eyes with the ends of his shirt. "But Leah, she can't keep hoping. It's easier for her if she tells herself otherwise. We agree to disagree on this."

"She really ran away?"

"She warned us for years that she'd do anything rather than serve in an occupation army, oppressing others. No, that she would never do."

My uncle holds up the two first fingers of each hand, putting his last lines in quotation marks. "As if it is so simple. Black or white. But we thought she'd grow out of it, mature. Maybe even skip the army, but get permission to do some national service in a hospital or with children. She loved children." He is proud of this last comment about his daughter.

I've never heard of Israelis like Yakira.

"I don't get it. Where is she?" I ask.

"I wish I knew. I spent every moment looking for her for a whole year. I phoned every friend, every friend of a friend she ever knew or went to school with and wrote to everyone I couldn't get on the phone. We even hired a private investigator, but all he said was some people don't want to be found, whatever the hell that means."

"I'm so sorry," I say. "Did she leave alone?"

"She married some older boy from her group off the kibbutz the day she turned eighteen to avoid the army." I raise an eyebrow. I can't believe I have a cousin who is married. To marry at eighteen takes guts.

"The army makes exceptions for married women. We prayed that would be the end of it." My uncle holds out his empty hands. His voice has sunk to a whisper. "I heard they were in England and then America. She sent this." My uncle reaches into his back pocket and takes out his wallet. He unfolds a deeply creased note and hands it to me. The bottom half has been torn away.

I will not take part in War, including the Occupation. The citizens of Israel are being fooled into believing they have free will when they are being used day in and day out by the government and its War Machine. There is no higher statement I can ever make with my life on this earth. The force the Israeli government uses against its own People will not stop until it has extended to the spilling of blood, deepening social inequality and an entrenched hatred of the Other. Any human being who takes any role in the army is another cog in the machine drawing us ever closer to Total Destruction. The army is a danger to the very citizens it wishes to protect and to the entire Middle East. I reject it wholeheartedly.

"She sent this to us. She sent it to the prime minister, too."

"This must be so hard." I don't ask him what she wrote on the missing bottom half, a personal goodbye or an expression of love and regret to her parents.

The tears return to my uncle's eyes, but he blinks them away.

I stand absorbing my uncle's suffering, twirling a lock of my hair. My first thought is that I'm selfish or at the very least too stupid to have considered before I boarded the plane that my life is not the only one with wounds in it.

Now I've ripped open Moshe's deepest wound and made it bleed. I'd have come anyway. My uncle is the only source available about my parents' past. I'll have to live with that. If it makes it hard to sleep here tonight, I'll have to live with that too.

"Well she's not here now, but you are." My uncle's smile is plastic, and I know he is lying because his daughter's desertion is very much here with us, like my mother's ghost. "And things can change any day. She could grow up, remember her parents. Hope, hope, hope." His voice fades. He rubs his eyes with his palms and takes a deep breath.

"We're going to have a great time. Rest and shower, and then we will eat and after I will show you around the kibbutz and you will tell me all about Hanan's ways in Canada, yes. And I have photographs of your grandparents. I bet you've never seen those. If I know Hanan he talks like he fell from the sky."

I swallow and Moshe winks at me. I can smell his candy breath. He's friendly, but I can't wait for him to leave. It's been forever since I've seen a double bed and it's all I can do not to fling myself under the covers, move my head from side to side on top of two pillows, clear the blue-green air of blood-related ghosts.

I shouldn't care what Moshe says about my father after what he'd done to me, but I do. I've never seen photographs of any paternal relatives, and I hope I didn't stare at my uncle too intensely.

Moshe's assumption is correct. To live with my father is to conclude that he parachuted into the desert in the 1956 war between Israel and Egypt and rather than hit his mark, he continued to fall, swooping through time and space for eleven years, until he landed in a tank in yet another war and drove without stopping until he finally reached Ottawa.

Chapter Twelve

WHEN I FEEL A WARM BREEZE ON MY NECK, I wake up. I
had meant to put my head down only for a moment in
the same way as I'd meant to eat only one of the date-
filled cookies, so as not to spoil my appetite for dinner.

But the cookies are all gone and so is the sun. Self-
centered girl that I am, my missing cousin didn't keep
me awake. I hear the soft tones of television rising and
falling in the living room, but no voices.

I notice the shower towels that I must have kicked to
the floor in my sleep and think of Dalit. My uncle must
subscribe to her shower-in-the-evening ideology.

Peeking out the bedroom door, I don't see anyone on
my way to or back from the shower, but the smell of
meat and cabbage is gone. It must have been a late lunch
they shrugged their shoulders and ate when they
realized I was fast asleep, or perhaps Leah prepared it
for a neighbor who is unwell or for a neighbor after a
birth, and not for me at all.

"Miriam?" I hear my uncle's soft voice accompanied
by a tap on my door. "It's time to go to the dining hall for
supper."

"Almost ready."

Ten minutes later we are walking up the windy path
to the kibbutz dining hall, near the bus stop at the
entrance. The dining hall resembles a large cafeteria and,

except for the noticeable absence of cashiers, people fumbling in their wallets, and the exchange of money or credit cards, it has many of the same properties: the salad area, the soup area, the meat and side dishes area, stacks of brown trays, bowls and plates alongside compartments filled with cutlery.

After a week of living on soup and pita and the occasional sweet mostly supplied by Arslan, my mood lifts, and before I taste one bite, I decide it is all gourmet. I want to ask where Leah is, but I hold my tongue. Besides, Uncle Moshe is too busy greeting everyone to answer any questions. He finally leads me to a corner where we put down our heavy trays and settle into cafeteria-style chairs.

"Eat, eat," he says. "You don't like soup?"

"I had soup every night this week," I tell him, trying to keep my voice light, as I dig into my chicken. I don't want my uncle to think I have come to beg or start leaking my envy of the other overseas students prancing in and out of the dormitory with pizza boxes and bulging delivered bags from Burger Ranch and McDonald's.

Somehow my uncle manages to eat, even though every few minutes someone stops at our table to greet him. It takes me a half an hour to figure out that I am a curiosity. Everyone knows everyone on the kibbutz, and nobody knows me. Here, a son of the kibbutz has brought a foreign niece, the daughter of a brother they've never seen. This is a miniature event.

We are in the dining hall for two hours between the nonstop introductions and greetings, but Moshe doesn't seem to mind. He is quiet and soft spoken, and if it wasn't for their identical coloring and shared bandy legs, I could easily be talked out of the knowledge that he is any relation to my father at all.

But it's impossible to know how similar they really are. Since I was old enough to ask, Uncle Moshe is a verbal road as blocked off as my mother. "It was another life, Miri, another time. Better you stay as you are." I want to dive into questions about my father's childhood, but I hold back. My instinct tells me it's an old rugged path best taken slowly.

"Come," Moshe says, after he's cleared off our trays, sweeping our chicken bones into the mouth of the garbage can and shooing me away with a flick of his fingers when I try to help. "Let's have a beer downstairs in the *moadon*."

A beer. My father flares his nostrils at alcohol and mutters about a lack of class. I should stop looking for similarities. It's doomed from the outset. They've been separated for thirty years.

What do I imagine? Some manner of invisible cosmic cord that knots them together, only discernible to the naked eye by similar eating habits? It's not as though I have a sibling of my own for consolation or even comparison. One paternal uncle for half a day, most of which I've spent sleeping, is all I've got to go on.

Soon we are in an out-of-the way spot in a roomy clubhouse on the bottom floor of the same building that houses the cafeteria. Moshe sips a beer, whatever they had on tap. I've declined and am nursing a hot Turkish coffee instead.

It's harsher than the one Valerie prepares and it bears some resemblance to the Druze coffee Arslan serves. A plate heaped with slices of yeast cake, baklava, and poppy-seed bars rests between us at our table for two. There is still no sign of Leah.

"Your father, he's in good health?"

"Yes. He works out every day."

"He always liked that. Being big."

I nod and try to keep the anger out of my facial expression. Uncle Moshe doesn't need to know the truth. The big brother he speaks of with such admiration threw out his only daughter. It hits me. Moshe would give his right arm to see his own daughter while his older brother tossed his daughter out like chewed gum.

"I heard about your mother. I'm sorry. She was a beautiful woman. Very pretty. You look like her. I really thought Hanan was lucky with her, especially after you arrived."

I cock my head to one side as I try to understand the deeper meaning behind his words. I avoid eye contact. I don't want to ask Moshe how he heard about my mother's accident and cling to my wish: *Please don't let him muster the courage to ask me about her.*

In almost six years I've mentioned my mother to my father a handful of times only to be rejected. I used to pray for her soul every night before I fell asleep, that she should stay near us, watch over us at the least, come back at the most, tell us it was all a big mix-up, another woman who happened to look just like her had been driving that car.

I'd ask a faceless God to wind time back, so that she slept all day or flew out of town or came down with a terrible virus instead of smashing into a telephone pole while I was having a typical day in grade ten. I remember racing off the bus and flinging open the front door, ready to pop a few instant waffles into the toaster and tell my mom all about the new substitute teacher. Instead I found a silent house, not unusual, but rare enough to set me on edge.

I sat there alone in front of the TV until my father walked in at 8:00 p.m. and told me he'd been at the hospital; my mother had wrapped the car around a pole and would never come home. Then he put his face in his hands and bawled, which frightened me more than anything he'd said.

Instrumental music filters toward us from the coffee counter. In the sky birds sail overhead like singing shadows in the night. They are too quick for my eyes to catch more than silhouettes in the darkness. Meters away people relax with cold or hot drinks and start-of-the-weekend talk, full-stomach talk. The atmosphere is so relaxed, so peaceful.

"Are you ready for a kibbutz tour? Or you are tired maybe. We have all tomorrow to walk around."

"Don't you have to get back to Leah?"

"Leah?" He shifts in his seat and speaks to the floor. "No. She prepared food for her best friend, Vered, who came home now from the hospital in a wheelchair. They are eating in her apartment. Her friend doesn't have a husband anymore, and her son is in the army, so she's alone, too."

Moshe says all of this too quickly. I play with my hair, take a comb out of my back pocket, and brush my hair right there in the *moadon*, a habit I'd picked up after my mother died. Whenever someone would bring her up I'd feel this overwhelming need to do something and somehow settled on combing my hair. It used to bother Neil, and I'd stopped doing it around him. Even now I was doing it less because I was smoking more. But somehow tonight my comb found its way into my back pocket.

After a pause Moshe adds, "Really, she hardly ever eats in the dining room. There are too many people she's grown to resent over the years in these close quarters. She's still a Jerusalemite at heart, one for the city."

"I can't wait to see Jerusalem," I say. "Maybe she'd show me around."

My uncle misses a beat. He rubs the back of his neck with both hands.

"She needs her cane for big walks, and she's never accepted the cane," he says. "You'll have more fun going with kids your own age."

I'm burning to ask how Leah ended up with a cane, but my uncle doesn't offer any more information, and I hate to pry.

"Besides, there's all tomorrow to be with Leah. I can have my niece all to myself for one dinner in twenty years, can't I?"

"Sure."

"And what does my big brother do without you?" He laughs, but I don't get the joke, and his shoulders rise and fall, which causes his chair to tip forward. I clear my throat. *He hangs out with an idiot named Jacquie who thinks she's French and is using him to get out of her rat-hole of an apartment that is only one notch above living in her Honda.*

"He fixes things and resells them. Televisions mostly and cars. But you're right. He doesn't have many friends, more like acquaintances."

"He was always good with his hands. He got this from our mother. Me? I am like our father. I cannot change a light bulb without looking it up in a book. He is like the gymnast who can stand on his head while I can hardly sit on my *tachat*."

He laughs at himself again, and I notice he has finished one beer. He holds his thumb and four fingers together, which I'd already learned in Israel means *wait*. He heads for the bar where he hands his glass to a man behind the counter, who tips it under a fountain on the counter.

"You know your father was popular in his youth," Moshe says, resettling into his chair. "Many friends. But it was not easy for him, Miriam. It was not easy here in those days. We didn't have anything, not like today when the kids have everything. And there was the tension with our father. Our mother was left with us all day and we were so poor."

He sighs and holds his glass up remembering things that happened years ago. I try to diminish myself in my chair, so he'll see his memories and share them instead of seeing me.

"I begged your father to run away to the kibbutz with me. So many young people were doing it then. There was no food in Jerusalem. But he was the oldest, and he wouldn't leave our mother. He didn't think much of me for going, I know. But she couldn't feed us, *b'emet*. I was one less mouth to feed." He crosses and uncrosses his legs and drains his glass. "But you are a young woman, what do you want with this old history? Here I will show you something and if you guess what it is, you can have it."

My uncle reaches into the miniature backpack he'd been carrying on his shoulder all night and produces a jewelry box. He tilts the top of the box open and reveals a green-blue stone in the shape of a Star of David on the end of a gold chain. The charm is thick, weighty.

"I don't know. Is it turquoise and something?"

"Aha, that's good enough. It does have turquoise in it. It's an Eilat stone, a real one, not the fake blue and green rocks they sell to tourists. Bend closer."

I lower my head, and my uncle clasps the necklace around my neck.

"It is genuinely mined in Eilat." My uncle looks proud. "It is time you learned something about the country your father fought so hard for, no? I don't think they mine any real ones in Eilat anymore."

"I love it. Thank you."

"It has turquoise as you correctly said, but also malachite and azurite. It's our national stone. They used to call it the King Solomon stone. You should wear it in good health, and it should bring you *mazal* and good things. It suits you."

I finger my new necklace, and I almost forget why I came. I cannot help but question why my uncle would present me with such a fine gift on our first meeting.

Maybe he wants to make up for his lack of a relationship with my father or he's just a generous person who so longs for his daughter's return that he's giving me the jewelry meant for her. I've always struggled with saying thank you when someone does something nice. I mine for ulterior motives instead.

"So, your mother struggled?" I want to steer the conversation back to where we'd been and I never knew my grandmother, which bothered me more after my mother died. If I ever have kids they won't know their grandmother either.

"Yes. She was a beautiful woman when she was young, but she married late and they didn't get along and, of course, the wars didn't help. And she was lonely for her parents, she was from Jaffa-Tel Aviv, not Jerusalem. In those days the distance was real, far, not like today when you hop on an air-conditioned bus. Surely that much Hanan has told you."

I nod and sip my tiny coffee. I don't correct my uncle. I don't want to say that if my father does talk about his childhood, he never fails to mention his *zevel*, good-for-nothing brother who turned out just like his father, someone who abandoned their mother for good, left her for dead, sick and in need of medical care with no way to pay the bills when she couldn't clean or bake pitas in her chicken-filled garden.

Besides my desperation for a place to stay on weekends, I'm hungry for any information about my father's past, and stirring up controversy seems misguided. I feel protective, unwilling to reveal the little he has ever shared with me. I shouldn't overdo it.

"What do you do here? On the kibbutz."

"I'm a genealogist at the museum. We have a museum, you know, for tourists. I work mostly with people off the kibbutz these days. There is much work in our country in my profession," he says. He bites into a slice of cake.

"Like what?" I ask.

"Survivors seeking relatives, other museums that need information, Jews forced out of Europe or Arab lands or who need to prove their religion before they can marry, or sometimes tribal ancestry. You know what that means? If they are Kohens or Levites. But my work sounds boring to you?"

"No, not at all. Just you are so different from my father working all day under a car or with his nose in the back of a TV."

He laughs and finishes his dessert. "Well, we all have our jobs in this world. And it was different for him, Miriam. He bore the brunt of the hard years and stayed on. Jerusalem is in his spirit after all the toil he did for it, no doubt until today. While there was food here for me." He picks up another poppy-seed cake and swallows half in one bite. A few crumbs fall on to the front of his shirt. He dusts them off with one hand.

"I didn't go back as often as I should have." He lowers his voice, and his smile is gone. "We'll never be brothers again, the way we were as kids. I'm no fool. Please don't answer," he puts his hand on my knee. "But I could still be your uncle. Leah would be a perfect aunt. We miss family."

"I appreciate that," I answer. "I'd love an aunt and uncle."

The black muddy coffee hits me, and I am wide awake when I'd felt myself nodding off only a minute ago. It must be my uncle's kind words combined with the deep sleep I had in the late afternoon mixed with the first red meat I've had in a week, and the caffeine and white sugar. I try to come up with another question that might open a door to my father's past but bring back the smile to my uncle's face. I am afraid of saying the wrong thing. The conversation has brought my uncle down. I don't want to remind him too much of things he regrets, to come to symbolize deep-down mistakes. His brother. His daughter.

"Excuse me, Moshe? Are you playing that game?"

I look up and lose my train of thought. Whoever this is, I can't take my eyes off of him.

"Take the backgammon, Guy. Have I introduced you to my niece from Canada? Miriam," my uncle says, inclining his head toward me, "this is Guy, fresh out of the army. His parents live next door and," my uncle pauses here, takes a deep breath, "he used to be a good friend of our Yakira." I have to strain to hear this last line.

"Shalom, Miriam."

"Hi." I play with my new necklace instead of reaching for my comb. Any thought I had of finding out more about my father takes flight. This is the boy next door!

"Guy, would you like to sit with us, or are you in a rush to play your game? It might be nice for Miriam to meet someone her own age." He looks at his watch. "What am I thinking? I missed the time. Leah must be fuming. Guy, my boy, you are my lucky charm tonight. Would you take Miriam around for me and make sure she gets home? I promised Leah something that I'd do for her." He turns color as he does every time he mentions his wife's name. "And I'm late. I am sorry for my rudeness. You forgive me, Miriam?"

"Of course. Is everything okay?"

"Yes, yes, you know just something. You'll be safe with Guy. He's like a son. Goodnight. See you later. *L'hitraot.*"

Moshe already has one foot facing the exit. He gives me a quick kiss on the cheek, shakes Guy's hand, and he is gone.

"It's nice to meet you, Miriam. Where you from again? I was planning to suggest a game of backgammon to a friend, but I always win anyway." He grins and shrugs at me.

"Canada. I'm new here." I try not to stare at my new companion, but my eyes embrace him from head to toe.

"So, the Mediterranean at night is new for you?"

I nod. I cannot remember what I look like, if I have any makeup on so late in the evening or if I stained my shirt at dinner. I don't know where to put my hands, so I hold them in my lap.

"Let's go then," he holds out his strong, bare arm, and I hesitate. I haven't linked arms with anyone new in two years.

"How's my English?" he asks.

"It's good." I take a deep breath and let him take my arm. "That's what my roommates keep asking me, too."

"You have roommates. Let me guess. You are a student. You can practice your Hebrew on me if you want."

"*Beseder.*"

I don't say I've had a whole week of practicing Hebrew at the university and I'm on a ten-month program. I lean in a drop closer. In spite of the warm night, he smells like the woods after a rainstorm.

In twenty minutes we are sitting on a wooden bench overlooking the Mediterranean Sea. Every few minutes people walking alone or in small groups pass us, but no one sits on the bench beside ours. My mind drifts to my uncle's story about leaving his family in the city to find a better life in the North.

"Tell me, Miriam. A pretty girl like you has a boyfriend waiting for her somewhere, no? Something is bothering you. I can tell."

"It's hard to explain."

He smiles at me. He takes two cigarettes out of his pack, lights them both and passes one to me.

"I had a boyfriend for a year or so. He's not the most exciting guy you've ever met, but he's nice and stable. You know what *stable* means?"

I cannot believe I'm revealing this to a total stranger. Maybe it's the sea. I never do this at home. Traveling seems more and more like the chance to inhabit a new body and try on a variety of images like teen girls let loose in a wig shop. No one had cautioned me about the effortless transformations in new places. And look at this guy? Thick black hair, creamy tanned skin, a dimple in his chin. The last thing I should be talking about is Neil.

"*Stable* means *standard* maybe?"

"*Predictable.* Like no surprises."

"Does that mean no fun?" he asks. He laughs at his own joke. "You want a drink? Anything you want I will get from the *moadon*. If not, what will your uncle say about my manners? I should have brought something with us. Beer? Cola?"

"Maybe a hot chocolate."

"Come on. It's the weekend. I'll get us some wine."

I shrug. No one as good looking as Guy has ever offered me a drink.

"I'll be right back."

Guy leaves, and I am forced to confront myself head on. I allow the sounds of the waves to relax my neck and shoulders and try to empty my mind. Soon I hear Guy treading back toward me up the path. I turn my head and see he is barefoot. He has a bottle of wine in one hand and two glasses in the other. I don't ask him what happened to his shoes, but his jeans seem slung lower than before and show off his flat stomach when he walks.

"So, you were telling me a story," he says, filling two glasses with white wine. "I like stories. *L'chaim*, or what do you like to say? Cheers?"

He clinks my glass with his own and sips.

Watching him put his full lips to the glass makes my own throat seem inordinately dry. He notices me staring and puts his glass to my own lips. They part. He tilts the glass, and I feel the cool wine on my tongue, sliding down my throat. He holds the glass now, only an inch from my mouth.

"More?" he asks.

I nod. My throat and stomach are already warming up. I haven't had wine in a long time. I've never been much of a drinker. He slips his hand around the stem of my glass and loosens my grip at the same time as he feeds me more wine. My stomach drops into my legs as his smooth skin brushes mine.

"Let's trade," he whispers, his mouth close to mine. I can feel his hot breath on my ear, in my hair. I try not to move, and I pray no one he knows will pass by, stop to chat.

"What did your boyfriend say when you told him you were leaving?" Guy speaks in a normal voice, maybe a drop lower than before. I clear my throat. I don't want to whine about Neil. I want my voice to come out just right, not like some overexcited, inexperienced little girl.

"The usual. How I must not really care for him. How he always knew I wouldn't be any different from his ex-girlfriend."

"Pshshshsh. Hard. He said those things really?"

"He might as well have."

"What will you do?"

"The usual. Nothing. It's a lifelong habit. He stopped talking to me six months ago when I told him."

"Lifelong habit? You don't look more than twenty."

"I am twenty. I mean, I'm not so good at standing up for myself. I'm one of those people who play back scenes after they're over and include all the things I should have said or done."

112

"Hmm. Not me. I can speak up for myself at the right time. Sometimes it's better to be quiet. I should work on that. I thought I'd meet a girl in the army at the end, but I felt tied down enough by my unit. I did meet a few nice girls in my last year, but no one that really stood out, you know? I mean, not really."

Guy looks away, as though he regrets saying too much.

I nod, trying to catch his eye. Did I stand out? He sure stood out to me. The 'not really' he threw in at the end was a dead giveaway. Someone had stood out to him along his route. He looks off into the distance, so I probe.

"Not really?"

Guy raises one shoulder. "There was a girl I dated all through high school. We thought we'd make it through army service, but you know, girls do two years and boys three usually." His voice trails off. I can hardly hear him.

"And?" I ask. I can hardly see him now. The moon has gone behind a cloud.

"And she was free you know while I was tied up the third year. She wanted to travel. India, Thailand."

"And?" Relax I tell myself. Let him reveal what he likes.

He raises both of his eyebrows.

"So far I got one postcard. Almost ten months ago now."

"I see."

"She always said she wanted to live overseas. Not me. This is my home."

I nod. Whoever this girl is, she's hurt him. Guy clears his throat.

"You want a chocolate?" Guy digs into his pocket and pulls out two heart-shaped chocolates. He tosses me one, unwraps the other, and pops it into his mouth. It is clear he wants to change the subject.

"Thanks. Can I ask you about Leah?"

"You can ask me anything. Who is Leah?"

"Leah Damari. My uncle's wife."

"What about her?" He finishes his cigarette and tosses it into the sand. The wind had burnt mine out. Guy notices and relights it for me, passing it again from his mouth to mine.

"She was very warm but didn't eat with us. My uncle said she was comforting a friend, but he wasn't so convincing."

Guy raises an eyebrow. "Seeing you rubs it in. Here comes the good girl first cousin. She comes *to* Israel instead of running away *from* it, not to mention the biological one."

A doorway opens in my mind, and I realize Yakira might be adopted. The blonde hair, the pale skin, the only daughter of two dark-skinned parents.

"I'm not sure you're right." I say this more to egg him on than anything else. I want to hear more.

"Yakira was a good girl, smart, but she got into this crowd, left-wing extremists. She forgot what her great-grandparents went through here under the Turks and then her own parents under the British, how they fought and died, so she could have all this." He points in the direction of the *moadon*. "Or she never bothered to find

114

out. Every one of their heroes became a terrorist in her eyes. What did she think the Jews who were living here in the forties should have done? Dive into the sea?" He shrugs.

"I take it you weren't in her crowd?"

"If you are asking me if I believe in mass suicide, no. I just finished three years in the army, believe me, I wouldn't wish it on anybody. I want peace for my kids one day, too, but until that day comes, we need to defend ourselves, and at the end of the day, history has proven that we are not safe anywhere. Jews deserve a tiny piece of land on this earth, too, no?"

I enjoy seeing him fired up, but I don't want him to overboil.

"Smart girl like you, nothing to say?"

"I feel as though whatever I say, someone tells me I have no right to say it because I don't live here."

"You're here now. It's worth trying to understand."

"Do you understand Yakira?"

"I think even the right value can be expressed in the wrong way."

I don't answer.

"You asked me about Leah. It's true she's not a typical kibbutznik, she works off the kibbutz, and you can imagine how it is around here. Her daughter refused to serve, ran away from the country. People talk. No doubt it makes her more withdrawn."

Guy draws in the sand with his toes. I watch the muscles in his calves while I think about what it might be like for Leah watching all of Yakira's classmates, the kids she grew up with all on the same block come home in uniform for weekends, while her own daughter is God knows where. This topic is beginning to put me off. I should just enjoy the evening with Guy. This mood is on its way to that place in my mind I dislike but that's so familiar and comfortable, I slip into it again and again, a recipe I only know how to spoil. Yakira made her decisions. No reason to ruin *my* night over them. If I haven't already.

I finish my wine. Guy finishes his glass and circles his forefinger around the rim. Silence settles around us, except for the reassuring sound of waves slapping against the shore. As the silence lengthens I'm convinced that I've made a fool of myself. I should never have asked about his close friend's mother or dug around in his love life. I don't know what I was expecting him to say.

"Isn't it the best down here by the water?" Guy changes the subject again and my shoulders relax. I thought he was about to suggest he walk me home as his way of letting me know I was about as fun as a used paper lunch bag. "What I really want to do is get a PhD in marine biology. That's my first love: the sea. I'm starting at the National Institute of Oceanography next semester. I'll be near you in Haifa. That might be nice, no?"

"Really? That's great." Is he kidding? That's the best news I've heard all week. He can be near me whenever he wants. I should just come right out and ask him when second semester begins. Guy refills both of our glasses and clinks his next to mine, but he pulls the same move and puts the rim of his glass to my lips before I have a chance to raise my own.

I sip again, but gulp deeper this time.

"Maybe I should have some water to balance this out?"

"Feeling out of balance?" He raises one eyebrow. I'm learning this is a signature motion.

"A little. Tell me more about the sea."

"The truth might sound corny to you."

"Try me."

His face brightens.

"Well, I grew up on the coast, and at the same time we are in the Middle East. Think about it. Right next door to Eilat there are millions of people in Egypt without enough food," he says. "Not to mention we have poor people of our own."

My brain scrambles to keep up with him. I'm definitely feeling the effects of the wine.

"I believe the best answer is the sea, a world of food. If we can farm fish more effectively and preserve our seas and oceans, we can eliminate starvation. It shouldn't exist. This is the true way to bring people together. Create enough food and prosperity for everyone."

I let his words sink in. They make me feel small, irrelevant. I never thought much beyond surviving the next day. I studied English literature because I enjoyed it, not because I thought it would help anybody else.

"How come you're not saying anything? Do I sound, what's the word? Cliché?"

117

"No!" My answer comes out too emphatically. "I mean, I admire that you have a dream that is so much larger than yourself. That's really something."

Guy's face lights up, and it's all I can do not to reach out and touch his skin, brush my lips against his. He has a five o'clock shadow that suits him, and I long to rub my fingers across it.

"I'm always hanging out by the sea here on the kibbutz." He settles his arm on my shoulder and little currents of electricity go off in my arms. "I do my own little water temperature experiments at the fish ponds, or I study the behavior of the fish. You know in Judaism, a fish is seen by some people as a symbol of good luck?"

"Really?"

"You didn't know that? Fish are said to have survived the Flood. Noah's Ark and all that. That makes them lucky."

The wine has gone from my head to everywhere else now. I put my glass down on the bench so I won't drop it, and when Guy holds up the bottle I shake my head. I'd better take a break.

Guy leans closer to me. His wine glass is still in his hand, but now his arm rests on my waist. "Did you hear what I said? You seem a little out to sea yourself."

"Every word," I answer.

"What's the last thing I said?" He inches closer to me.

"It had to do with luck. My uncle said this necklace should bring me luck."

"I would feel lucky if you'd let me kiss you."

"I would feel lucky if you kissed me."

But Guy doesn't kiss me. He steps behind me and pours a couple of drops of wine down the back of my neck, and I straighten as the cold liquid drips down from my neck to my spine. He pours more until his glass is empty. Then he kisses the back of my neck where my skin is wet and slides up my shirt at the back with his fingertips, tracing the wine with his lips all the way down to my waist. I close my eyes and feel him behind me. Soon he kisses my back in reverse, starting at my waist and kissing me softly up my spine until he reaches my neck.

I turn to face him with my mouth already open and pull his lips down on mine, my hand at the back of his neck. His lips are warm and soft, and he tastes like the sea and sweet wine. His arms are around my waist, and my free hand moves to rest on his shoulder. He feels so different from Neil, who always had a bit of stubble around his chin and dry lips, and there's no way I ever would have been so forward with him.

He pulls his head back and smiles at me, and all I can think is that he's this experienced ex-soldier who's kissed dozens of beautiful women, while I've had one real boyfriend my whole life and we weren't what anyone would call adventurous. Even at the drive-in Neil kept his eyes on the screen until the last credit rolled.

Guy might have kissed me for three minutes or thirteen. I've lost track of time. We sit down on the bench holding hands, and he kisses me again. I am aware of his mouth, hot now, tasting of wine and chocolate, and the cool sand beneath my feet and nothing else. There is the sound of people laughing not far away. It grows closer and Guy begins to pull away. There must be other late-night strollers.

"Hey, you live near the beach in Canada?" Guy lets me go, stands up, and removes his shirt all in one movement, but I am in a daze, circling the sand beneath the bench with my toe and don't notice. I don't want to break this mood by looking up, and I don't want any of the passersby to notice me either, just in case my uncle is searching for me. They don't appear to be aware of us. I wait until they pass to speak.

"There's a small beach on a river, but it's nothing like this, and the winters are long so the river's ice half the year."

Finally I glance upward, and he's taken off his pants. He wears nothing but black trunks.

"Let's go for a swim."

My mouth drops.

"Don't worry, I'm a lifeguard. You're safe with me. Miriam is the one who sings the 'Song of the Sea' in the Bible, no? So you must like my first love: water. Come on."

He turns and races toward the Mediterranean. Splash. I am left holding my empty glass in mid-air.

"Join me," he calls. "It's great in here." He swims beyond the shore until he is a dot on the water. "You're missing out."

His voice is closer and then farther and then closer again. I look both ways to see if anyone else is around. It's late. Most people have turned in for the night.

I glide to the shoreline almost on tiptoe. I'd slipped off my sandals when I noticed Guy returned barefoot, allowed my feet to play in the sand. I watch his strong body swim in perfect strokes toward a giant rock a distance from the shore. I feel him kiss me along my spine all over again, lick off the wine.

Take off my clothes and swim with someone I just met on my uncle's kibbutz? What if people see us and it gets back to him? What will he think of his niece? A cheap slut who comes from overseas to embarrass him? And if he never invites me again? Or tells my father? I don't know if this is a normal thing to do here. I don't know the rules. I've never been on a kibbutz.

Guy sings now in garbled Hebrew I cannot make out. Then he's under the water again. I watch him until he reappears, smoothing his black hair down, naked in the water from the waist up. I don't want this moment to end.

"You afraid of the cold? I thought you are Canadian?"

That's it. I strip down to my bra and underwear. I'm certain my two glasses of wine are the source of my decision. A voice in my head protests: *This is crazy!* This is not me at all. I'm giving him the impression that I'm a slut. I've never undressed in front of a stranger. I'm the type who goes into a cubicle at a woman's gym.

I hesitate at the edge of the water, and the part of my mind that's not wine soaked urges me backward, but my body can still feel Guy's warm arms and longs to give in for once, to be free of my nonstop sense of maternal abandonment and paternal guilt. I leave my new Eilat stone necklace on. In a minute I am in the Mediterranean. Free. This is fun.

I look around, but the only light comes from the moon, and the one light above the bench about 30 meters away casts dim patches of pale white on the water. I don't know where Guy is. I lie on my back and close my eyes. Let him sneak up on me if he likes. Maybe he will bring the bottle of wine into the water, pour the rest of it over my bare shoulders into the sea. Then he could taste it on my collarbone and down my chest.

I feel as though I have discovered a new part of me, one that is not always apprehensive and apologetic, afraid people will discover that my parents are nothing more than longed-for ships at sea, my mother dead, my father a hollowed-out rock.

"Miriam Gil! Is that you?"

Oh no. There are only two people besides Guy who know me on this kibbutz, and it's a woman's voice. Maybe I'm wrong. My ears are half submerged. I must be imagining a voice.

"Miriam, why don't you answer me?"

I move to the edge of the water and crouch, leaving the water to cover me up to my shoulders, bare except for bra straps. In the dim light I make out the profile of my aunt Leah. Did she follow me?

"What are you doing? Guy, for heaven's sake. It's the middle of the night. What if something happened to you out here? Who would hear you?"

"You know, I'm a lifeguard, Leah," Guy's voice is light as air. He eases himself out of the water and unselfconsciously slips back into his jeans.

I splash out of the water with no grace, like a skidding stone. Now I am on the beach struggling to put my T-shirt back on against my wet, salty skin, my new necklace twisted down my back. I want to crawl under the sand, but I follow Guy's lead and force myself to dress at a normal pace. I can't imagine what Leah's doing at the beach at this time of night.

"I will take you back to our place." Leah waits, her arms folded across her chest. She taps her foot on the stone path, making a percussive noise.

"It's okay, Leah. I am a professional escort."

"Thank you, Guy. No. It's out of your way."

Guy shrugs, winks at me.

"It was fun to meet you." He picks up my hand and brushes my fingers with his lips. My stomach drops. Neil would never do something so romantic.

"My room is easy to find, near the cow shed. Visit me next time you come, okay?"

Then he is gone, the bottle of wine and both empty glasses still on the shore. I resist the urge to clean them up, to take any ownership of them in front of Leah. We hike in silence and in spite Leah's attempt to hurry, she's not capable of striding, so the walk is endless, double the length of time I remember walking with Guy. Maybe she'll throw out her cheap niece.

By the time we are in viewing distance of the dining hall, Leah stops and turns to me. "What if something had happened to you? Do you have any idea how dangerous it is to swim at night and mixing it with alcohol? We are responsible for each other on this kibbutz and that includes Guy, and responsible for you while you're here.

We'd be liable. Do you have any idea the risk you were taking now? You think no one's ever drowned on the coast?"

I burn with shame and mumble an apology, but my tongue feels heavy in my mouth. Bird-song fills the night, but I am not soothed by their melodies, all I can hear is the beating of my own heart.

Chapter Thirteen

MY EYES SEARCH FOR LEAH the next morning at breakfast, but I haven't seen her since she let us in without a word last night and disappeared into her bedroom, not even turning her head to see if I'd locked the door behind me.

I am reluctant to ask for her, and my uncle and I pass the morning reading on the beach, which is all but deserted except for one other family with three small children. Uncle Moshe explains to me that the beach gets crowded only after lunch in the late afternoon on Saturdays, and by that time we would be long gone. I look around for him, but don't dare mention Guy. My uncle said few kibbutzniks come down to the beach in November, even though it is unusually warm. If Leah had said anything to my uncle about Guy, I couldn't tell. I wish I could relax about it and stop feeling like a naughty child.

By noon the sun has warmed me through to the bone and I doze on the lawn chair my uncle brought down in a wagon at the end of his bicycle, a common mode of transportation on the kibbutz. The squealing of happy children jars me awake, and when I have both eyes open and pick up my head, it is Leah I see perched in my uncle's place. I don't know where he's gone, but sitting up and taking in a wider view, I am dismayed to realize he's nowhere around.

"Your uncle's gone to his crossword puzzle meeting as he does every Saturday morning before lunch," Leah explains, reading my expression.

I pray she doesn't say anything about last night that will humiliate me in this lawn chair. My stomach churns. I suck in my cheeks, but stare past her at the sea, it almost looks black. I busy myself with sunblock, rubbing it into my legs. I can't think what to say. I'll hide in my novel if my uncle doesn't return in a few minutes. My fear of my aunt is tangible, towering over me, stronger than the Middle Eastern sun. She had been so warm and welcoming, and I had acted irresponsibly and scared her.

"You had a nice time last night with Guy?"

Oh no. She's cut right to the chase. I clear my throat.

"It was fun."

"It looked it." I am surprised to see out of the corner of my eye that Leah is smiling at me. "He's a nice-looking boy, a good boy. I was pleased to see him having fun with a girl. He had a girlfriend for so long. Everyone was convinced they were an item from now until eternity and then poof! Gone."

I nod. My fear descends a few degrees. Perhaps I've been misreading her. Maybe she's forgiven me.

"Here. You'd better drink. You slept for a while." Leah leans over and places a tall glass of lemonade in my hand. I thank her and take a sip. It's good, not too sweet, not too cold.

"I'm sure Moshe will get himself busy with lunch as soon as he's done comparing crossword puzzles with his gang. It's a ten-year-old bet they've got going." Leah chuckles.

126

I want to hear more about Guy, but I don't want to be presumptuous. Maybe Guy isn't her main topic of interest.

"You look like your mother," she says.

"That's what Uncle Moshe said."

"I just thought with your father being so dark, you'd come out more like him. Not that I don't see a resemblance, I do. You've got his beautiful hands for sure. Lovely shaped nails wasted on a man. Why don't you do yours? I've got plenty of polish. Take what you like."

I hold up my hands and look at them as though for the first time. No one has ever known my father well enough to compare my hands to his. I don't feel comfortable asking her why she would remember my father's hands so well. Some people notice everything. I don't ask her if the polish is hers or leftovers from her long-gone daughter.

"Your father was a good-looking man in his day. Well built. Does he still enjoy that sort of thing?"

"Sure."

"I guess it's been a while since your mother, he has no trouble with women."

An alarm bell goes off in my head. Is she asking me if my father dates other women since my mother died? Is this a Saturday afternoon girls' gossip session? Well, I suppose it's been thirty years, she's entitled to some curiosity about her brother-in-law. I clear my throat.

"My father's not interested in dating." I change my tone, try to sound less defensive. I can't seem to arrange my arms or legs properly.

"I think he's—" My eyes are shinier than I'd like them to be. I swallow. "I think he's still in love with my mother. He's never taken her photograph down off the wall in his room or out of his wallet for that matter."

All of this is true. Jacquie's only a blip on a screen. For all I know they've already parted ways and my father's alone in the evenings again. Either way there's no chance he's doing anything more than using her for company after so many years of puttering around on his own. I refuse to believe he could have any true feelings for that bloodsucker, and I'll be damned if I'm mentioning her to Leah. With luck my absence had doused my father in cold water, and Jacquie's a memory.

Leah clears her throat, and I see her face has fallen flat, and now it is she who looks as though she might cry. I've said too much. She must always be on the cusp of loss. I've never told a soul my father still carries my mother's photograph in his wallet. It seemed to me the most natural thing in the world until now that I've actually uttered the words. I've never given a thought to my father moving on, getting over her. I assumed this was the ground he'd stand on until the end.

"That must be hard." She doesn't say for whom—for him or for me. Neither of us speaks for a moment. She takes out her own sunscreen and busies herself applying it to her face and neck, rubbing in wide circles, so it's hard for me to read her expression.

"About the swimming with Guy, you need to be careful, Miriam." She says my name with the accent on the last syllable. No one's ever pronounced my name that way before. All her *th*'s and *w*'s come out sounding like *v*'s or *d*'s: *svimming, wid*.

A shade paler from the cream, she eyes me, scrutinizing me, and a shiver runs up my spine in spite of the warm weather. "Israeli men are not the same as the Canadian men you are familiar with." She speaks what I can describe only as gravely, and I try but fail to read the meaning beneath her words. I play with the sand, allowing it to fall through my open fingers. We're the only ones left on the beach besides two amateur surfers, who are spending more time in the water than on their surfboards.

"I'm not familiar with guys, really." I hope she doesn't think I'm being coy.

"Of course, you're young, a girl. Nevertheless, I want to warn you, Miriam. I want you to be careful. The men here can be so alluring. They have something warm, something passionate for life. Maybe it's the army, the threat hanging over them all of the time. And a young, innocent girl can fall so hard so fast and then—" She spreads her arms wide, her palms open, and shrugs. "And then bam! Like a sniper. You go down. Okay? You hear what I'm saying?"

I nod, open-mouthed. I can feel sand on my teeth. The wind picks up. Maybe she thinks this is what really happened to Yakira. She didn't fall in love with an ideology, but a man behind an ideology. I wouldn't dare ask.

"We were just clowning around, me and Guy."

She holds up a hand, all five fingers together: stop.

129

"I'm not trying to be like a mother hen or something like that. Just that you hear me. It's enough. Come now. I'm starving. Let's see what your old uncle's put on the table for the girls." She holds out her hand, and I let her pull me up. She's strong for a middle-aged woman with a limp.

For the second time in less than twenty-four hours, we walk home together from the beach without speaking, but this time I am lost in thought, puzzling over her words. We will be sharing lunch on the spacious balcony that is double the size of the living room. I am grateful when Moshe switches on the radio. Within a few minutes he's tuned into a news program and Leah's busied herself with a puzzle, making no effort with lunch. I assume Saturday lunches are my uncle's department, as he motions me into a chair.

As he listens Uncle Moshe lays out a cotton tablecloth with a colorful coconut palm decor on which he sets out a bowl of hard-boiled eggs, purple cabbage salad, shredded carrots, sliced bread, cherry jam, and triangular doughy cheese pastries that he calls *bourekas*.

"The dining hall is not to my taste on Saturdays," he says. "Pancakes." He sticks out his tongue like a child.

I'm afraid to say pancakes sound delicious. I can see why they seem far too American to appeal to Moshe; my father would have turned his nose up at them, too.

"If you'd lived overseas, you'd have eaten pancakes like everybody else," Leah snaps, as if to say her husband would never stand out wherever he went, he'd fall into line already populated by the wishy-washy, the everyday, be indistinguishable from any crowd.

A sense of anxiety passes over me. But then my thoughts really don't sound far-fetched. They share an only child who looks down her nose at them so hard she's taken flight. It's bound to cause waves in any marriage.

"Because you're so adaptable doesn't mean it's for everybody," Moshe murmurs, retreating. "You know, Miriam, your aunt lived overseas when she was young."

Leah glances hard at Moshe, as though he's stepped on her naked toe with his shoes on.

"That's nice. Where did you live?" I ask.

"I saw New York and stayed in Montreal for a while." Leah's mouth is full of hard-boiled egg, she stuffs in a *boureka* and covers her mouth with a serviette while she chews.

"It was a long time ago, before you were born even," Moshe adds. "Shush, now the news. I think Yitzhak Shamir is still burning over his loss to Rabin, no? The Left is getting somewhere he never got to." Leah eyes him, her expression sours. She grips another hard-boiled egg in her hand, and it cracks. We fall silent while the news comes on.

"You think any Israeli with a brain believes in the peace Rabin's talking about?" Leah asks.

"I think you're still a Jerusalemite at heart, not a *kibbutznik*. Rabin's on to something. Many people are exhausted from wars, and where are they getting us?"

"We're still here, that's where."

Moshe shrugs. "True, but maybe the other side is tired, too. How many years of fighting?"

Leah scoffs. "I can tell you something about Arabs. They have the patience of crocodiles. If you know anything about crocodiles, you know they wait for their prey as long as it takes, even until they are starving themselves."

I turn to face her. Fascinated. Uncle Moshe rubs his knees with his palms.

"And what do they do while they're waiting? Study the behavior of the other side, their victims, always watching and learning. For them forty-two years is nothing, we're still in a cradle compared to them. Shamir knows this. Rabin pretends he doesn't."

Moshe looks annoyed. He cracks his knuckles and stretches his legs. Each time he opens his mouth to respond, his eyes dart toward me and he stops. "Do you want me to turn the channel?" Moshe asks Leah.

"No, let's wait for the weather to come on."

There's no more conversation after that.

After lunch I leave them both nibbling on thick slices of halvah and comb through the library. Leah has an extraordinary number of books on policing, public administration, national security, and emergency management both in Hebrew and English. Her name is written on the inside of all of them. There are no cookbooks, novels, or fashion magazines, which is all my mother had on her bookshelves.

In my bedroom there are four different nail polish bottles on the side table next to my bed. I assume Leah put them there for me to use. Soon I'm sprawled on the double bed, painting both my finger and toenails a caramel color, which reminds me of the beach at night.

I begin writing a letter to my father but tear up two false starts until I lift my hands and fill in the postcards Uncle Moshe had left on my bed along with the two towels, writing paper, and two pens. I write one to my father to tell him I'm having a great time, with three exclamation points after the word *great*.

Hugging the pillow, I review everything Moshe told me about my father after only one meal together. He is the first person I've ever been frank and honest with about him, it's not something I take for granted, but it's not the feeling of lightness I anticipated. No. I'm heavier than before.

It turns out I'd been judging a man who had lived through horrors I could never imagine, and Moshe had said it in a way I couldn't gloss over as I do at home. An ill mother. A poverty-stricken city. Starvation.

Why did I find it so easy to give my uncle a pass, not judging him for choosing the kibbutz over Jerusalem, and so hard to cut my father even the slightest slack? There's a photograph of Yakira in the top drawer, and I take it out to study it. She asked a similar question about her parents, whether she should cut them any slack, and gave her answer. No. Abandoning my father. Letting him wonder if I'm alive or dead. It's not the answer I'm prepared to give.

After a light dinner, it is time to go. In the semi-blindness of dusk, Moshe somehow senses my hesitation about next week.

"I will see you next week?" he asks. He puts his hand on my shoulder.

"Are you sure?"

133

"Of course, you must come again. Tell me, do you have anywhere else to go? I went to university. You think I don't know it shuts down on *Shabbat*. Speaking of going, I want to give you a few things. Come."

Uncle Moshe leads me down the well-kept paths toward the dining hall. I keep my eyes on my uncle and my mind off Guy. It is ridiculous for me to expect him to say goodbye. It was just a spontaneous swim out of thousands of swims he must have had living on the seaside, nothing more.

But it had already been more for me. I couldn't stop thinking about his muscular arms and smooth back, his passion to feed the Middle East. I feel his tongue on my neck. I shake my head.

"Let's start with fruits and vegetables. And then move on to the dry foods." Moshe leads me into a storage room filled with fresh produce. I inhale the earthy smell. "We take as much as we need for ourselves, for our households. You might as well take."

In one night I had become an extension of the household. It's something I want to take back to Haifa with me and a warmth I attach to my Eilat stone necklace.

Forty-five minutes later I stumble back to my uncle's home under the weight of his gifts. I peer into the night seeking his terracotta-colored door, which is one in a row of identical white stone houses with terracotta-colored doors and matching red roof tiling.

The neighborhoods look so similar I have to follow him closely to avoid walking up the wrong path. Fresh fruits and vegetables bulge through my backpack. Under the cucumbers, tomatoes, onions, eggplant, zucchini, tangerines and pears, I have a kilo of white rice and white sugar, a tin of coffee and another of black tea. In one hand I have three loaves of plain sliced bread banging against my knee in a heavy plastic bag and two dozen eggs that my uncle promises he can find a container for, so they won't break on my bus ride back.

I repack the food as best as I can after I've sprawled it out on the dining room table, praying the eggs won't crack on the bus.

I am ready to go. Leah has vanished for good it seems. Moshe squeezes my shoulder.

"You thought I might be upset with you because Hanan doesn't take my calls. He has reason to be upset with me, Miriam. True he might have gotten over it in thirty years, but the heart is a fragile thing."

"Moshe, what are you babbling about to the girl?" Leah appears in the doorway and for the first time I see her with a cane. There is an edge in her voice, an admonition. I resist asking him the same question.

"Nothing, Leah. Just saying goodbye."

"Goodbye, Leah," I chime in. "Thank you for your hospitality."

She gives me another bear hug, and I lean down so she can kiss me on both cheeks. I kiss her back and inhale her meat and cabbage smell.

"Please don't be a stranger," she says. "And if you need anything, call right away."

"I will."

I had already made it clear to my uncle that I could find the bus stop on my own, and I scurry toward the

135

dim semi-circle in the road with the broken lamppost, ignoring the weight of my backpack.

A car stops in front of me and a woman I don't recognize offers me a ride. She must be one of the people my uncle introduced me to in the dining hall because she calls me by name. I thank her and walk on. I don't mind the walk, and I might spot Guy somewhere.

There's surprisingly little light, but I notice a drugstore near the bus stop. Kibbutz stores are not for profit, ideal for my budget. My backpack's too full for anything more than weightless items. No one will steal it, but I shove it into a dark corner near the bus stop just in case.

As I examine the eyeliners and mascaras, my mind wanders back to the conversation about my father. I need to get more out of my uncle. The gap between Israel and Canada is still too wide. I hear a familiar voice, and I realize it's Leah with a female friend. I watch as they inch toward the shampoo section, but for some reason I don't call out. I itch to hear what Leah thinks of me after last night with Guy.

"She is beautiful," I hear Leah saying. They're in the large baby section. "Of course, no one can compare to my Yakira, but twenty is twenty."

Vered? I thought my uncle said she's in a wheelchair. If it's the same Vered, she's recovered quickly.

"We were, too," Vered says.

They're talking about me. My heart races. I creep along one aisle over from them trying to listen and look natural to any passerby at the same time.

"Are you kidding? Before the accident they used to stop me on the street," Leah says.

"I'm sure," Vered answers. I can see them through the shelving. Vered looks about the same age as Leah with wavy, white hair, but it's hard to tell from the back.

"She's Hanan's daughter through and through, let's not kid ourselves," Leah says as they enter the soap aisle and Leah pauses to read labels. "One hundred percent devil."

I jump at the word *devil* and force myself to freeze.

"The monster. One week. Seven goddamned days after our divorce, which he insisted on doing through lawyers. After ten years of eating my heart."

"It's terrible. There's no excuse," the friend says.

"Go skiing, they all said. It will take your mind off things, a change of scene. Blahblahblah. I didn't even see that boulder," Leah says.

"You didn't die," Vered answers. "That's what matters."

"I could have. Three weeks in hospital and the pain. Agony. And the first thing the doctor said to me when I woke up," Leah says.

"You'll limp the rest of your life," Vered finishes for her, chants in a way that says she's heard this story dozens of times. "No phone call, no note, not a flower, not a breath. Might as well have been dead and buried. I hear you, darling. Poor thing."

"You're the only one who understands. A decade I served him on my knees, and I could have bled to death on a mountain of snow for all he cared." Leah slams a box of cookies back on the shelf. "The apple doesn't fall far from the tree."

"Rotten to the core, no question," Vered says. "Moshe understands. He's an angel. I'm not the only one. And when Yakira's been married long enough, she'll understand, too."

"Hah. You'd think Yakira was Hanan's," Leah says. "If I thought he was smart enough I would suspect *him* of luring her away," she says.

This conversation is surreal. It can't be true.

"Maybe it's not so good that this girl should visit. She's like a golem, a spook," Vered says, shaking her head from side to side.

I realize I've been holding my breath and race out of the store. A monster, a golem, a spook.

The rumble of a bus pulls my attention away from the drugstore where no doubt Leah and Vered are still involved in their agonizing tale. I turn, grab my bag, grunting under its weight and run to catch it. I need to get out of here.

Chapter Fourteen

ON BOARD THE BUS I am thrilled to see Valerie.

"Hey! Awesome. Our coordination worked. I told you we could figure out the damn bus schedules."

I tumble into the seat beside her. I'd forgotten all about our plan to get on the same bus Saturday night. I need to think about what Leah said when I'm alone. It doesn't make sense. The most obvious answer is to question my father, but he's not someone who takes well to questioning.

"Check you out: You're loaded," Valerie says.

"We'll eat like queens this week," I answer.

I look around for Maayan, which seems counterintuitive. She should be someone I can't avoid seeing.

"Maayan stayed at home an extra night," Valerie answers without me saying a word. "She wanted to shop with her mom. She's a regular mall rat. Hey, did you notice the driver?"

"What?"

"He was looking at me before. We could use a driver once in a while stuck up on that hill. I'm going to get up when the bus slows for the next stop and chat him up."

I shoot her a puzzled look. She wants to become friendly with the bus driver?

"You look like you've been on the beach. Lucky. We spent half the day cleaning out Maayan's fridge. You know she has a mini one in her room all to herself? Her parents are divorced, and she gets whatever she wants as compensation." Valerie draws the edges of her mouth downward, remembering. "Now I stink like expired hummus, shrunken cucumbers, and clumpy date honey. Yuck. I could hardly breathe with the smell of disinfectant."

"Mmmhmm."

The rhythm of the bus is making me sleepy. I had too much sun, and Leah's conversation has freaked me out. With each stop the bus becomes increasingly crowded until the number of passengers plateaus on the highway. I am surrounded by soldiers in their khaki-green, white, and khaki-beige uniforms returning to their bases after the weekend.

"Why not just tell Maayan that you came to Israel to have fun and travel, not to clean her room?" I have no idea what Valerie is talking about anymore, and I realize I'm overdoing it. She'd lost me after the mini-fridge story, but she's enjoying the complaining, so I don't stop to ask what she really did all weekend.

"You're right. I should," she says, sticking her hand into her open backpack. "Then I had to put up with a whole weekend of this bogus friend of hers." She takes out a plastic container, opens it, and removes a white plastic fork. I smell a mixture of chocolate and peanut butter.

Valerie sticks her finger down her throat. She's really lost me now, but I smile at her antics. I want to tell her about Guy at the right time, when I'm awake.

A piercing siren fills the air. The bus had been half full when I boarded, but it is now standing room only. The passengers with any access to windows crane their necks almost as one limb, as their eyes search for the source of the sound. The bus comes to a screeching halt.

I'd been just about ready to break through Valerie's narrative, show off my new necklace, when I feel it fall. My palms instinctively cover my ears. I inhale deeply but don't smell smoke.

Valerie, a forkful of food halfway to her lips, looks toward the front of the bus with large eyes. She squeezes my knee but refrains from competing with the alarm. The shrieking stops.

I lean into Valerie and catch a whiff of chocolate mixed with fresh deodorant and Colgate. I notice her face is still frozen, so I smile then crouch down on the floor, my fingers feeling around for my necklace. Got it. I sit back in my seat. Valerie hasn't offered to help me or even asked what I'm doing on the floor.

"Some super high-tech theft alarm must have gone off. Maybe in one of those buildings off the highway."

No sooner do I finish my sentence when the blaring of police sirens sound, followed by a voice booming through a megaphone, "Stay back. Clear the area. *Hefetz hashud*."

"What does that mean?" Valerie asks.

"Suspicious object on the road."

I marvel at how calm the Israelis around me remain at the sounds of sirens, alarms, extraordinarily loud noises. I fill with envy at their composure, close my eyes, and imagine what my father would say: *Nothing scares me. Don't be soft, Canadian like your mother. Be strong.*

More honks mixed with low rumbles. The murmuring inside the bus is all at once loud and I realize the other passengers are not only composed, they are no longer the least concerned and have resumed their conversations and laughter. The bus driver might have lowered the volume on his radio for a minute or two, but it's back at regular volume now.

Boom. Rumble. Boom. There's a secondary explosion.

"If it's two booms, it was a real bomb," the woman in front of me says to her partner.

"God protect us," he answers.

Valerie has been silent since the first abrupt blast. In the dim light, she does not take her eyes off the bomb squad clearing the road in front of the bus, her neck craned at an unnatural angle to see through the crowd. Behind us the traffic is already backed up for as far as I can make out in the darkness, twisting myself around in my seat and crouching on my knees.

In front of the bus there are six sappers, soldiers trained to clear mines, in state-of-the-art body armor on the highway. I note one of them is female, her ponytail sticks out of her cap. The area is sealed off in minutes, halting traffic in both directions. The bus is becoming overheated, and a few passengers have pushed the windows open in spite of the air conditioning. Then it is over. In half an hour the highway looks like any other highway on a Saturday evening anywhere in the Western world.

Momentarily stricken, Valerie pales against her freshly applied pink gloss, the one she reapplies countless times a day. She packs away her snack, stands up, elbows her way forward a step then flits back to her seat. She wanted to approach the driver but realized it's too soon since his route's been interrupted. Surely, he is more concerned with getting his bus back on schedule than with some young American student. I hope she'll forget all about him now. She's fearless of strangers, but this bomb scare has clearly thrown her.

"Someone must have phoned in with a report or something," I offer. "I heard on the news with my uncle today that Dan Quayle, is in town, so they're taking all precautions. It's routine here, I think."

"That was a real bomb we could have driven over," she answers.

Valerie is reapplying her lip gloss with a trembling hand.

"That was a bit of a scare. I won't pretend I've ever seen a bomb squad in action before. But danger? Looked like top security. I reckon where I'm from it's more dangerous to drive on icy roads, and how many months a year do we do that?"

The color returns to Valerie's cheeks and she laughs. A few heads turn to stare at us. I pretend I don't see them.

"You're right. I almost got myself killed last time I drove in a snowstorm. My brother wasn't too happy about his car. My only compensation was that it was totaled. Hey, you haven't told me anything newsworthy? Anything cool happen?"

I breathe deeply as I consider what to tell Valerie. I show off my new necklace then I plunge into my midnight swim story about Guy.

"You must be wigged out! Swimming alone at midnight. That's awesome. You should put that in your letter to dipstick."

"You think that's common on a kibbutz?" I ask her.

"I have no idea. It's not common in LA, but you said he was a combat soldier, right?"

"I think so."

"Duh? What's a midnight dip to him? Nothing. I should have gone with you instead of playing maid all weekend."

I smile and I hope it's enough of a response. I want to leave Valerie with the image of me on the beach at night in the water with an irresistible guy, not with my chin at my chest, with my tail between my legs, burning with embarrassment behind an aunt I'd known for twenty-four hours who thinks I'm the spawn of a monster. Somehow, I know she's talking about my father. I don't know how I know it, but I do, and she said that part so convincingly, she must believe it.

Chapter Fifteen

I<small>T'S LATE WHEN</small> I <small>STICK MY KEY INTO THE LOCK</small> and open the door, which creaks louder than ever. My shoulder hurts from lugging all of the food my uncle had sent with me. Valerie hadn't even offered to help me carry any of it, which I could only understand in the context of how much that bomb scare had let her imagination run wild, had concretized for her that we're actually here, live on scene—not watching Israel through a camera lens thousands of miles away.

Only a short while ago, I'd been a hair's breadth from a bomb squad called to dismantle a real bomb. A bomb! The meaning of this experience cloaks my shoulders, sinking them closer to my shaky legs, and I slow down as I lock the door behind me, take a deep breath, and command my knees to steady themselves with silent pleas.

I'd expected a greeting of silence topped with semi-darkness, with the only light coming from the moon and the campus glow outside, and that matched my needs perfectly: the expected darkness to bathe in until I could regain my composure. Instead, all of the entrance and kitchen lights are on, and Dalit sits straight-backed at the table, with her nose in a history textbook.

I immediately see myself whizzing past her, even on wobbly legs, picking up momentum and gliding into my own bedroom with the grace of a figure skater. I don't want to show Dalit how frazzled I am. She might ask why and I don't want to have a conversation about bombs on highways and who they might have been planted by.

Our eyes meet, and I feel a powerful sense of hopelessness. Maybe if I'd had an everyday bus ride home, I could have made it to my room undamaged, but the way my knees are shaking, I don't have a chance.

"Something is wrong?" Dalit asks. "You don't look like yourself."

Her hair has been cut, and it reaches only the bottom of her ears now. Since the last time I saw her she has streaked her hair blond. Her lipstick has worn off, and the rust-colored liner remains, giving her an unusually unfinished appearance. She pats the plastic chair beside her and pours tea from the small teapot on the table, an item she stores in her room, into a glass cup with no handles.

"Where did you say your uncle's kibbutz was?" she asks. At this moment I am sure she can read my mind. She continues before I have a chance to speak. "In the North, no? What's it called? *Yalah*, come and sit down. You need a drink, but the bathroom first. I'll wait."

I nod and let my bags drop to the side of the front door. The sound of their collapse rings in my ears. After I use the bathroom, I splash lukewarm water on my face and neck and comb my hair with my fingers.

"I have food to put away." That's my only response as I re-enter the kitchen, stretch my arms behind my back, and slide my bags across the floor with one foot. I sense trouble as I open the fridge in the nearby kitchen and begin to clear space on my shelf. The kitchen smells of bleach as it does whenever Dalit comes near it. She refills an oversized bleach bottle on the top shelf regularly. Normally, I recoil at the smell, but now it is making a welcome dent in my foggy mind. If only I could bleach my thoughts.

"Galim, that's it. I heard about the suspicious object on the road now on the radio. The bomb that blocked the highway. I come in from the same direction. I was only a little ahead of you. Were you there?"

I nod, but I don't look at Dalit. I stop organizing my food and make a cup of tea.

"This scared you, yes? No such things in Canada."

I concentrate on the space I share with Simona in the fridge. It's the barest of all three shelves so far, but now I begin to cram it with food, starting with the cucumbers, onions, and tomatoes. I then put away the white rice, white sugar, and white bread I'd sliced myself in a kibbutz slicing-machine. There's nowhere to put all of the eggs besides a plastic cereal bowl that barely holds more than six. I'll have to boil up the rest in the morning. The container Uncle Moshe used is impossibly big for this fridge, so it's useless now. I can hear Farzeen's radio playing from their room, a song in Arabic. For the first time I wish she'd burst out of her room and interrupt us.

"Well, have you nothing to say?" Her brown eyes dance now.

"Civilians should never be targets."

Dalit has picked a bad night. There was last night's humiliation with my aunt and then the crazy conversation she had with her friend in the drugstore and to top it off the bomb scare on the highway. I'm too worked up.

"I think God sent you this message, Miriam, so that you can see what we are living with here. Why do you think we need those bomb squads? To protect us from the Arabs. Now you see they want to kill us. Maybe you understand my little request better now?"

I don't respond. In my head I tell her to bug off, but in reality, I can't speak. It's been a long evening. I don't know what she heard, but she knows something. To avoid speaking, I fill a second plastic cup with water from the tap and drink. It tastes like the bleach all over the kitchen counters. I feel sick.

"The tea is much sweeter. Sit, Miriam. You've stuffed that little shelf, and bananas should sit on the counter with the tomatoes."

I collapse into a chair.

"You know there was a big terrorist attack on Kibbutz Galim once. It's famous for Israelis who remember." I drink the tea she makes me. It is warm and sweet. While she speaks I keep my eyes closed, my head on my arms on the cold table. It's late. I'm tired. I can't believe I threw a cup of coffee at another person, and I want Dalit to stop and continue at the same time.

"Terrorists came up from sea one night about ten years ago and opened fire right on the beach. They killed a pregnant woman right away. I don't remember exactly now, all the details. Murderers."

She's talking about the beach where I just spent the evening with Guy. In the last twenty-four hours I'd enjoyed myself in the spot of a terrorist attack and then climbed on a bus that was stopped by a bomb squad. This information rinses through me before it settles in my throat. This isn't a game.

"So, you see what I mean?"

I don't see what she means. I'd tuned out after the part about the murdered pregnant woman wondering now if anyone had witnessed it. Leah? Moshe? How old would Guy have been?

"Miriam, are you listening to me? Now you see why you have to sign that paper?"

I look at Dalit. Tears well up in my eyes, and I am overwhelmed with emotion. A bomb might have detonated on the highway. My father would be truly alone then. I imagine him, from an aerial viewpoint, as he stamps snow from his boots after yet another funeral, his face gray underneath his eyes, motionless air straining through his lungs.

Dalit reaches out and puts her hand on my shoulder. She slides the tissues on the table over to me, and I wipe my eyes and blow my nose.

All at once with my knees just calming down and the sugar from the tea in my blood, Dalit makes sense. What do I need this for? There's no glory in being blown to bits or shot? There's just blood and bone and waste. I shouldn't tempt fate. Things happen for a reason. Maybe the bus incident was a warning for me to wake up.

Dalit smiles and excuses herself, holding her fingers and thumb together, which I know means wait. In a minute she returns from her room with a side plate filled with two thin pieces of chocolate cake and two large oranges. As she peels her orange, the letter arrives as though by magic. My eyes are so heavy now I must have missed something. It might have been on the table the whole time, or she might have retrieved it from her room with the cake.

It has cooled off in the apartment, but I don't have anything warm to wear in my bag, nothing I could reach down to grab and wrap around my shoulders for comfort. Outside the campus is still, except for the occasional shrieking of cats, which seem to inhabit every corner and garbage can in Israel, the way squirrels roam Ottawa. Dalit takes the deep purple wrap from her own shoulders and places it around mine, a big smile on her face.

I finger the complaint letter, fumble with the pen Dalit has placed alongside it and sign my name: Miriam Gil.

Chapter Sixteen

Haifa, November, 1992

IT IS A TUESDAY MORNING and I am in line with Valerie at the Ministry of the Interior on Palyam Street. The university administration had told me I could apply for an additional bursary as the daughter of an ex-pat, but I need a copy of my father's birth certificate, which of course, he doesn't have.

It took me four phone calls and long, detailed explanations, accompanied by a lot of begging to get him to any place he could fax me permission to request it from the Ministry of the Interior. My father has a strong aversion to any sort of bureaucracy or paperwork.

Valerie had a faxed replica of her father's birth certificate notarized by a lawyer, stating it was a copy of the original, within twenty-four hours, once her mother heard she was eligible for more money. She was just as eager to apply for extra cash as I was.

Now, two hours had passed while we sat on hard plastic chairs, clutching our numbers and protecting ourselves from the bursting crowd with our knees and elbows. We have a view of the busy street in the heart of Haifa's business center.

Off of Palyam is a major tourist attraction; the history of Haifa engraved into the pavement. There are rows of ornamental arches with reproductions of old maps and city sketches.

In class we learned thousands of visitors come here every summer, but we are past the height of tourist season now, deep into November.

We learned about the Arab leader Daher-el-Omar who was in charge of the Galilee and Acre back in the eighteenth century. There is a likeness of him, as well as an image of Haifa a century later. By that time, the rulers were the Ottomans.

The artist's positive energy is palpable in these drawings. There are caravans pulled by camels meandering along. Haifa Bay is in the background and the predictable scenes of Bedouin tents.

A few students in the class invited the rest of us on an optional trip south across Israel's border to Sinai and mainland Egypt. The trip is not an official school trip, the students are organizing it without the school's help, and Valerie and I are pooling our resources to go.

I came back with so much food from the kibbutz that I think I can manage the travel expenses with what I saved. I also picked up a translation job from the advertisement I saw on the bulletin board.

I got lucky because the student is one of Simona's friends. She struggles with her psychology textbook in English, and more so with her essays. I'm sharing the work with Valerie.

Between our dictionaries and our grammar school Hebrew we plan to stay up nights in my room when Simona's away. Language is another thing that separates us from the rest of the overseas students, who can't speak a word of Hebrew.

"Hey, Valerie. It says here a thirty-day visa to Egypt is only fifteen dollars American, but you can get it at the border crossing." Valerie had lost interest in thumbing through the information booklets scattered on a back table, but I needed something to do to pass the time.

Before she can respond, my number is called. Finally! I double-check the number in my hand and spring through the crowd to the counter and immediately spread out my papers and identification. Already I can feel the guy behind me in line over my shoulder, waving his number in the air. I hear who I assume to be his wife asking him to take the screaming baby from her arms outside for a walk, but he doesn't budge. The infant's wailing continues.

"Where is your Israeli passport?" the clerk asks, oblivious to the crying baby behind me. He's wearing those glasses without frames that have recently become so popular. The Interior Ministry clerks, like all Israelis, even politicians, are dressed informally. He wears a T-shirt that stretches across his broad chest and faded jeans. His baby blue collar matches his eyes.

"I only have a Canadian passport."

"That's fine for Egypt. But I recommend you get an Israeli passport while you are here. It will take a week to find your father's birth certificate anyway. We're overloaded."

I nod and wait while he processes my request. The man behind me asks me if I'm almost done and I nod. He mutters something that sounds like people with babies should get priority, but I'm not sure if I translated properly and I'm not about to respond.

"Here is the passport application. Fill it out now so you can skip another morning in line. I'll put a note on it and phone you next week when it's ready."

"What's the extra cost?"

"Less than you will pay when you miss your flight home after they refuse to let you board."

"Really?" I ask. I play with my Eilat stone necklace.

"The next time you go to the airport they will want to know where is your *p'tor* from the army. You know what that is?"

"Not really."

"The paper that says you are allowed to leave, that the army has given you permission. Without that you go nowhere. And army exemptions from the Israeli army go in Israeli passports, yes? And there's the leaving tax, too, that all Israelis pay when they travel."

I lift my hands open-palmed. I don't fully believe in the fugitive scene he paints for me.

"I'm trying to help you, Miss Gil. You don't have to take it." He holds the application in one hand. I choose the path of least resistance.

"I was told the clerks here aren't so friendly, but it's nice of you help."

"Who told you that? Someone who has never been here?" He raises his eyebrows. "They are friendlier in Canada? Here. My name is Yaron. Fill out the paper and give it to the guard at the entrance with my name on the top. I'm writing it in Hebrew for you. By the end of the month it's ready. You'll thank me when you don't have airport headaches."

"I guess I should thank you now," Miriam says.

"Know there's an exit tax, too."

"Excuse me?"

"Israelis have to pay one hundred dollars at the airport to leave. Make sure you have it."

"What?" Miriam asks.

"Is she almost done? It's been forever." The man in line behind me is right beside me now.

"Please get back in the line, sir. You'll have to wait your turn like everybody else."

"But the baby —"

"Please go behind the red line."

He steps behind the red line, but not before he glares at me. I give him my back, but I feel his eyes on my shoulders.

"Your number please?" the clerk asks.

"I live in a dormitory. No phone."

"So, you phone me. Please." He scribbles his number on a piece of paper. Who wouldn't phone this guy back? "Remember, I'm Yaron. I'm here every morning until noon. No Fridays."

I take out seven precious ten-shekel bills and hand them to him, my fingers touching the ends of his making me stand up straighter, as I add two more passport photos from my wallet. I can tell he's used to explaining things repeatedly as he asks me a final time if I understand his instructions. I understand. Phone him one week from today. Two weeks before the class is unofficially scheduled to go to Egypt. Before I can replace my wallet in my bag, the man behind me is elbowing me out of the way. His wife and baby take up all of the available space, and it's all I can do to double-check I have the right papers in my purse and make my way back through the crowd to Valerie.

"I'll meet you outside," I say to Valerie, who was done first and is sitting near the security guard by the door, filing her nails. "I need the washroom first." It was so hot in Israel I'd taken to carrying around an extra deodorant in my bag and freshening up, much to Valerie's amusement.

"Did that guy say anything to you about an Israeli passport?" Valerie asks when I finally emerge.

"Yes. He's not the first. He's the third. At least." We head back to the central bus station on foot.

"At least your dad's really Israeli. Mine just stopped here for a couple of years. I didn't have the extra seventy shekels, so I left the form and applied for the grant. I'll come with you when you pick up yours. Maybe you'll get that hot clerk again."

"Maybe," I answer.

"Think about how crazy this is, Miriam. How could they keep us here when we have tickets to go home and we're not from here? What's the deal on the army permission? My mom's freaking out already. She wants me back for winter break. She's springing for it. A miracle."

"You're leaving next month?"

My longing to stop and buy a cold drink has been replaced by Valerie's verbal wake up call. She might leave me here after I'd already formed such an attachment to the extent that I had made no effort to befriend anyone else, not beyond an introductory level.

"Just for the break. I'm registered for the year, like you."

I look at her. Am I hearing what she's really saying?

"If your mom's so upset why would she let you come back and pay another ticket?"

"Chill. There's no damage so far. She might flip out on something else tomorrow. What else did you find out now?"

I slow down to gaze at the display window of a shoe store. Israel is full of shoe stores and bakeries. I've never seen so many pastries in my life. It is no wonder Maayan can so easily supply Valerie with baked goods.

"Hello? You with me?" Valerie links her arm into mine.

"He told me they might hassle us when we leave about an army exemption and that all Israelis have to pay an exit tax at the airport."

"An exit tax?" Valerie drops her backpack and takes out her water bottle. She wipes the sweat from her upper lip with her sleeve. It should be cooler at this time of year, but it's not. "I thought it was a free country," she says.

"It's steep too. A hundred bucks," I answer.

"A hundred bucks to go home?"

"That's what he said. I handed in the grant application now. Yaron said to phone in a week."

"Oh. Yaron, huh? Yeah, he was giving you special attention."

That evening I phone Uncle Moshe to ask if I could invite Valerie with me to the kibbutz for the weekend. She'll be good protection against any future public Guy incidents, which had lost me points with Leah. I couldn't help but worry that she'd talk to my father about it one day. The fact that they hadn't spoken in thirty years didn't make me feel any more secure.

"Shalom, Miriam. How was your week?"

"Good. We have a lot of trips planned." I lean against the wall and play with the telephone cord with one hand, twining it between my fingers.

"Well, that's why you came, no? To see the country."

"I guess so. I'm calling about the weekend."

"Ah, the weekend. I wanted to talk to you about that. Look this weekend's not so good," he says.

I straighten up and let the phone cord hang loose, winding it between my fingers with my free hand.

"No? Are you going away?"

"We never go away. You guess why."

In case Yakira comes home.

"So, what is it?"

"Leah's not feeling well." I hear the crinkle of a toffee wrapper. He clears his throat. Then my uncle speaks while chewing. "She doesn't want you to catch anything from her. She's a worrier. I'm sorry to disappoint you. Please tell me if you're still there," he says.

"I'm here," I answer. "There's nothing to apologize for. I hope she feels better."

"Look, skip this weekend and come next week, okay? Yes? Call me first. I'm sure she'll be in mint condition by then," he says.

"I'd better go now. There's a long line of students for the phone in the evenings. Goodbye." I hang up and stand quickly, dart out of the way of the next caller, and walk toward my room.

"Hey, there you are," says Valerie.

I turn and see her with a stack of papers in her hand.

"You should be proud. I finished that paper today. Dinner and a work out?" she asks.

"Is Maayan out for the evening?" I answer.

"Whoa, did I deserve that? Did she?" she asks.

I avoid catching Valerie's eye and take a deep breath.

"No. You didn't. She didn't. Let me help you with all of that," I answer, taking half of her pile into my arms. "I'm sorry. I just got dumped that's all."

"Dumped? What that gnarly ex of yours had the guts to get on the horn?" she asks.

We've arrived at my room. I want to work out in my own room for a change, without Valerie's roommate around. The door is unlocked. No one is here.

"He might have dumped you, but you're the one on the other side of the world and not just any side, the Mediterranean side. He's freezing his tuchus off over a beer somewhere with a dart-board in the background, checking out the tractor pull scores," she says.

I laugh. We dump her schoolwork on my desk.

"You really think I'm from Hicksville."

"I know you're from Hicksville."

"I was talking about my aunt. Supposedly she's sick, so I have nowhere to go this weekend," I answer. I don't say that I overheard this crazy conversation between my aunt and her friend. It was late, and I was listening at a

159

distance. It was a conversation out of context. They could have been talking about anything or anyone. That's what I've been telling myself until now. But now my uncle's told me this clearly bogus story that Leah's not feeling well, poking holes in my theory that it must have been some grand misunderstanding and what I deserve for eavesdropping.

"And no gorgeous combat soldier. What was his name? Guy?"

I flutter my eyes at her and pretend to swoon. "No Guy for more than week."

"Hmm. I can't help you with that, but what you're really saying is you've got no place to go this weekend?"

"Yes."

"That's not a problem." Valerie grabs my hand and cha-chas me out of my room down the empty hallway and back. "That's an opportunity. We'll find a few others or not, get group take-out or not, hit 'The Square' for sure."

"The what?"

"That's where all the clubs are. Maayan's been promising. Don't worry."

"How will we get home? A taxi on a Friday night? That's for the rich."

"If you'd forget about that doorknob, you'd attract enough attention to get us a ride home," she answers. "Though I've lost ten pounds if I do say so myself on our vegetarian diet." She puts one hand on one hip and the other behind her opposite ear striking a model pose. "Come on, smile first for once."

I stick out my tongue. Valerie does look slimmer in spite of her chocolate and pastry addiction and all I can think about is Guy, not the doorknob she's referring to.

"As a just-in-case," she says, collapsing on my bed, "find someone who needs a paper translated and can pay in advance. It's only Tuesday."

Chapter Seventeen

THE NIGHTCLUB VALERIE TAKES ME TO is at the end of a long line of nightclubs on a dingy road in what Valerie calls "The Square."

Valerie became quiet the minute we stepped onto the bus and grabbed the first seat behind the back door. At first, I thought she was nervous about getting to the right place, mixing up the address, but after a while a different sort of mood settled on her, a coating over her eyes I couldn't identify.

Twice she'd begun to speak to me, hinting that there was something she felt I needed to know and then stopped. I ran ideas though my brain trying to pinpoint what she might want to say. Maybe she's the type who has one drink and turns into a slut, or someone who clams up in a bar next to good looking men. I knew that it was common for people to take on different personalities and behaviors in bars, lose inhibitions, especially after a few drinks. People said and did things that they wouldn't anywhere else, certainly not in daylight, and I suspected that was what she was trying to confess, to prepare me for. Well, there was no need. I swam in the sea in my bra and underwear with a virtual stranger after two glasses of wine. I patted her knee, but she only looked out the window.

There is no line-up, and after passing by the two bouncers at the door, we climb a darkened staircase and we are in. The club doesn't look or feel different from the nightclubs I've been to at home, though it's a rare pastime. Loud, vibrating music, crowds, hot, stuffy, energy, this is what hits me as I enter. The barmen are more muscular than the ones I remember, but otherwise they have that same I've-seen-everything transmission around them. I don't see any female bartenders.

"I'll get us two screwdrivers. You sit right here next to the bar, so I know where to find you," Valerie says.

"Hard liquor?" I am surprised.

"You planning to be a buzz-kill from the get-go?" I shrug and she's off, lost in the crowd.

I notice the plump black and green olives placed in small dishes around the bar and on our table for two. I couldn't imagine a bar in Ottawa with small dishes of olives on the counter and an empty dish beside them for the pips.

"*L'chaim*!" Valerie hands me my drink and knocks hers back. I sip mine, wrinkle my nose at the acerbic taste.

Maayan gave us directions and bailed. I don't know how Valerie feels about it, but I am relieved. I had this fear last night that Maayan would saunter off with Valerie, leaving me stranded by myself in a strange nightclub. The fear of abandonment haunts me, and I push it away, back on that shelf in my soul that I never dust or want to look at.

The ten pounds Valerie lost increases her confidence, and there is no doubt there is something magnetic about her, which I can describe only as optimism. She is one of those overweight girls that people look at and think: *If you ignore the weight, she has a pretty face, bright brown eyes and bow lips and well-tended hair, if you don't mind the feathered look all the way to the shoulders.*

We are not at the table ten minutes before someone who introduces himself as Khalid approaches me.

"Remember me?" he asks. "I didn't think I'd see someone like you here."

I draw my eyebrows together and study him. I don't recognize him. And what does 'someone like me' mean?

"The post office at the university. You come in for aerogrammes and Bezeq cards and never have change. Haven't seen you lately."

"Oh." I nod. Khalid drags two more chairs to our table and sits down. His female companion sits in the other chair, next to Valerie.

"I work there one or two days a week when things are slow with my dad in construction," Khalid explains. He shrugs his wide shoulders.

We have to shout at each other because the music is loud. Khalid moves in closer to me.

"What do you mean 'someone like me here'? A tourist?" I ask.

"No, not a tourist." He winks. I give him a half smile.

"Am I missing something?"

He clears his throat. "It's not my business. I remember you said you were writing your boyfriend. So, I was just surprised to see you in this type of place, you know?"

I told everyone I ran into my first week here that I have a boyfriend, even the post office clerk. It seems so long ago now. Another life. And I don't know what he means by this type of place. I raise my eyebrows.

"But maybe you're like me and you came to watch out for your friend. For me, my cousin, or at least that's what I'm hoping, that and maybe your boyfriend won't mind." He winks again and wiggles his shoulders. I laugh. It's only a few minutes later that I understand the meaning behind his words.

"Do you want to dance?" he asks, before I can digest everything he's said. He stands up and holds out his hand.

The DJ is playing Prince's "Cream." I hesitate. Valerie kicks me under the table, so I take his outstretched hand and let him pull me toward the dance floor. Khalid's female companion offers Valerie a sip of her own drink, which Valerie accepts. It's something in a short, wide glass on the rocks. Their eyes lock and they both giggle, sipping deeper from the same glass with two straws, draining it, falling all over each other.

All at once time slows down and events come together in my mind: Valerie's hemming and hawing on the bus, her slowed pace down the dark, cigarette butt-filled street—bit by bit like a safe cracker turns a dial this way and that, and even with the most sensitive ear and delicate fingers, the click is unexpected. I stop dancing and slap my head in recognition. This is not an ordinary nightclub. And look at Valerie, ten minutes and she's smitten. So much for worrying she'd saunter off with Maayan. At least Maayan would have been returning to the dormitory. Now she's into some girl who might invite her anywhere anytime. Great. It's been a quarter of an hour, and I'm on my own. Totally.

I try to focus on Khalid, to breathe easier. He is basketball tall with a trendy haircut, short in the front and sides and long at the back. Here he blends in with the crowd. I would have kept an eye on him at home. He's wearing a soft yellow T-shirt with an extra short-sleeved black and small checkered button-down on top. His top two and bottom three buttons are open, revealing the crew neck of his T-shirt, which also extends a couple of inches underneath the tightly checkered sleeves. I recognize the layered look from the guys I've seen on campus. His gold cross necklace is hard to see against the yellow background of his T-shirt, but I'm close enough now.

Vanilla Ice's "Play That Funky Music" comes on as we hit the dance floor and the vibrations bounce off the wall. Khalid shows off his stylish dancing skills, but the dance floor is so crowded with both genders, I can hardly follow.

When the song ends I drift toward Valerie. She could have just told me she's gay.

Khalid disappears, after pointing to the bar. He returns with two fresh screwdrivers and hands me one. I am about to say I'm still on my first when I look closer at the table and see two empty glasses. Valerie drank for both of us. The four of us move to a table at the back. Still, we need to shout at each other to be heard over the music.

"Christian Arabs," Valerie whispers in my ear.

I put on what I believe to be a normal facial expression, though inside I wish she'd slow down. I can see it's too late. Valerie's already drunk.

"This is Re'em," Khalid says. "She's my favorite cousin." I don't know if he means real blood cousin or close as a cousin.

Re'em reminds me of Arslan, the same skin coloring, eyes like inkwells and long, black, wavy hair, only hers is streaked blonde. Her features are not as fine, and her skin is rougher than Arslan's. She wears pale gray linen shorts and a matching T-shirt, black sunglasses that are clearly for fashion or decoration and black nail polish. I'd already noticed on my uncle's kibbutz that people here wear shorts all year round.

"How do you like the university?" Khalid asks me. "I never saw the dorms." I strain to hear him over the music. "What are your roommates like? I don't think I'd like roommates." I bristle. Imagine if I tried to explain. I flip a mental switch to my default reaction: pretending.

"It's my first time living with roommates. They all seem so busy." I play with my Eilat stone necklace. "I thought we'd spend so much time together at first."

"And you don't spend time together?" he asks. Out of the corner of my eye, I see Valerie fingering Re'em's necklace. I let my necklace drop. Re'em and Valerie have all but melted into one another's eyes, and I'm trying not to stare. It's obvious Valerie has forgotten my existence. Jealousy runs through me followed by fear as a close second. I'm on my own for the rest of the night, like it or not. Khalid clears his throat, and I have to remind myself what he asked me about.

"When I first arrived, I had this so wrong idea that these are the women I'd see all the time, but their schedules are packed. They study round the clock."

"An Eilat stone? Right?"

I nod.

"It looks real. Someone likes you."

I don't correct him. I don't say that this someone is the reason why I am here with him instead of on the kibbutz with Guy.

"So, what do you study?" he continues.

He takes out a pack of cigarettes, Marlboros. I've only been in Israel for less than two weeks, and it seems the entire country smokes and that American cigarettes carry prestige.

"The students are serious, older, and it's very competitive here. It's not for me, but you, do you enjoy it?" Khalid's English is broken, but understandable, if I tune out the music and concentrate.

"I'm studying Middle Eastern studies. I love it, actually. The teachers are great."

Khalid sits on the edge of his seat. If he is anything like Neil, the presence of gay men makes him nervous. I sense this is the reason he looks at me so intensely. It's a loud message: I'm into women. Normally, this would unnerve me, but tonight it works. His focus on me makes it easier for me to ignore Valerie ignoring me.

"Is Valerie your roommate?" he asks.

"No," I snap. His expression changes. "Worried?" he asks. Then he laughs. "Listen, if there's anyone who needs to worry about being seen here, it's me. You can just hop on the next plane. My society is very traditional."

He inches closer to me and speaks into my ear. "If I wasn't so protective of Re'em. She's had some rough times, ended up in an ambulance once, and she's like a little sister to me. We all live in the same house, you know. Arabs live many generations in one home and..."

He stops talking and lowers his eyes. His eyelashes are thick and black.

"I see."

Neither of us says anything for a minute.

"You asked about Valerie," I say finally. "We're in the same program. The first friend I made here."

I try not to stumble on the word *friend*.

"Would you like another drink?" he asks.

I shake my head and pop a few of the pretzels from the bowl on the table into my mouth. I'd better not drink. Khalid's watching my every move with green cat eyes, and his hands move quickly, he'd already demonstrated that on the dance floor. I don't want to get carried away on my first time in a club in two years. I need to take it easy.

Speaking over the music strains my vocal cords, and the motion of the strobe lights is dizzying. Even though he and his friends were older I never knew Neil to club it. He preferred restaurants without menus, the drive-in, doughnut shops, and the racetrack. If someone asked me about it right now, I'm not sure I could say any of those places ever existed. Khalid places his hand on my knee and whispers in my ear that he'll be right back. I nod. I realize that I'm in way over my head. I am so rusty I squeak when I move. I don't know how to read unfamiliar guys in bars any more than I know how to read unfamiliar girls in my own program.

I should have just showed up at Guy's door and announced I'm his guest for the weekend. I put a hand on my stomach, but I might as well be at the table by myself. There isn't a sniff in my direction from Valerie or Re'em. The vodka and orange juice aren't mixing well, but I don't want to undo the button on my jeans. It might be taken the wrong way.

Khalid's obvious desire for my attention makes it difficult to sort out my feelings about Valerie and Re'em. At least she's having a good time. Isn't that why I came? I close my eyes and consider what I was seeking when I agreed to come here. A new entry for my journal about my trip abroad? Proof I could occupy myself on weekends without my new family? Was I still in line to prove something to Neil? Perhaps I really am naive enough to think Guy is missing me somewhere, maybe gazing out at the sea and remembering last weekend.

Re'em stands and takes Valerie's hand in her smaller one. Valerie follows her without a glance back at me, and I see Valerie barely saying goodbye on that first night we prepared dinner together after Maayan had come into their shared room, led her outside by the hand. Where the hell is Valerie going? I am too much of a coward to ask or to follow.

By the time Khalid returns I've lost sight of Valerie and Re'em.

"Where's Valerie?" I ask Khalid.

170

"I told you Re'em likes her. Re'em has places to go with people she likes."

What? I look around. This nightclub is vast. It has two floors and three sections. Valerie could be anywhere. Now Khalid smells of liquor scented with mint.

"How old are you?" he asks. "I'm twenty."

"Me too."

My birthday's coming up. I'll be twenty-one. I want to ask him why he didn't enlist in the army but hold back. Those conversations have never gone well. It hits me that I no longer think like the girl who got off the plane only a short time ago.

"Think Valerie will come back soon?"

"She can take care of herself."

"She drank too much."

"How do you like Haifa?" He inches closer again.

"It's pretty."

"So are you." He brushes my neck with his lips and mumbles into my ear, "You smell good."

"Thanks. Want to dance again?" I need to get him up, get him moving.

"American girls. They like to dance." He smiles and looks younger.

We dance. On the dance floor he offers me one of his mints, and when I nod he pops it into my mouth for me, fumbling with it in his fingers. I note the strength in his arms and chest. He pulls me close to him with one arm. "You want to go somewhere where there's no audience. I have a car."

Then he's kissing me on the lips.

Khalid hasn't done anything wrong, but I need to find Valerie and a taxi and get us back to the dormitories. I pull away from him.

"We just met." I laugh to take the edge off my rejection.

"I could come and visit you in the dormitories."

This is the first time it occurs to me how easy it is to find me. There is only one dormitory building at Haifa University. It can't be hard to walk in and ask for Miriam or just sit outside and wait to spot me. For the first time in my life I am grateful my name is such a common Jewish one. Khalid's face relaxes when I point to another couple tripping over themselves on the dance floor and giggling. The more relaxed he looks, the hungrier he is for me.

"I'm really worried about my friend."

"Re'em's got secret spots, but okay. If it will calm you down."

I want to change the tone, water down his appetite. What did I expect in a nightclub? That some guy would offer me tea with milk and honey and a game of crazy eights? It occurs to me that it will be like this everywhere I go as a tourist in Israel, unattached. There will be assumptions about young women holding alcoholic drinks in nightclubs, on kibbutz beaches. I will be the one standing behind these assumptions, like it or not.

Khalid weaves his fingers through mine, and we wind around the nightclub. I realize I haven't had one cigarette all night. I haven't needed to. The place is thick with smoke, and my throat feels raw and scratchy. Now I know why Khalid carries mints in all of his pockets.

There is no cover charge, so the club attracts all types, and there's an obvious devil-may-care attitude toward drinks, which overflow on the tables in neon colors. I don't think there's anyone in here over twenty-five. I look at my watch. We were late leaving the dormitories and only arrived at 11. It's nearly 1:00 a.m. I don't get why they're still serving drinks.

"When is last call?" I stand on my tiptoes to shout into Khalid's ear.

"What?"

We are shouting at each other, and I don't want to give him reason to pull me closer. The vodka and orange is wearing off.

"Last call?"

"What's that?"

"You know the bartender announces it's the last round of drinks because it's illegal to sell alcohol after a certain time of night." He looks down at me with a puzzled expression.

"I don't know where you're from, Miriam, but there's no such thing here." He laughs. "What a crazy idea. If the club is open, it's selling alcohol. Why else? To give a free dance."

I nod and his words sink in. The rules are all different here.

"What time does it close?"

"When everyone goes home. Maybe five. I'm not sure."

He squeezes my hand. We've combed the place.

"I told you Re'em knows what she's doing. She's a regular."

For me it's time to go home. I can't believe Valerie has done this. I don't know if I should give up. Abandon Valerie in a nightclub on a Friday night. I've got enough money to get home, but I don't know if she does.

"Your friend is a big girl. She'll be okay. They're having a blast. Re'em knows how to party. Why do you think your friend left America? To have fun. Forget troubles." He twirls me around. "Are you always like this? Anyone ever tell you you're too pretty to be so serious?"

I smile close-mouthed and step back from him.

"You're right. She'll manage. I'm thirsty."

Khalid brightens and leads me through lines of people to the bar. He orders two more screwdrivers. I hold up my full glass, and he kisses me on the neck again, but I pull away and pretend to sip. He downs his drink, and I hold up two fingers. He orders two more. He has a healthy supply of money for drinks. I excuse myself, go to the bathroom, and pour my drink down the sink to the amazement of the short blonde beside me. I put my finger to my lips and wink at her. I don't reapply more lipstick or fix up my makeup.

I play this game for another half an hour until Khalid must be seeing double. A couple of his friends show up, and he chats with them in Arabic. He's in good shape and holds his liquor well. I can see construction work is great for bodybuilding. There is still no sign of Valerie. I vacillate between anxiety and antagonism. I have not allowed my mind to venture further, that she has gone off with a stranger and could be anywhere. I feel like a dunce. Khalid trips over his own feet, and his friends howl uproariously. It's my signal to scram.

I lean over to the bartender and whisper, "How do I get a cab here?"

"There's always cabs waiting through that side door to the right." He points with his chin, but he keeps drying glasses with his eyes fixed on them. "I'll offer him another on the house. Chicks always need the bathroom. And hey, cabs want to rip off tourists, especially on Friday nights. Don't pay more than eighty, wherever you're going, unless it's outside the city."

I raise my eyebrows instead of nodding my head.

"What's with the bartender?" Khalid turns up at my side. "Bothering you?"

"I want to know what he puts in these drinks that make them so addictive. Must be the Jaffa oranges."

I am still hesitant about Valerie, but it's her or me right now.

"Hey, brother. Something special for you and your lady friend?"

Khalid turns to the bartender, and I indicate the direction of the bathroom with my head and lose myself in the crowd.

Chapter Eighteen

BACK IN THE DORMITORIES it is eerily silent. The guard eyes me over the top of his magazine, but doesn't say a word as I step in. I can hear a washer and dryer spinning in the basement and climb down to the bottom floor to peek. I am overwhelmed with a desire to know I'm not alone in this whole building. The half-asleep guard doesn't seem to count, and even the laundry room is empty.

I turn and head to Valerie's apartment, one floor up. Stupidly, I knock on her apartment door with a shred of hope that she somehow made it home before me, but it's locked and there's no sound on her entire floor. The clattering of my heels hitting the tiles is too loud, and I'm aware of my own breathing.

The stillness of the place is getting to me, and I imagine Khalid will pop out of the shadows when most likely he's having a good laugh with his friends over the American girl he danced with tonight and he's already on to the next cute smile. He's right. I take everything way too seriously. Girls are a dime a dozen. So are Friday nights in clubs.

I put my key in my own apartment lock and turn. The door swings open with a jarring sound. We haven't fixed the loose hinge yet. It hits the back wall with a bang that makes me jump. I lock the door behind me and leave the key in the lock. I shower off the layers of smoke and sweat, put on sweatpants and a sweatshirt, and fall into bed.

Someone bangs repetitively on the door of my apartment. In order for me to hear it at the end of the hall behind my own closed door, they have to have been banging for a while because, until a moment ago, I was in a deep sleep.

I drag myself to a sitting position, rub my eyes. My sweatshirt is damp in the armpits. I throw it on the floor and put on a T-shirt. It takes me a moment to realize that with the blind dropped, my room will remain in darkness no matter how much I rub my eyes. I lift the blind, and I am thankful that it is cloudy, that I have not been assaulted by sunlight because my head aches and my throat is dry. There is black mascara all over my fingers. It must have leaked onto my hands without my noticing when I rinsed my face and neck last night in the shower. There must be thick black streaks across my pillowcase.

Bang, bang, bang. Someone's kicking in the door. The hinge is already loose on the front door, a few more swift kicks and who knows if it will lock again.

I open my bedroom door and stare down the empty hallway. I'm trying to focus.

"Please open," a male voice says. Oh my God. Maybe Khalid did follow me here. I never should have led him on. I'm such an idiot. I breathe deeply.

"Who is it?"

"Sorry to disturb. Please open," the voice says again. I detect his Arabic-accented Hebrew, just like Khalid's.

"It's very early," I say. There's a tremble in my voice. "Who are you looking for?"

"Please. I'm sorry to wake you," the man says.

He doesn't sound drunk or angry. He sounds panicked. There is no peephole, but there's a guard at the entrance, and I can scream with the best of them if I have to. Still, I open the door as little as possible, bracing myself for an angry drunk guy who thinks I tricked him. But the person in front of me is a handsome man who looks about forty, wearing an Israeli army uniform. He rushes past me.

"Excuse me," he says in Hebrew, turning back to face me. "Sorry to be rude. There is no time."

"Who are you?" I ask. "Can I help you?"

But he has already disappeared into Arslan's room. I follow him and find him throwing Arslan's clothes into a duffle bag.

"I am Arslan's father. She'll be okay. Please God. With the help of Allah," he says.

"What do you mean?"

He stops throwing shoes into the bag for a moment.

"You didn't hear? It was all over the news," he says. "You must pray for my daughter. Everyone in our village is praying right now." His eyes fill with tears, but he blinks them away.

"Pray for Arslan? What happened to her? I haven't heard any news. Please tell me what happened," I answer. My pulse speeds up, and I steady myself against the wall.

"A few hours ago, four petrol bombs were thrown from Jerusalem's Old City walls at a bus stop. Four

178

bombs, four dead women. Innocent, just waiting for a bus, and Arslan," he says, but he can't go on.

"My God, she was there?"

"Yes," he says. "It was God's will."

He's regained composure now and zips up the duffle bag.

"Can I get you some water? Anything?" I ask.

I can't believe this is happening. It doesn't feel real. A petrol bomb. It sounds like something sinister homemade in a basement by crazy people. Poor Arslan.

"Just pray. Please," he says.

He accepts the tissues I offered and wipes his eyes.

"What was she doing in Jerusalem?" I ask.

"She had only just arrived. A cousin moved there, and they went shopping in the Arab Quarter, but now she has burns," he says.

"Terrible," I say. It's painful to look at his face. He must be screaming inside.

"She fell backward from the blast," he adds.

"Did you speak to her?"

"She's unconscious. That's all I know. I must go to her and her mother."

"I'm sorry. I'm so sorry," I say as I follow him down the hallway.

"Her mother wanted a few of her favorite things. I don't even know what I took."

"I'm sure it's all there," I answer. He's cleared out her whole closet. "I'm Miriam. If you need anything, phone the dormitory and I'll do whatever I can."

"Thank you," he says. "God should protect all of us."

He flies into the corridor with the duffle bag over his

shoulder, and he's gone before I even get a chance to ask him what hospital Arslan is in. It will take him two hours to get to Jerusalem from here. He has two hours to wonder if his daughter is dead or alive with only a stranger's voice on the radio to update him. And the other four women, there's no more hope for them. He said they were dead.

Before I can lock the door Valerie bursts in. She is still wearing her clothes from yesterday, and the smell of stale smoke clings to her.

"From the look on your face I should shower, huh?" Valerie says. "How was last night? Were we amped up or what?"

"Did you see that guy leaving?"

"The guy who knocked me over, yeah," she says.

"That was Arslan's father."

I look her up and down. I make a vague gesture with my hands. She leads me to a chair at the kitchen table. I collapse and she takes my hand in hers.

"Whatever it is I'm sorry to hear it." She runs her hands through her limp hair. "Take your time."

"You heard the news on the radio?" I ask.

"You know I try not to," she says.

"There was a terrorist incident in Jerusalem. The Old City. Terrorists threw petrol bombs at a bus stop, and Arslan had just arrived," I say.

"No, please no," she says. She puts a hand over her mouth. "Tell me she's okay."

"I don't know. Her father came for a few things. He says she was burned, but he doesn't know how badly. She hit her head from the force of the blast," I say.

"Those bastards. Oh my God. We have to stay calm, not freak out," she says, though she's pacing around the room, wringing her hands. "Maybe there's an update on the radio. Or maybe that's the last thing we want to do, hear more of this shit."

Valerie puts water in the kettle and flicks the switch. The primary colors she's still wearing from last night hurt my eyes. She prattles on about all of her mother's dire predictions as she lights two cigarettes and sticks one in my mouth, fills both of our mugs with tea and sugar and milk. She pours us both glasses of water and begins to boil eggs, chop a tomato, scrub the kitchen table, anything to keep her hands busy.

My leftover anger at Valerie for ditching me goes down the drain with the water. I can think only of Arslan now. She was here yesterday, gorgeous, eighteen, whole, alive. She was right here. My friend. The worst thing that ever happened to a friend of mine was a broken arm playing baseball. A teacher broke her leg on a skiing trip once. Nobody got firebombed at bus stops. Nobody I'd ever known. All at once I want to be by myself.

"Don't you think you should sleep now?" I ask. "It's been a big night."

"I'm too jacked."

"At least shower."

"You want to be alone?" she asks. "She's going to be fine, you know. Israel has the best doctors in the world."

I nod.

"I read you. I'll go."

She kisses me on both cheeks and lets herself out, so that I can cry alone.

181

Chapter Nineteen

ON SUNDAY MORNING four overfed suitcases block the door to our apartment. I notice them only after the sounds of raised, tense voices wake me, leading me into the hallway and finally into the kitchen. There in the bleak morning light Dalit has lost all composure. Her shouting has transformed into an edgy growl directed at someone I've never seen, a short woman in a pants suit with a fixed expression, who doesn't look like a student. The woman responds to Dalit in an equally low voice, but as I watch them from the edge of the room the tone of their conversation becomes increasingly explosive, their Hebrew so rapid-fire, I can't grasp more than the odd word.

Finally, the woman turns on her thick heels and stomps out of the apartment, inelegantly climbing over the suitcases to get out.

Dalit is left alone, looking shamefaced and sad, an expression I've never seen in her usually self-assured and resolute eyes. If she notices me at all, she makes no indication of it. I have been eavesdropping on sensitive territory, and I ready myself to be told off, to mind my own business, but nothing comes at me from her direction. She is dressed as though she hadn't had time to turn on the lights. Her buttons are mismatched and her wrinkled blouse hangs lopsided over pants that are smudged with pen.

There is a light chill in the early morning air, and I am self-conscious in my sweatpants and flimsy undershirt. I return to my room, praying Dalit will continue to ignore me, at least until she calms down. But my prayers are unnecessary. No one missed a beat when I appeared in the hallway or in the kitchen, and there is no vibration in the apartment when I shut my bedroom door behind me. I stand in the middle of the room, my eyes running up and down over my daily schedule, not comprehending the words, while my heart pounds in my chest. Everything's going wrong.

I can hear Farzeen and another Arab student I don't recognize in the hallway outside my door, their voices rise and fall. I cannot understand their conversation, but it is obvious they are both angry.

Unable to hold it in any longer, I use the bathroom without looking left or right, and I float past without a flicker from either of them. I return to my room to dress. I'm never up this early in Israel. There's more than an hour until my first class.

By the time I organize my backpack for the day, fold my dirty laundry into the bottom of my cupboard, freshen the water in Simona's vase, make my bed, and lock my bedroom door, the apartment is empty, odd for 7:45 a.m. There isn't even a used coffee cup in the sink or a wet spoon in the drying rack. There is no fresh salad and no smells of bitter coffee and sweet sugar with milk, and for once the radio is silent in Dalit's room. I'd always imagined I'd be grateful for one quiet morning without the blaring of bad news in the background. But instead of a gentle calm, I sense a deep absence, and I feel unusually guarded, double-checking the sink and swinging open the refrigerator door to confirm my suspicions: I've never seen the shelves so bare. It's as though Arslan got hurt and wounded everybody.

After my last afternoon class, I cannot resist the urge to jog back to the apartment, but the place is still deserted when I breeze in, the air uncommonly stale, and the only light leaks in through a half-raised blind. The suitcases are gone. Both of the other bedroom doors are locked when I rattle the doorknobs, and the smells of fried onions, garlic, mint tea, and Nescafé are absent, too. There is only the now familiar scent of bleach.

I wish I knew where everybody was. Surely, Simona will pitch up mid-week weighted down with fresh food from Tel Aviv's shuk, sporting an updo and clutching a new bouquet of luxurious flowers as she does every Tuesday. Of course, with Simona it's not unusual for her to show up for only one night or to miss a week. Her heart belongs in Tel Aviv.

I have no doubt the next time I do see her she'll be wearing her usual know-it-all expression that will follow a revelation I should be smart enough to figure out on my own now. But I'm not. I miss my evening lessons with Arslan. I'd phoned the hospital twice once I heard on the news where the victims had been taken, but they give out information only to families, so I glued myself to the hourly newscasts. She's stabilized is the only detail they're giving out. Thank God for that. It could have been so much worse. She could be the main part in one of the four funerals the radio broadcast today. The thought sends shivers through me.

I unlock my door, half expecting someone to be on the other side, but that's preposterous. There is no one to come into my bedroom and lock it from the inside. As far as I know only Simona has a key. Still, a tiny ray of hope fills my heart as I swing the door open. A moment later, I am disappointed, standing in the middle of my dark room alone. The exotic, foreign apartment at the top of Mount Carmel, a mere stroll to a nature reserve, kissing the blue sea, all at once seems merely flat and stifling, the wad of lecture notes on my desk burdensome.

I raise the blind, but it's a cloudy winter evening and I'd forgotten to replace the broken bulb in my bedroom, forgotten to even pass by the overseas office and put in a request. I flick on the hallway light and check the apartment again. Not a soul. Something's wrong, and I'm more alone than I've ever been.

Chapter Twenty

IT IS AFTER MIDNIGHT when I finally hear the door groan
open and I stick my ear to my own door immediately,
leaving it ajar to listen. I make out the mumbles of Dalit
and a female stranger, but no clear words. Something
prevents me from waltzing into the kitchen and
confronting Dalit, or even asking her in an ordinary way
how she is doing, what's up, where is everyone,
inquiring if her connection had finally failed her and if
she's been forced to receive a roommate after all, or if she
is just entertaining a midweek sleepover. Maybe this
stranger was part of the bargain. Farzeen's already
moved. Her room is stripped clean. She never said
goodbye.

Dalit and her friend go about their bedtime rituals of
teeth brushing and face washing in record time, and then
the apartment is once again plunged into darkness. No
nighttime Nescafé with vanilla wafers or mint and lemon
tea with chocolate cake. No peals of laughter recounting
what must have been long day's events. Nothing.

I cannot resist the urge to speak to Dalit, and I leave
my bed, tiptoe down the hallway and knock on her door.
I lack the nerve to ask her my real question: Will she
come with me to visit Arslan? I'm afraid to navigate an
Israeli hospital. Ever since my mother was killed, I have
a terrible fear of hospitals. The smell of them speeds up

my heartbeat.

No one responds to my second knock or my third. Maybe someone yelled a muffled goodnight, or maybe they were snoring or pretending to be asleep. It's clear Dalit's ignoring me. I sigh and return to my bed.

I force my eyes shut. I need to get a good sleep or I'll be tired for our class trip to the North tomorrow. I'd already scratched out my own name from the printed-out sheet taped to the door of our classroom, the one with the list of overseas students interested in the trip to the Sinai and Egypt. I had no appetite to go without Valerie, and I'd spotted a red line through her name this morning. But that was an unofficial trip organized by the students themselves. I need to attend the class trip if I want full marks for the course, and I may want these credits some day to apply to another degree.

My eyes open again. I have to stop thinking about Arslan covered in bandages in a hospital bed, replaying her near death in her mind. I distract myself with what I've packed or may have forgotten to pack, mentally double-checking my bag. But my focus on reviewing my packing list is counterfeit, a dam to keep back my wave of bewilderment in this altered apartment, where my voice echoes off the walls and the locked bedroom doors.

To calm myself I rise, drape one of Simona's shawls over my shoulders, and review the itinerary. The plan is to spend two nights in the Golan Heights, an area that borders Israel, Lebanon, Syria, and Jordan, and I already know that I will stay as close to the professor as I dare and force myself to focus on the beauty of the waterfalls, the mystery of the ancient Roman aqueducts and abandoned railroad bridge I'd read about in my history book. Our last night is planned for Safed, a small town in Israel's north I have yet to read up on.

By the time I fall asleep my shoulder muscles are sore from hunching over the translation notes I'd jotted down for yet another essay. In the morning I have to rub them, as though I'd already completed the five-hour hike with a heavy backpack across craggy terrain scheduled for the morning.

At 7:50 a.m. on the dot, I'm waiting in line for the phone in the foyer, picking at a scab on my knee through a hole in my jeans. December is around the corner. I must call Yaron at the Ministry of the Interior before I board the bus and I'm taking the chance that he'll answer at 8:00 a.m. and I'll still make it to the parking lot, where the professor said we all had to meet in half an hour. Yaron had made a point of saying I had to speak to him personally, so I pray he hasn't taken the day off or missed his bus.

My backpack and sleeping bag are at my feet, I have a phone card in one hand and there's still a smudge of chocolate spread on my wrist from where I'd spread it on a pita in a rush to leave the seclusion of my kitchen and then stuffed it in the outside pocket of my backpack as a snack on the bus. If I can get this bursary I won't have to kill myself translating half the night and I might be able to tour more, maybe even invite Guy to tour with me if I can muster up the courage. Just imagining what it would be like to explore Israel with someone as daring, outgoing, and handsome as Guy makes my knees weak. Yes, I'm counting on this bursary.

After what seems like twenty rings, Yaron picks up and I recognize his silvery voice right away.

"Allo?" and then "*Khen*, Miriam Gil. *Mah shlomech*? Of course, I remember you. I remember all of the American girls who come in." I no longer correct Israelis or even other Americans when they call me American.

He puts me on hold while he checks my file and cautions me not to hang up or I will automatically be at the end of the queue. In the background, I hear the sounds of telephones ringing and raised gravelly voices. I imagine Yaron's broad chest underneath his tight T-shirt. Every man is an open door these days. One year of loyalty has crumbled with one drop of salty water from the Mediterranean and a pinch of Middle Eastern sun. I remember reading that people's personalities are often similar to their climates. There is no question there is a heat that is foreign to me here, it gets under your skin, steaming you up, influencing your judgment, informing your thoughts.

Valerie sails by me in the foyer, her back bent with a bulging backpack, a badly rolled sleeping bag half slipping off the bottom hook. Her hair is streaked with copper and blonde, something she must have done without me. She doesn't see me with her face in her bag of doughnuts. Hanukkah is two weeks away, and the red, jelly-filled doughnuts covered in powdered sugar are already on every cafeteria counter and bakery display window.

For once the foyer is empty. A series of beeps tells me I need to deposit more tokens and I feed the slot all of the tokens I have left. I'm starting to sweat about catching my bus.

Finally, Yaron returns.

"Miriam, you still there?" His voice has transformed from silvery to matter-of-fact.

"Yes."

"It's Miriam Gil, right?"

"Yes. You said you remembered me. The bursary and the passport application."

He clears his throat. There must be something wrong with his line.

"I am sorry to tell you. Unfortunately, I could not process your passport application, and it goes without saying I could not process your bursary application for children of ex-pats."

"What? Both of them rejected? You're the one who told me I should get an Israeli passport."

"You're right. I did. But I thought you were Jewish."

"Excuse me. You thought I was Jewish. Is that what you said?"

"Are you Jewish, Miriam?"

"Of course, I'm Jewish."

"I mean are you Jewish according to Israeli law? Do you have at least one Jewish grandparent? More importantly, do you hold Syrian citizenship?"

"What kind of crazy questions are these? I'm Jewish. My father's Israeli. Aren't ex-soldiers on record somewhere?"

"Do you hold a Syrian passport or not?"

"What?" My mouth drops open.

"According to our records, Miriam, it says your mother is a Syrian Christian and your father is *bilty*

190

yaduah."

"He's what?"

"I'm looking it up for you in English. One second. I want you to understand. We shouldn't be doing this over the phone, but you said you are a student. I want to believe you."

I tap my foot on the side of the wall, angrily. The way he said he wants to believe me tells me that he doesn't. This is crazy. I hear him shuffling pages in the background.

"Unknown. Your mother is a Syrian Christian and your father is unknown. That's what we got back from our application to the main office in Jerusalem. Come down as soon as possible before anyone else phones you. You must because we cannot continue over the phone."

"Is this a joke?"

"No."

"You think my mother is Syrian Christian and my father is some kind of alien. Give me a break." I force a laugh into the receiver. "Isn't this one big joke?"

He doesn't laugh with me, and his voice deepens an octave.

"Come down. Bring some proof about your parents."

"Proof? Like what?"

"Your parents' marriage certificate would be a good start. Birth certificates. Any other documents. You need to prove you are Jewish, Miriam, and who you are in general. It's very important. I'm here for you every day from eight to twelve. Shalom."

Yaron hangs up, and I am left with the receiver mid-air in my hand until another student snaps his fingers and I realize I'm holding him up and about to miss my bus. The foyer doesn't stay empty for long.

I race out the dormitory entrance. Nothing has been as it appears ever since I set foot in this country. And maybe I am stuck here. Now that I've gone and put myself on the Israeli radar screen, I don't know how I'll get out. *Unknown.* I have no idea what that means. My father with his soldier's walk and his guttural Hebrew is an unknown man married to a Syrian Christian. All anyone has to do is take one look at him. This is nonsense. My mother was Jewish, too. My head spins. I don't know what I'll say to my father.

***

I gaze over Safed from my seat on the bus. I thought I would be exhausted by the third day of our trip, but I'm exhilarated. I'm falling in love with this tiny country. It's as though I'm not seeing something for the first time, but remembering something precious I'd forgotten and given up for lost, every new mountain or waterfall seems foreign and familiar at once. When I leave here there's no doubt in my mind a piece of me will stay behind, waiting for me to return to Israel.

The small town of Safed is asleep at the summit of the mountains, the highest city in Israel. It is our last stop on another one of our dawn outings. Not long ago I would have been thrilled at the thought that I don't have to worry about where to spend the weekend. Now that worry seems girlish, infantile. I don't know what's happening in my apartment, my friend has been firebombed, and each time we pass a police car my stomach clenches and my toes curl. Part of me believes they are combing the country for me, eager to catch the Syrian imposter, who came in to the country on a Canadian passport. I shake my head to scatter these thoughts, willing them away, just as my professor announces that we're sharing a prepaid breakfast at a popular café and then we're all free to go in our own directions, if we don't want to spend the Sabbath here tomorrow.

"There is only a small Muslim Arab and Maronite Christian community in the Galilee's predominantly Jewish town that is also considered by many to be Israel's largest haven for visual artists," says Professor Malkah. "Many residents prefer to sleep away the afternoon, tucked away as so many are in cul-de-sacs amid rows of art galleries enmeshed with small eateries and centuries old synagogues," says the professor.

"What about all of the art galleries?" Sender asks.

"Who cares about art galleries, where's the funky klezmer music?" Richard says. "And the cool kabbalah stuff?"

"There's all of that coming up," says the professor, standing in the bus aisle, clutching a microphone.

On the bus I'd sat in my by now customary position with the professor. Today all of her hair is pinned at the sides, and there are circles under her eyes and redness at the edges of her nose. I inch toward the window. If she's got a cold, I don't want to catch it. My throat is continuously dry in this chill. It is a cold winter day, my first cold day in Israel. The air here is dryer than in Haifa and penetrates more to the bone.

Once the class disembarks, I follow behind the

professor down Safed's cobblestone streets in Israel's hilly north to the Maximillian Café in the heart of the Artists' Quarter, where we have a pre-booked breakfast table. I inhale the smell of plum tomatoes, basil and onion, forcing myself to ignore the fact that Valerie is in costume with all of that makeup on and she's laughing with a whole group of new friends. I've become way too sensitive since I heard about Arslan. Valerie should make other friends.

My breath catches when hands cover my eyes out of nowhere. I peel them aside and tilt my head backward. Farzeen comes into focus. I almost don't recognize her out of context, off campus.

"Surprise!"

"What are you doing here?"

"The foreign students aren't the only ones who go on school trips. We've been in Tiberias, but some of the different university groups are meeting in Safed for lunch. We're early."

I don't know what to say. I'm happy and embarrassed to see her. There is an eager quality in her voice, and I picture her surveying Tiberias with its centerpiece, the Sea of Galilee, with a cross face. No doubt her temperature would rise at the idea of Jewish control of the lowest freshwater lake on Earth.

"How are you?" I blurt.

I bite my tongue. Anything I say sounds patronizing, as if I didn't sign a letter of complaint about her. As usual, I cannot read her expression. Questioning her about Arslan is way out of line. The last time they were together her eyes were shooting flares. I imagine an

194

angry red line of fire launching from her mouth and hitting me right between the eyes in front of the whole class, only a few steps away.

"I'm starving." Farzeen pats her stomach. "I only had half a roll for dinner and nothing yet today. The restaurant smells delicious and it's good." She lets her hair out of its long ponytail. The elastic band she takes out of her hair is thick and all the colors of the Palestinian flag: green, red, black, and white. She wears it now as a bracelet. It matches her sweatshirt and scarf. "I've been here before with my family. Try the garlic bread. Delicious."

She steps closer to me and whispers in my ear. "I know you signed the letter."

I rush in with a garbled apology, but she holds up two hands.

"I forgive you. I'm content in my new place. It even has a small space to tutor, so I don't need to go out all the time."

I struggle meeting her gaze, and she continues to hum into my ear as I glue my eyes to the cobblestone path.

"Look, I know how the Zionists work. It is me who should have warned you. They wear you down until you're sedated." She squeezes my arm.

I don't correct her assumptions. I don't tell her I'm not sure who the Zionists are in her mind. The university administration? Dalit? Simona, the up-and-coming world-famous psychologist? I don't tell her no one injected any serum into my arm, hooked me up to a mind-numbing machine. Rather something happened that made me realize how close every single one of us is to the butt of a gun or the tip of a homemade rocket. Not far at all. There's still a scab somewhere in my body from the first time we'd met and I'd challenged her. My lips feel glued together.

Everyone else in my group has entered the café. I can see them out of the corner of one eye sitting at the table. Some have scattered to the bathrooms, to payphones, to demand water from the waitress.

"I'm glad I ran into you." I clear my throat. "I really believe I owe you some sort of explanation and, so you like the new place?"

"I told you, I know what happens here. It is me who needs to explain things to you or rather enlighten." She stretches out the syllables of this last word and switches to her normal authoritative voice. "I'm not so far from you as you think on campus, and we're all master's students. No babies. Soon there will be a break for Hanukah. What will you do then?"

By then I might be thrown out of the country or in jail, but I don't say that.

"I don't know." I notice she doesn't tell me where her new apartment actually is. I don't begrudge her.

"Well, you'll think of something. You have time. There is much to see in Nazareth, where I am from." She pauses. "If you are interested. Nazareth Village, the ruins of Megiddo."

"Farzeen, that's something I hadn't thought of. It's nice of you to mention. Thank you. I can't say I've planned anything yet."

I swallow a laugh at the irony of the situation. As a

Syrian Christian, Nazareth should be top on my list. If anyone from the government is looking for me, it sounds like a good place to start searching, and hanging out with Farzeen there, perfect. I won't have a leg to stand on. My imagination is getting the better of me. The word *Arslan* is on the tip of my tongue, a milk tooth hanging by the root.

When I try to meet Farzeen's eyes, gauge her true feelings, underneath her stony persona, I see she has become absorbed in my professor's lecture. The class has moved back outside. The professor talks unfalteringly about the history of Safed. She is on to the Crusaders' rule in the twelfth century when the city was called Saphet. It is obvious that she does not care if anyone is listening or not. She has a picture of life to present for anyone who wants a view of it.

"You got one of the better professors this semester. An Egyptian." Farzeen nods her approval. I'm about to correct her: She's an Egyptian Jew who was expelled from her home in the 1950s along with about 75,000 other Jews—an entire community with deep roots, who had come to be seen as a fifth column. On the bus ride she'd told me in low tones how her family's property had been sequestered, about the 1948 bombings and riots.

"I'd better return to my group," Farzeen says.

She's forgotten all about her invitation for me to spend the holiday with her, or at least she doesn't press it. My last chance to ask about Arslan is slipping away. But just thinking about how Farzeen might react fills my mouth with the taste of failure.

I'm utterly taken aback when I feel Farzeen's lips brush first one cheek—half a brush on the cheek and half an air kiss—and then the other and then another brush and air-kiss on the first cheek, and she is gone. I touch my face where she has kissed me, trying to decipher the meaning behind the expression and for a split second I consider if someone has seen her kiss me, Farzeen, with her Palestinian flag emblazoned sweatshirt and matching scarf and hair elastic and wonder what they might think.

A cat yowls in the distance and an engine backfires. The noise brings me back to the moment. I need to make an overseas call. I'm in trouble. My professor arrives out of nowhere, takes me by the hand, and leads me to the table. She nods encouragingly and piles wide noodles smothered in buttery white sauce on my plate. I eat without tasting the food and avoid looking at my watch, counting down the minutes until it is a reasonable enough hour to wake up my father. I don't allow myself to expand this thought. I won't think about whether or not it's a good time to wake up my father and Jacquie. The image that provokes in my mind makes me sick to my stomach.

I'd spied a bright orange payphone just outside the restaurant, and I've got two new phone cards in my pocket, both full, so I think I can manage a long-distance call. If I'm going to enjoy my first weekend in Safed at all, I need to speak to my father now.

Fifteen minutes later when I pick up the receiver it's sticky with hummus, and the area around the public telephone smells of urine. Revolted, I sift through my pockets for a serviette or tissue. I come up empty and have to use my shirtsleeves. I dial my home number with my clean hand, try not to inhale deeply and after five rings my father picks up.

"Allo?"

"Abba?"

My father's familiar voice reverberates through the line. My heart lifts, and I struggle to get my emotions under control, reminding myself that his familiar voice might placate me, but it's the same one that threw me out of the house.

"Miri? You calling me? Why you wasting your money on the phone? You can write me a letter. I'll write you back."

For my father a long-distance call is a shopping spree.

"No, Abba. It's okay. I have a job. I translate papers for an Israeli student."

"Smart girl you are. How is Israel?"

"It's exciting. A lot of action." I have my back to the restaurant where the ten students who have decided to stay for the weekend have ordered double chocolate biscotti.

"Yeah, Israelis like action. They are not half asleep like over here."

There is a pause between us while I strain to hear if he misses me, if there is any longing behind his words. But I hear the same message I heard last spring: He doesn't want me wedged between him and his new love life.

"You saw my brother, Moshe?"

"Yes." I take the comb out of my back pocket and run

it through my hair. I switch hands and comb out the other side.

"It was okay?"

"He's friendly. He gave me a lot of food."

"He'd better be friendly. You're my daughter. If his daughter comes here, we'll be friendly, too."

The muscles in my neck tighten. He knows about Yakira? I didn't know she existed before I came here. What else has he kept from me? Maybe everything Leah said was true. It can't be. My father would never discourage someone from fighting in the army. She was talking about something incomprehensible.

"You know about her?"

"I know they have a daughter a bit younger than you. Young people like to travel, also Israelis, not just Canadians. So, I'm saying if she comes, that's all. Why? What's to know?"

This makes more sense to me. I can't imagine my father mentioning an Israeli who ducks out of army service without adding a few choice curse words before or after her name.

"Nothing, Abba. I'm asking you about Leah. Do you know Moshe's wife?"

"Which one?"

"Did he have more than one? I don't know. This one is Leah. You know her?"

"Leah." My father says the word as though his mouth is filled with wet paper towels.

"Yes. Leah. She's very friendly, but kind of a loner."

"What do you mean? Did she say something to you?" His voice has changed. It was relaxed and easy, and now it's tense.

"Just to come whenever I like."

The pause between us lengthens. This isn't entirely true. She looked at me barely dressed the first night I ever met her and then she pointedly warned me about Israeli men, but the whole picture's not fitting my narrative right now.

"So that's how she is I guess. As long as she doesn't bother you, you get a free place to eat and sleep. What do you care?"

This business with Leah will have to wait. My father doesn't like long phone conversations.

"Abba, I need to ask you something."

"Go ahead. Ask me because I need to get to work. I don't like you wasting money on the phone. Buy yourself something you need instead or better, save it. So many TVs to fix you wouldn't believe, but who knows about tomorrow?"

"I applied for an Israeli passport."

"What for? Canadian is good enough. It's better."

"They said it would be easier for me to leave the country. When I called to ask when it would be ready they told me they could not give me one, that my mother was a Syrian Christian and my father is unknown."

"What? What kind of *shtuyot*? Who told you?"

"The Interior Ministry."

"They're a bunch of dummies. What kind of a country is it there now? Who is running the place?"

I cave into the phone box, forgetting about the hummus. The urine smell is harder to ignore with each passing minute.

201

"I need papers to prove who I am now. Do you still have your marriage certificate?"

"I don't have nothing. Your mother was in charge of those things. You already drove me crazy with a fax. You wanted Israel. This generation knows everything. Now you've got Israel."

I dig my heels into the ground. If I talk back now, he might hang up.

"Could you look please? I'll call you in a couple of days again."

"Miri, it's a crazy mistake."

"I know that, but I need to prove it now. They're not taking my word for it."

"You don't worry. I'll look. It will be all right."

His voice is reassuring, but he's not the one I'd choose to find official papers about anything. He writes phone numbers on torn serviettes, recycles dental floss, and pays for everything in cash.

"I need to clear this up."

"We'll clear it up. I said we would."

"Will you look right now?"

"Of course. I'll go now and you call me again. Bunch of idiots. You take care of yourself. *Yalah.* God bless you, Miri."

"Shalom, Abba."

I hold the phone to my heart for a few minutes before I replace the receiver. I didn't expect the tears that run down my cheeks. I wipe them away with the back of my hand.

Chapter Twenty-One

THE QUIET IS BROKEN when there is a knock at the front door of my apartment. I sit in a wet towel on my bed and look around for something clean to throw on. I've been back from Safed for only an hour, after a quiet Sabbath spent writing down everything my professor had said, so that nothing would be lost to me later on for the final exam. This was preferable to worrying about Yaron's last instructions: Come down to see him with documents in hand. Documents I don't have.

The knock is louder this time. My first thought, stuffing myself into a pair of jeans, is that it must be Arslan, finally healed, returning from her northern village. She's lost her key or is too burdened with packages of sweets from her mother to reach it. My heart lifts. I ignore the obvious fact that none of my roommates ever return on a Saturday night and no doubt Arslan would return with a team of family members to help her.

It has to be her. On the radio they said she'd been released. If it was Valerie she'd be calling through the locked door, announcing herself to the entire dormitory.

I realize the jeans won't do up because they are Simona's and peel them off. I spy a pair of sweatpants, yank them on, and grab a sweatshirt to wear over my long-sleeved cotton undershirt. I run down the hallway and open the apartment door a crack. My face falls. It's Boaz, the dormitory security guard.

"Phone call," he says, and turns without a backward glance. There's no way my father could have found anything so quickly. Still, a possibility has opened up and with it my mood lifts. Maybe this passport problem will all be over this week, if I can convince my father to pay for first-class mail.

I run to the foyer barefoot on the cold tiles. If it's my father long-distance he won't be happy that I kept him waiting.

"Hello?" I gasp into the receiver.

"Hey. Shalom, beautiful Miriam. I'm glad you're still up. How was Safed?"

My mind draws a blank, and there is an awkward pause.

"Miriam?"

"Guy!" I can't believe it. I am making such a mess of this. My palm meets my forehead. I let him think I didn't recognize his voice. I'm a complete idiot. "There must be something wrong with my end of the line. How are you? How did you know I was in Safed?"

"A little bird told me," he says. "How are you?"

"I'm good," I lie. I'm not about to tell him that I'm alone, friendless in my apartment and that a clerk from the Interior Ministry has let me know the Israeli government doesn't consider me to be Jewish.

"How are you?" I ask.

"I broke my hand, actually."

"You broke your hand?"

"Lifting weights. I was stupid and a weight fell on me."

"Oh. I'm sorry."

"It's okay, could be worse. I have a cast."

He sounds relaxed, and I wonder if he's taken any pain medication for his broken hand. I imagine what he must look like, lying on his bed in one of those bachelor apartments on the kibbutz, one hand in a cast at his side. My uncle told me the single rooms were more like lofts, or at least the bedrooms were merely lofts in one large room built with a high ceiling. He must have climbed up the ladder one-handed to his loft and slid under the covers, his head on one of those long narrow pillows that stretch the length of the mattress.

"Tomorrow I have a get-together with my new class in Binyamina. Do you know where that is?"

"No."

"It's near Caesarea, close to you. I thought you could meet me there."

"Tomorrow? I'd love to."

"Good. There's this nice little park. It's called Alona. Are you writing this down?"

"Of course." I turn my face to the wall, so I won't be distracted by any of the other students. I need to memorize whatever he's about to tell me.

"Alona Park. Ask for Mei Kedem. That's where I'll be waiting. We'll be done by noon at the latest. Do you think you can find it?"

"I'll ask at the bus station."

"You might have to take a cab from the bus stop."

"I'll be fine."

We say goodbye, and I return to my room dreamy-eyed, but I know I need to perk up, not go off on a mental tangent about what might happen tomorrow with Guy. If I'm to miss my Sunday afternoon classes, I'd better finish the paper that's due the following day. I'm still an enrolled student whether the Interior Ministry thinks so or not.

***

Mei Kedem is an underground water tunnel stretching over hundreds of meters in Alona Park, an hour from Haifa University. Guy forgot to mention that small detail. That it's a water tunnel. I groan. I should have known he'd choose a water-related outing. I'm wearing a soft pink long-sleeved cotton T-shirt with a popped-up collar, jeans, and running shoes. Not water shoes or flip-flops, and I didn't bring a change of clothing.

It had been easy to board a bus to Binyamina, but I took a cab ride to the park. There weren't any direct buses that I could find, and I didn't want to be late. I buy a flashlight they are selling for four shekels at the ticket counter. That's another detail he didn't mention, the flashlight. I would have brought that, too.

It's a hot December day, but it's not tourist season and the park is quiet. The landscape is beautiful. All around me are green hills dotted with agricultural settlements. I'm the only one here at the Mei Kedem tunnel, besides the girl with her nose in a book selling tickets. I sit at one of the ten or so picnic benches, in a shady spot near the ticket counter, adjacent to the almost empty parking lot.

"The Mei Kedem water tunnel extends nine hundred and eighteen feet to Caesarea and was built more than two thousand years ago in the time of Herod and Hadrian. The water tunnel was part of an engineering system designed to supply water to ancient Caesarea."

The brochure goes on to tell me that the water level reaches the average adult's knees and that the tunnel walk is always accompanied by a guide and shouldn't take more than an hour. I put the brochure on the table and fold my hands under my head, soak the sun into my hair. I check my watch. He's fifteen minutes late. Well, Guy's not getting points for being on time, but he gets five stars for originality. I've never walked through a 2,000-year-old tunnel on a date before. This gives me pause for thought. I wonder if Guy considers this our first official date. Is he late on purpose as some sort of message that he happened to be in the area and thought he'd make a day of it, nothing more? And if he doesn't show? Then I've skipped all of my afternoon classes for nothing. Another ten minutes passes and I take out the bus schedule I grabbed, review the return times to Haifa with a cross face.

"Miriam. Shalom! I'm so sorry. Do you forgive me for being late? I couldn't get away."

I glance up, and there is Guy with a cast on his left hand. He leans over and kisses me on both cheeks, but I've noticed that's a standard greeting here, it doesn't signify anything special. He's sporting the grunge look today, a red-and-white checkered flannel shirt and worn jeans.

My heart skips a beat.

"You thought I would leave you stranded here and after you took a taxi and missed classes, right?"

I smile blithely. He sees right through me. It frightens me and thrills me at the same time. I always had to spell everything out for Neil.

"I didn't mean to scare you. Not sure if that's the right word. To make you nervous. It was supposed to be a *gibush*. Do you know what that is? To meet and become familiar before the course starts, especially this one specific course where there will be many excursions, and there was this one woman who just wouldn't stop talking and there's no car insurance for driving with a broken hand, so I had to get a friend from the kibbutz to drop me off. If you can believe it there was no gas in the car when we arrived, so in short, I missed the first forty-five minutes and had to catch up."

We look at each other and break out laughing. It feels good to be with him. It feels safe.

"It sounds as though I'm reporting to a teacher, no?" He grabs both of my hands in his. His fingers stick out of his cast. "I just don't want you to think I would ever have left you alone here. So, come." He pulls my hands toward the tunnel entrance.

"There's just this one thing, Guy."

"I know what you're going to say, and the water won't come past my knee. It will be fine with the cast. *Yalah*. We want to go now at the hottest part of the day, and you're going to love this water hike."

"I meant that you never told me I'd need water shoes and a change of clothes."

"Ah. I thought I did." He frowns, but only for a moment, looks down at my feet. "It's okay. Running shoes are fine. It won't ruin them. Most of the time the water is only to your calf." I try not to show that my body tingles when he takes my hands. I don't want him to think I melt the minute he touches me.

Guy purchases two tickets at the counter and another flashlight and we are led into a small, cozy room with a movie screen at one end.

"Hebrew or English?" asks the guide.

"What?" we both ask at the same time.

"I can show you the movie in Hebrew or English."

"English," says Guy.

"It's about twenty minutes. I'll come back at the end. You're the only ones here today, and I don't have any reservations, so we might as well start now."

In another minute I'm sitting alone with Guy in a small, dark theater.

"Starting in thirteen B.C.E., Herod spent twelve years rebuilding an earlier Phoenician city to honor Caesar Augustus. Since there was no fresh water, Herod build this aqueduct to bring water from Mount Carmel, nearly ten miles away."

I turn my head and catch Guy eyeing me. He reaches over and takes my hand with his one good one, holds it lightly in his lap, playing with my fingers, making it hard for me to concentrate on the film.

"There's a really nice beach here, too. It's great to come in the summer. Beautiful sunsets," he whispers into my ear. I nod. I don't know how much longer I can sit in this dark room with him looking so handsome and at ease in his long flannel shirt. He can't be that comfortable in a cast. He came prepared with water shoes. He notices me looking at them.

"I'll owe you a pair of shoes if yours never dry," he says, grinning at me. "And you'll be all right if your jeans are damp, no?"

The color rises in my cheeks, and I'm grateful the lights are off. The tour guide could return any minute, and he does. He flicks the light switch.

"Now, we're heading into the tunnel. Follow me."

The Roman aqueduct is in excellent condition. In one minute I've gone from a charming theater to a dark, enclosed tunnel, sloshing forward in water up to my ankles. I hadn't thought about how claustrophobic this might make me feel. I've never walked through an underground water tunnel before, and I grip Guy's good hand.

The guide is laid back, relaxed, and tells us to go at our own pace; he stays in the lead.

The look on Guy's face is one of amazement. He's in his element, and I remember that he's a lifeguard, too. I relax my grip and shine my flashlight on the ceiling.

"One of the most fascinating aspects," Guy says, shining his flashlight on the ancient walls. "A second channel was built as the city grew and more water was needed. The Romans built these massive structures without power machinery, and often the stones were fitted together without mortar."

I press my lips firmly together, so I won't interrupt him. It's nice just to watch someone so excited about something.

"Hundreds of thousands of people were dependent on this aqueduct for survival over hundreds of years of Roman rule. If they could do that, think of what we can do to enable millions to survive with our technology."

I could listen to Guy for hours. I've never met a man who had such vision so young. My few university courses have left me ill-prepared for this discussion, and I'm hoping he assumes I have to concentrate hard on not slipping on the wet stones.

We continue forward through the murky water, and after sixteen feet the guide cautions us to be careful of the drop coming up in the tunnel floor. The guide stays at a respectful distance, close enough for safety, but far enough so that he doesn't appear part of the conversation.

I slip on a jagged rock and Guy grabs my forearm, steadies me. With his fingers wrapped around my arm I suddenly don't mind that I'm walking around in squishy, water-logged shoes and drenched socks, the ends of my jeans sticking to my legs. Guy had left his jeans at the ticket counter. This time he is wearing long blue board shorts that reach his knees, not the trunks I recall from the beach. He'd looked at me sheepishly as he'd undressed.

"I shouldn't have phoned you so late. I was half asleep, and they'd given me something for my hand, for the pain. I thought I'd told you."

"It's no big deal."

"I don't actually mind seeing you in wet clothes," he said with a grin.

211

I would have stuck my tongue out at him, but the ticket seller was watching us.

Now we are at least halfway through the tunnel and my eyes have adjusted to the gloom. The tour guide points out that there are stairs and an exit here at the halfway point, but there's no other way to get out from here on until we reach the end. He's experienced with claustrophobic guests and good chance more than one parent has brought a child into the fresh air at the halfway point, but Guy doesn't give the exit a second glance and I'm not about to tell him enclosed underground spaces aren't my first choice. I do enjoy ancient history and water activities, above ground.

"One of the reasons I like it here so much is it reinforces the history, you know what I mean?" Guy asks me. Because we are walking side by side I can't look into his eyes, but I feel his breath on my cheek as he talks.

"Mmm," is the best answer I can muster. I'm not sure what he means.

"When you love the land, you want to learn as much about it as possible. It's never enough. Israel is such a big part of me, of us, our roots."

I'm not sure what he means by "us." He might mean the two of us or all Jews or Israelis. He moves elegantly through the water, never missing a step, not at all intimidated by the variations in depth, though admittedly this is a tour for five-year-olds and up; it's me who's not used to Roman aqueducts. One minute we tread through water to mid-thigh, the next minute it's shallow again and the rocks are slippery. By now we've been underground half an hour and the air is thicker. I don't allow myself to spoil our time by thinking about the lack of fresh air, the exit maybe a half an hour away.

"You're okay, right?" Guy asks. A look of concern on his face.

"This is great. I just get claustrophobic sometimes." I force myself to smile. He reaches out and guides my chin toward him so that we can see into each other's eyes.

"I messed this up. No notice about the clothes, and I didn't dream that you might not like being underground for an hour. Last time I came with a buddy and it wasn't more than thirty minutes, but he wasn't moving in heavy shoes and I had both my hands for balance." He holds me under my shoulder, and our pace picks up.

The guide shines his flashlight on a black metal staircase, and in a minute all three of us are back outside. We'd been much closer to the end than I'd calculated. The tour guide lets us know where there's a bathroom area and refreshment stand before he thanks us for coming and leaves. We walk back to the picnic tables and sit down.

"You liked it though?"

"Yes. I learned a lot. Thank you for taking me here. I wouldn't have come on my own."

Guy leaves to retrieve his pants, and I take off my dripping shoes and socks, roll up my jeans, and then think better of it. They won't dry that way.

"Why don't you wear my pants?" Guy asks.

"Your pants?"

"They'll be big, but dry. I'll stay in my bathing suit."

"Why not?"

I return from the bathroom barefoot in Guy's pants rolled at the cuffs. They keep slipping down off my waist, showing my midriff, not a look I usually adopt.

"I like them on you," he says. He's bought two bags of chips and two colas, and he's already eating his. The area is peaceful and green. I can see why he enjoys this park.

He stretches out along the bench, and I sit opposite him, sipping my soft drink.

"Tell me, Miriam, what are you learning in university?" Guy asks.

"We're learning about the early Zionists in one of my classes," I say.

"And what do you think?"

"I don't really have an opinion. I don't know anything about them. There's a test coming up, so I'd better learn something."

But when I glance at Guy he's not laughing at my small joke.

"You mean you don't know enough about them to call yourself a Zionist?"

"Not really, no."

He looks at me, his head cocked to one side as if considering.

"Well, I'm sure your professor knows how to teach and you'll have a clearer understanding of your roots soon enough. It's very important to me."

"That I understand my roots?" I ask him.

"That I'm with someone who shares my passion for Israel. My last girlfriend, she felt suffocated here I think. She kept telling me she wanted to live in a country that

214

was finished. She's not a builder, but she was young, we were young. I figured she'd change, grow up. I was wrong."

I eat each salty chip one by one, grateful to have something to occupy myself, keep my facial expressions less readable.

"But I admire that you've come all the way from Canada to learn about your country, your heritage. It takes guts. Many people would just bury their heads in the sand in such a comfortable country as yours."

I stiffen and drum my fingers on the table. I never came here out of duty to anything outside of myself. I lack the external compass that guides Guy. The moment my father asked me to leave, I needed to go at once. I longed to throw off his command and if my destination would unsettle him, all the better. If I had the money to go somewhere more glamorous, London or Sydney, I might have forfeited my journey, but those countries weren't handing out free scholarships.

But I don't respond. I drink my cola as if I've just trekked through the desert in August instead of a cool, refreshing water tunnel on a temperate afternoon.

I'm afraid if I speak my voice will give me away.

It's only our first official date, and already I've taken on the role of the imposter. I'm allowing Guy to think I'm here with Zionist motivations. There's no chance I'll breathe a word about my Interior Ministry problem, the one that might get me thrown out of the university at any moment for pretending to be a Jew. Something like that might stain Guy's view of me forever. He's such an idealist. I suppose that's how builders have to be.

Guy sits up and flashes me a smile that melts my heart and floods me with guilt.

"Want to get some real food?" Guy asks, breaking my train of thought.

"Dressed like this?" I look down at myself in Guy's jeans, and yank them up until they reach my bra, which I pray he can't see.

"I guess you're right. You do need to get back to your apartment." He wraps his arms around my waist, careful not to get his cast wet on any stray damp clothing. "Please forgive me. Maybe what seems unlucky is luck," he says, kissing me on the neck. "This way I owe you a lunch date. Yes?"

Instead of answering, I kiss him on the lips. His kisses are so soft and gentle, and he tastes of the chips and sea and the sweet aftertaste of Coke. I rest my head on his shoulder, inhale his woodsy scent, and keep my eyes averted. Next time, I think. Next time I'll be prepared and I'll find a way to reveal who I really am without losing him.

Chapter Twenty-Two

I ENTER THE HALLWAY and breathe deeply. The door to the bathroom is partially open, and I edge it open farther with my toe and stick my head in, taking Dalit by surprise. The unwritten rule in the apartment is the bathroom is owned by whoever happens to be occupying it at the time: no sharing.

"I guess everything went well with your paper," I say, shoving a high note into my voice.

Dalit raises one penciled-in eyebrow. She continues brushing her teeth with her eyes on the mirror. She grunts.

"Farzeen sure is gone, and it seems you were right. There's no reason to live in tension," I continue.

Dalit spits into the sink. She clears her throat and spits again. The room is humid and damp from the hot water, and I feel the sweat at the back of my neck, but I smile and wait with my hands knitted together and finally sit down on the toilet while Dalit flosses each tooth and spits again.

"Your point?" she says.

"I'd like to visit Arslan. I've been calling the hospital every day, and I heard she's released. I just need her address or phone number."

Dalit winces or perhaps slips on the wet floor. She grabs the squeegee and pushes the water under the sink uphill, toward the shower drain.

"Did Simona put you up to this now? The psychologist with her nose in the air is using you to pass a diagnosis?"

"Simona? I haven't seen her either. I don't know what you're talking about. I bought Arslan a card and a gift. If you think she won't see me you might give it to her," I answer.

"You're half white yourself. Think I don't know an Ashkenazi Jew when I see one? And by the way, your card interests my tachat."

The squeegee hits the back of the shower wall hard, and the bottom detaches. Not bothering to screw it back on, Dalit slams the bathroom door. I return to my room and can't close the door fast enough on Dalit and her anger. I struggle to make sense of it. I signed her letter, Farzeen's gone. She should be delighted. I'm missing something she's pinning on me.

"Shalom," Simona says, opening the door wide.

When I don't answer she sits down beside me on my bed.

"What's wrong around here *now*? Didn't you enjoy the Safed trip last week? I admit it was weird here without you for a night," Simona says, standing and strolling the length of the room, her eyes on my every move. "And Dalit creeping around in the dark like a burglar or a deranged cat. She gets worse with time. But Safed is pretty, no? It's beautiful if you can ignore the weirdos who actually live so far from civilization year-round."

Simona is her usual talkative self. That's good. I've been alone in the apartment for three days since my return from Safed Saturday night, excluding the post-midnight arrivals of Dalit. I glue my eyes to the history book I'm pretending to read and debate whether I should tell Simona about my confrontation with Dalit in the bathroom.

No, I look into Simona's blue eyes. I'm not ready to share this with her—not yet. She'll burst out laughing, and I'm not ready for that. I never thought I'd be so happy to see her and anyone to speak to is better than no one.

Today's she's playing the part of the amateur psychologist out in the open, wearing huge tortoise-shell glasses that match her necklace, and she has an extra long pen topped with a feather tucked behind one ear. Only Simona can pull this off and still look trendy.

She's settled in: lying on the bed in a paisley tunic, studying as she does when she's not in class or waiting in line for the phone to speak to her boyfriend. This week she has replaced the wilted orchids with a handful of miniature purple violets.

"It's not your boyfriend, is it?" She stands up and begins to rummage through her cupboard.

"Simona, I don't have a boyfriend anymore." There's no chance I'm telling her about Guy and the regular phone dates we've had since our date on Sunday. How much I look forward to his voice on the other end of the receiver is none of her business.

"So, what is it?"

"It's hard to explain." I hate how brittle my voice sounds, and I don't want to push her away. Even her company is better than none.

"All right. You don't have to tell me. You clearly don't want to make progress in your life, and it's a shame because I'm right here with open arms. Maybe you are homesick or you feel regret about Arslan or something went sour with your girlfriend upstairs?" Simona digs.

"Valerie isn't my girlfriend!"

"Hey, you don't have a boyfriend. You don't have a girlfriend. Meet Miriam Gil, the girl with no friends. Better?"

Simona groans. She returns to her bed, plunks her long body down on her stomach, reopens her book. As the minutes pass the rest of her words take root and break through the fog Yaron put me into with one phone call. Maybe I'm regretful about Arslan.

"Oh, someone came by for you not long ago," Simona murmurs.

"Who?" I pick up my head. "Wait a second, what about Arslan? I know she was in that horrible attack, but the hospital said she's gone home. With luck she'll be back any day."

Simona laughs and it's not a laugh I like. She props herself up on one elbow on her side.

"She's not coming back."

"What? In the newspaper it says her injuries weren't that bad. A few burns on her leg and some bruises."

"She'll recover. Yes. But she's kicked out, bye-bye. As for your visitor, I'm trying to think. I *am* studying for a big exam. He is tall, thin, older. Yemenite. I would say fatherly. I asked him to leave you a note. Here." She reaches over to her desk and hands me a square of off-white paper with a personalized message printed in gold at the top: *From the desk of Simona Rosenbaum.*

I don't look at the note. I've been stunned into silence by Simona's words, winded. Dalit's words make sense all at once. She thought I'd come to gloat for two: me and Simona.

"Simona, please explain. What did you say?"

"I said he left you a note."

"What did you say about Arslan?"

Simona kicks off her shoes and rubs her ankles with her hand. She has manicured toes that match her fingers. "I told you that Moroccan *tembelit* was nothing but trouble, always swinging her tachat around in those pumps that went out with the Six Day War, like everyone else should watch out from the bulldozer."

"And?"

"Do I have to spell out everything for you?"

Suddenly the room feels warm, stifling. I jerk open the window, letting in the cold winter air.

"She sent her little letter, and it went as I predicted thank you very much. Her connection must have been the janitor she'd mistaken for the university president." Simona scoffs. "In short, they threw them both out. They won't leave one Arab student. It wouldn't be fair, three against one."

My mouth drops. I never should have signed anything. I should have followed my instincts and stood my ground. This is what I get for losing control. Farzeen didn't even hint at this. Maybe she tried to and I didn't get it. All that gibberish about anesthetizing me, enlightenment.

"Shocked, huh? I told you they don't distinguish between Arabs."

"Oh my God. She was traumatized by terrorists, and now she's not coming back to the apartment."

"She refused the new room they offered her with five Muslim Arab students. No surprise because Farzeen was one of them. It's too far to travel every day and too exhausting. Maybe she'll have better luck next year."

"What?"

"She's lost the year."

I feel sick to my stomach. I'd never dreamed this could happen when I signed the note. Not in a million years.

"She maybe can get some credit for what she's done, but no space in the dorm, no studies. Dalit's connections, hah. Serves her right." Simona performs now, speaking with her hands, her voice animated, snapping on her gum. "All Dalit wanted was a promotion for herself. Arslan's father won't be running to her with it." She sticks out her chest and huffs, but stops when she notices I'm not smiling.

Poor Arslan. She studied so hard to be at the top of her class. She's been injured in a horrible incident and now this. And I've done this to her. Dalit must be too embarrassed to speak to me after she bragged about how she can fix everything through her *protectzia*. I thought I felt badly this morning, now my head sinks into my hands.

The breeze blows something to the ground. It's the note I'd been holding. I pick it up and read the Hebrew: *Shalom, Miriam. I hope the Sabbath was pleasant for you. I had to come to Haifa for work. I will be in the cafeteria on campus for the next hour in case you get this note. In the humanities building. Your Uncle Moshe.*

"It's from my uncle."

"You have an uncle here? I thought you were alone. The only thing you've successfully hidden from me so far."

I ignore Simona's intrusive comment. Besides it's fake. I know she read the note, but I'm in no shape for a confrontation I won't win. Dalit might never look me in the eye again, her gross miscalculation must be a mountain of embarrassment she might not have the legs to climb, and I need someone in this apartment who is a source of information.

"I have to catch him."

Maybe my uncle can help me with my passport problem.

In the humanities building, I race down two floors to the cafeteria

I scan the empty tables. It's not busy at 4:00 p.m. I spot him, blowing on a bowl of red lentil soup, reading some papers in one hand.

"Uncle Moshe?"

He glances up from his meal. There are hand-written papers scattered in front of him. He looks more professional off the kibbutz, although he's dressed in the same manner: tan dungarees and a yellow T-shirt. I notice a bright blue sweater crumpled over his chair. The pastoral background of the kibbutz might make anyone his age look retired. Here he looks busy. He wipes his chin with his napkin and stands, offers me his hand. It is smooth and cool in mine.

"I'm pleased you got my note. Sit. I want to buy you lunch."

I try to remember if I ate today, but I cannot. He gets up without asking me what I want to eat or if I want to eat. It is the first time I've sat down in a university cafeteria since my dinner with Farzeen when that Arab man confronted us. I look around, half expecting to see him lurking in the corner, still wagging his finger at me.

Moshe returns with two large pieces of pizza on a tray, a small purple cabbage salad, and two bottles of orange juice.

"You prefer apple? Cola?" He holds out the bottle to me. "You were far away."

"Orange juice is fine."

"You look tired," he says.

"I am." I open the bottle and drink half of it in the first sip. I should ask him if Leah hates me. But then I would have to confess I was eavesdropping. He might forgive that, but who knows where it would lead. As her husband, good chance he'll take her side or he might be so humiliated he won't want to see me for a while. I need help with my passport, and there's no one else. It's not worth the risk.

"It must be noisy in a dormitory. You don't sleep well. For you," Uncle Moshe points to a large duffle bag on the floor. I hadn't noticed it. "I hope I chose the foods you like. Leah put in some shampoos and soaps."

"That's very generous of you, thank you. I'm sure you both chose well." I lean over and kiss him on the cheek. His skin is like my father's.

"Don't worry. It's packed very well with ice packs. Eat and relax, nothing will spoil. You won't have to shop this week. I brought bread, eggs, cheese, many fruits and vegetables, everything. There are some sweets, too, of course."

I nod, mumble something about how he shouldn't have, and bite into my pizza.

"So, how are your roommates? The studies?"

I consider telling Uncle Moshe that I'm a dunce, that I thought I'd flown to Israel to meet students my age from all over the world, but I cut myself off before I ever left Canada with my brilliant letter to the administration asking to be put in the regular Israeli floor of the dormitories, and that he wouldn't believe what a mess I've made of that. To top it off, I didn't realize that most overseas students come with a large budget, so they can travel and frequent Israel's restaurants and concerts.

In short, I can't afford to party with them in the evenings or eat out with them in the daytime. I don't even have another student from my program on my floor, let alone in my room. I'd isolated myself in all of my classes with Valerie, sitting with her at the back or on top of the professor at the front. My roommate Simona needs to hang a sign on my door: *Arslan's evicted thanks to you*! And that's after Arslan was a victim of a bombing attack, something I can barely absorb. For some reason knowing that Simon also signed the letter relieves none of my burden. My signature tipped the scale.

But I say nothing approaching what is weighing down my heart.

Instead, I tell my uncle it's nice to see him, that I am feeling more and more as though I was cheated of something that was rightfully mine as I tour around Israel, that I have a history that was never given to me. He gobbles this up, and in spite of my troubles, I smile.

I get up to wash my hands at the sink at the cafeteria entrance before I eat, unconscious of the clattering of trays and cutlery around me. While I'm pressing down on the soap dispenser and searching for a paper towel, I debate if I should stick with my discoveries about my connection to Israel that seem to please him so much and avoid my insecurities and inability to grasp the nuances in this culture. He might have formed his own opinions once Leah got through telling him about finding me half naked in the water with their neighbor, who I'd met only an hour before. She must have told him. I can't blame her.

I find myself in the women's bathroom when I meant to return to the table where Moshe shuffles through his work papers and waits. I'm more distracted than I'd realized.

"I'll be happy to get you seconds," Moshe says when I return. "Eat slowly. You've lost weight. I'll have to report that to Leah, who is getting better."

Moshe slurps his soup. He clears his throat a few times and shifts in his seat.

I stuff a large bite of pizza in my mouth and pick up my juice. I am all at once famished, empty inside. Sauce runs down my chin, and Moshe hands me a napkin.

"It's good she's better. I want to ask you about the Ministry of the Interior?"

"Ministry of the Interior?" His hand knocks his orange juice, and it lies on its side, its contents dripping to the floor. "A problem?"

Moshe's mood is altered. His facial expression clouds, and his lips are pressed together. He looks as though he might bolt. I might as well have accused him of shoplifting our early supper.

"Sort of." My voice is high, almost a whine. I dislike the way he's looking at me, as though he doesn't know where to put his eyes.

There is no more food on my plate. Moshe springs up.

"Some dessert. You have room."

He sprints away before I can protest, and I watch him dart around the food area, examining the cakes under a glass window.

My father's words slither into my mind: "Even my mother never liked that son. *Ben-zonna.*"

I throw a few more napkins over the spilled juice. The napkins are the cheap ones I've seen all over Israel, thin and waxy, not absorbent at all.

I should have called him on it, asked my father what he meant. But it always brought on a black mood. I can't hold it against someone that decades ago they were so hungry and exhausted they chose to run away from their family, to save themselves. I know so little about Uncle Moshe, not enough to fill a page of a book. I need to learn more.

He returns with a second tray, filled with three kinds of cake and a dish of ice cream. "You like apple? Chocolate?" He pushes each plate toward me. "This one is good." He points to all three of them.

He concentrates on his pizza. When he finishes he stacks the sugar and Sweet'n Low packets into a small tower.

"Have you heard from my big brother?" Uncle Moshe asks.

"I spoke to him. Yes." I run my hands through my hair.

"It wasn't easy for you growing up with him as a newcomer over there. I could have made it easier. Phoned you. This food is the least I can do now."

"You don't owe me anything," I answer.

My uncle takes a long sip of his drink.

"My father did do some difficult things when I was a kid, but there's no point in trying to improve your life story, is there?" I ask.

"No. I bet he had you involved in his business plans. When we were young he was always scheming, asking every friend and neighbor to stick a few liras into his ideas."

I told my uncle then about my Sunday afternoons growing up. How my father would rifle through the classified sections of the free newspapers that crammed

228

our box on Sunday mornings with a blue-ink pen in one hand.

"Hmm, here is my advertisement," was how he always began, looking straight into my twelve-year-old eyes.

"I want to check it. Read the English, Miri. It's good?"

I bent toward my father as close as I dared. He would still be chewing the last bite of his salad. I could smell the onions and the Thousand Island salad dressing on his breath. The scent of Vaseline Intensive Care hand lotion I knew he had rubbed into his hands that morning would still be there. I'd read aloud: *Electrolux. Ten years old. Best offer.*

"Yes, Abba. It's fine," I chirped. He disliked it if my voice was low, so I put as much singsong and butterscotch in as I could muster. I always wished at those times that I'd have gotten to the classified section first. But so what if I had? I never had the guts to tear it up, set it alight, pour corn oil over it or egg yolk or ketchup. Anyhow, it was free, delivered to the door, and replaceable like the twist ties for the garbage my mother never used.

"Miri? Where is your head? I'm talking to you and you're dreaming. Look how many advertisements I've circled. Let's get on the phone for these TVs. Let's be the first to get the money, not like those last-minute Canadian dummies."

I was his reluctant partner. He was certain that his guttural Hebrew-accented English might put them on the scent, make them suspicious of cheaters and bargain hunters. Maybe they didn't like selling to immigrants or refugees or darkies or foreigners.

My uncle looks at me now through the same eyes as my father's. If I look too deeply into them I'll blush. I've never shared that memory.

"I could have visited or invited you to Israel, to meet your own cousin. Maybe that would have been good for her, too. Who knows what effect one person has on another?" he says. He scrapes the chocolate frosting off of the cake with his fork and shoves it into his mouth. "She might have taken some pride in having you here by the beach for a summer or two, taken some pride in her country."

I sense his despair.

"I'm sorry about it. Sorry about many things. Believe me, it couldn't be done. I can't explain it all."

"I'm here now," I say, though what I want to say is "Why can't you explain it all? What's with all these secrets?"

"Yes, you are." He reaches across the table and puts his hand over mine. Squeezes. "And I want to tell you something that might make more space in your heart for your father. Did he ever tell you about the war in '48?"

I shake my head.

"In those days he was my champion. I was a boy, seven or eight, and I worshipped him. Remember, you saw the house where we grew up when you were in Jerusalem?"

"Yes. I phoned you from my class trip to ask you if it was the right place, remember? I photographed the whole row just to be sure I got the right one."

"I'd love to see them."

He doesn't add "on your next kibbutz visit."

"They say a picture is worth a thousand words, but I want to tell you some things about this house you won't learn from photographs. When I was a boy this house was at that time like an airport for Israel. My father, your grandfather, he rented it to the army in 1948. They built a shack on our roof with lights to help the planes land and take off. Whoosh." Uncle Moshe motions now with his hands, as though they are single engine airplanes zooming over the cafeteria table.

"The Arabs across the way, in a village called Sheikh Badr, disappeared like this." He snaps his fingers. "From one night the war starts and they are gone. The village was empty. So, the workers come to our house, block the windows and the doors with sacks filled with sand. Water and electricity there is none, and the city is surrounded." I can see Uncle Moshe has traveled back half a century into his boyhood.

"Food, medicine, and so on can only come from the air. This is why the planes were so important. They needed an instant airport, and our place was it. Tractors came, flattened the ground, and soon they are bringing sacks with food and other basics, everything, even cigarettes. Meanwhile on the roof are soldiers who stay there and cover the shack with wire, so you can't see them."

"Camouflage," I offer, and my uncle nods. "I was scared. I was just this big." Uncle Moshe motions with his hands extending his right arm to the floor with his fingers stretched out. "Food and water was rationed, but we were lucky, the soldiers brought us leftovers from their military kitchen, so many were hungrier than us. But in no time the bombs began. Everything closed, schools, work, and everyone had to help fight the war. It was for survival. Across from the house, the dead were in crates one on top of the other. All day we heard the screams and the cries of parents and families who went behind the trucks. I can hear it now. I will always hear it. The situation worsened, and we received coupons for food and water. But your father, he never cried or complained, and he himself was not yet bar mitzvahed."

My eyes widen, but I can't say this surprises me. I've never seen my father cry, except the day he told me my mother died. But he didn't cry at the funeral or later, when they took the house away.

"He didn't hide like so many others or sit around kvetching. He built himself a wagon with proper wheels, and all day he picked olives in *Emek Hamatsleva*. He learned from our mother which plants we could eat, and he picked those, too. You know, *khubeza* — in English you call it mallow — and other roots."

I know Emek Hamatzleva is the Valley of the Cross. I'll have to look up mallow later.

"I begged to go with him, but he wouldn't let me. He wanted me near the house in case of bombs, at least the bathroom was a shelter.

"At night he would hold me while the mortars flew above us, through the sky night after night. Taka, taka boom. It gave me nightmares and I couldn't sleep. One night he woke me to see a twin-engine airplane, very rare. It was very exciting for us. When the mortars were sounding close, we ran to the bathtub and he held me the whole time. Our mother was not so strong, and it was harder for her to comfort me. He told me not to worry, we were okay, nothing could touch us, and I believed him. He was so confident. He must have understood so much more than me what was happening, what could happen, but he never showed fear. Nothing. He was a big help to my mother waiting all day in line for our water rations, bringing her more food, and for me a hero."

"Where was your father?"

"Oh him. He spent the war in the hospital. The only hospital was run by nuns. He had a broken leg, shrapnel from a bomb, so the responsibility of the family fell on Hanan. They only had student doctors available, so after six weeks of lying there, they had to break it all over and set it again. Three months in total he was there. Hanan was the father, in that sense, really."

I digest this while my uncle laughs, almost a giggle, at the end of his story, as though he has relived the sounds of the mortars whizzing so close to his ears, and he needs to release nervous energy. A comfortable silence settles between us as I review the words, savor them like the rationed water he described, the first time I've ever heard from a relative about my father's youth.

"Thanks for telling me that story, Moshe. I never imagined what it must have been like. He sounds as though he was a real big brother to you."

"Oh, in those days he was. For sure. Things happen as you grow up. People change, get in the way. What can you do?"

233

I notice the large clock on the cafeteria wall. I'm running out of time. I need to drive the conversation back to the present.

"Listen." There's no choice but to bring up the Interior Ministry again. "A strange thing happened. I came on a Canadian passport, but I applied for an Israeli one and my application was rejected because of something crazy." I lean forward as close to my uncle as possible across the table. "I need help with some bureaucracy. Or maybe Leah has the time? What does she do, anyway?"

Uncle Moshe reaches for his glass of juice.

"Leah works for the Interior Ministry."

"No way. Unbelievable." This is great and terrible at the same time. Part of me fills with hope. Maybe Leah thinks I'm the devil, but she was kind publicly. Even if it's an act for her husband, I'll take whatever help I can get. I clap my hands. This could be fixed in no time, unless I heard every word correctly and she despises me, wouldn't lift a finger. I don't see what I have to lose. I wasn't supposed to hear that conversation, so the dumb act it is.

"She'd help me, right?"

This explains her book collection and her penchant for reading topics like public security.

My uncle shuts down. His face is no longer readable. I twirl my hair around my fingers and bite my lip. Instead of answering, my uncle folds his arms across his chest and inches his chair back. The light in the cafeteria is white and highlights his bald head. He is balder than his older brother. He says nothing. There is no one else to turn to. I can wait.

It is untimely dark in December at only four o'clock in the afternoon. Israel switched to winter clock in early September, in time for the holiest day of the Jewish calendar, the fast of Yom Kippur. The lights in the cafeteria glow against the darkness pouring in from the windows. I see the new moon over my uncle's shoulder through a large window at the back.

Now he looks at his watch. The last time he did that he disappeared on me.

"Oh my goodness, Miriam. I'm so late. I have to go."

I can't believe it. Is it some kind of signal?

"I hope I didn't make you late for anything important."

"I have a big meeting on the kibbutz and with the traffic and everything. I don't want to rush you, finish, and what you can't eat, take back to your room."

"You're not rushing me. Ask Leah, okay? I'll call you later."

"Good idea and take this please." He slides two 100-shekel bills across the table. "Buy yourself earrings to go with the necklace, yes?" He leans over; I smell the sea. He pecks me on the cheek.

My uncle stands with his tray and glides across the floor as though I may chase after him. Mid-way across the room he crashes into a woman with a yellow beret tilted over one eye. As they collide, both of them attempting to dump their trays through the mouth of the bin at the same time, her cap falls to the floor. I watch as he apologizes, not turning once to look at me. He takes the lady's tray for her while she brushes off the spilled crumbs from the front of her blouse and dusts off her cap. His one clear desire is to leave the cafeteria.

I review our conversation, searching for the bump in our dialogue that set him off. I push the apple pie to the other end of the table. The pistachio ice cream is melted. I wouldn't have insulted him by telling him how I dislike pistachio, it was my mother's favorite and I can't even stand the smell of them. I clear my tray and stack it with slow, steady steps, as though its weight has doubled.

The cafeteria is empty. The staff prepares for the dinner rush, wiping down and resetting tables. Instead of leaving I return to the empty table. I grip the sides of my plastic chair. I should leave, but I fold my arms and rest my head on the cold surface. Someone wiped up the juice. There is more privacy here than I'll have in my apartment now that the sun has set and classes are over, a time of hunger. I half smile at the irony that the two people left in our apartment are Simona and Dalit. I'll have to confront Dalit at some point, break the ice. It's not her fault her plan blasted in her face. I can excuse Dalit, but for myself I'm filled with guilt about Arslan. I wish I had a chance to explain, say goodbye, but she won't want anything to do with me. I remember she nailed me as a betrayer when I refused her request. She thought she was doing the right thing by signing, but I knew it was wrong and should have stood by my instincts.

It's obvious my uncle is on Leah's side and at least part of what I heard is true, the Leah-hates-me part. The way my uncle bolted, said it all. I'm on my own. A quarter of an hour passes before I realize I'm still clutching the money my uncle pushed toward me before he raced away, as though an old fiery demon were after him.

Chapter Twenty-Three

Haifa, December 1992

"ABBA? IS EVERYTHING ALL RIGHT? Did you find the papers?" I wait, not breathing. Please say yes.

"I didn't find the papers yet. Don't worry. I asked the guy who helps me with the TVs, remember him?"

My shoulders sink. It must be 2:00 a.m. at home. The guy who helps my father with the TVs stinks of beer and whiskey. He won't be much help.

"He will come tomorrow. I'll mail them first-class. You know I don't read English like you."

At least he didn't say Jacquie was coming to act as his assistant. Either she found a guy with deeper pockets at the bingo hall or my father wants to avoid confrontation.

Fifteen minutes ago, a classmate came panting into my history class with a note: *Your father's waiting on the line.* I am still catching my breath. I've always been a runner, but I'm out of shape.

"It's nice to hear your voice." I start off cautiously with my father. Baby steps.

"Yeah. I know. Listen, Miri. You saw my brother?"

I can't tell from his voice if the right answer is yes or no.

"A little."

"He's telling you something? About the past maybe?"

"Something?" I feel guilty for sharing my teenage memories with my uncle. Maybe there was deceit in my voice. My father has clearly sensed disloyalty.

"He brings me food from the kibbutz and talks about his work, his daughter."

"Food? That cheapskate. Well, it's free for him. Good for you. Take it. I want to tell you a few things about the past. It sounds strange I guess, but there are things I want you to hear from me, not from him."

Leah's words run over me: *I could have bled to death on a mountain of snow for all he cared.* I don't know if I want to hear anymore.

"You don't have to —" I begin.

"You have time to talk now? You busy? I want you to hear it from me because I don't trust that big mouth brother of mine to tell it right, and his wife, she thinks so much of herself, *prima donna*. I wrote down some notes to read, so I don't get mixed up, you know with the crackles on the line and what do you call them? The echoes."

I'm troubled. Whenever I'd asked my father about his past, I'd received the sort of look that freezes you to your core, makes it crystal clear you've passed a border and the territory below is packed with minefields so old they might go off with the touch of a toe, a deep exhale of breath, or a light stumble, and he's never asked me if I had time for him. If he needed me it was understood I had time. The notion of my father writing out notes to

239

speak to me is so far afield I can't get my head around it. Distance changes people. I see that now.

"Of course, Abba. So many men here remind me of you. I have as much time as you like."

"Remind you of me?" My father chews over that for a few minutes, and my heart goes out to him. What should be natural for him is disquieting, a wife you can trust with your wallet, a brother who knows how you are, a daughter who sees your shadow from thousands of miles away. I hear my father take a breath and the rustling of papers. He's written a story for me!

"In my day in Jerusalem, the Yemenite lived with the Yemenite and the Sephardic with the Sephardic and so on. It's nothing like today. Now everyone is mixed up, so scrambled they don't know who they are anymore."

I hear my father sip his tea. I know it's black and steaming. He will eat his usual with it: one third of a banana and half an orange. He will store the rest of the banana and the orange in their original, natural packaging, careful not to disturb the peel beyond the part of the fruit he plans to consume.

As my father speaks in a storyteller's voice, I can see some faceless grandfather picking up his newborn son from Mount Scopus, in his 1932 Ford and driving him to their home in Jerusalem, which Moshe had described to me when I'd phoned him from one of my class trips to the Knesset. He'd told me I was right by his childhood home, and also described the only family car he'd ever known. When I sought out the house, it was still there: A quarter of an acre plus a big garden, but the 3-meter high fence had been replaced by stone walls and a modern gate.

My father hates talking about the past. Possibly he's not feeling well. Perhaps, it's the solitude. I've been gone for a while. His voice is melodic, his usual mixture of old-fashioned Hebrew and street English and soon I can see the series of unpaved dirt paths that led to his childhood home. By the end of the day, all of them had turned into puddles of water, thick with clay-like mud in the rainy winter season my father remembers.

I've stretched the phone cord so that I can sit on the floor in the foyer. The room is deserted smack in the middle of the morning. My father is frightened of something his younger brother might say to me. I've never seen or heard my father frightened of anything.

My father's voice sounds tired now. It's the dead of night for him and anyone born in Jerusalem in 1936 can only rave about his childhood for so long, sooner or later it transforms into the horrors of war. I'm not ready to hear about that. Moshe's memories from when he was eight-year-old were painful enough, and they can't possibly compare to my father's as a twelve-year-old.

"The war, we will talk about later, Miri. I will write to you about it. It's Moshe I want to get to. I'm tired now."

My father pauses and I sense his hesitation. I feel his wave of fatigue from here, a lifetime of fighting fueled by his tremendous desire for change, like a man who has been carrying a bulging sack of coal over his shoulder for so long, he cannot tell if his hands are black because the sun set long ago, or if his eyes are closed.

241

Finally, he speaks.

"Leah, I knew her before your uncle Moshe. She's from Jerusalem, too, same neighborhood, not Yemenite, but same area, you know? Sephardic."

"Okay." I steady myself for what I fear is coming next. My mouth runs dry.

"When I first came to Canada, I was working at the embassy in security."

"I know, Abba."

"Let me finish. At that time Leah, she was the secretary to the ambassador."

"You met her working at the embassy?"

"No, I came with her. We came together, you understand?"

I don't understand. They worked together in Israel in foreign affairs and were transferred together. This is how Moshe met Leah, I guess. His brother introduced him to a coworker, but Moshe wasn't in Canada, too. Or maybe he was. She'd mentioned Montreal over lunch.

"She was at that time my...wife. We were very young when we married, teenagers, still in the army, but I needed to get out of my house after my parents' divorce. It was best to move out."

"What? You were married to Leah? Leah, Moshe's wife?"

"Hard to believe. I'm talking about a different person, really I am. Leah, she couldn't have children. It's not like today, the medicine. And her mother never saw me without telling me how dark I was. *Snobeet.*"

"But she married Moshe."

"Her mother was dead by then."

242

"Wait a minute. Your brother married your ex-wife?" I'm stunned trying to put this together with the conversation I overheard between Leah and Vered on the kibbutz. But my father needs no recovery time.

"After the army she got a job working with the foreign ministry, and she got me a job, too. She was the ambassador's secretary. She still works there maybe. She was worried I'd leave her because I couldn't imagine never having a child. She was right about something."

My fingers close around the phone. I press my forehead against the coolness of the wall.

"I don't think any of this has anything to do with you, actually. Nothing whatsoever, really, but that idiot brother of mine I don't know what he's going to say. If I could, one kick in the teeth and he'd be shut up good, but I'm over here."

I recoil at the image of my father kicking his brother in the teeth. It's making it hard for me to process. They were both married to Leah.

"Where did you live?" I ask.

"Who? Me and Leah? We lived on the bottom floor of a house. The top three stories were the consulate, and we had the ground floor. I was security, you see, so I was there all the time. But she never took her eyes off me, so I had to get out sometimes. That's how I met your mother."

"Mom knew you when you were married to someone else?" I ask. My head swims with this new information.

"We were kids, soldiers. *Ze'hu*. Finished. But I don't trust them, you see? A brother who marries his brother's wife? *Yech.* Two snakes, they deserve each other as far as I'm concerned. Now you're with them, and at first I thought okay, but the longer you're there, the more I don't like it. You're *my* daughter. You remember that, Miri?"

I can hear my father rubbing his prickly cheeks to stimulate blood flow. He'll shave in the middle of the night, his razor scratching into his dark skin in short, shallow strokes. I always leave the room when he shaves and ask him to close the bathroom door; the sound of the scraping of the razor on his skin makes my own skin crawl. Such absurd thoughts to be having now in the middle of a university foyer on Mount Carmel. Such unbelievably dead-end thoughts when my father has just told me my aunt used to be his wife—or that he had a first wife at all, that alone would have been enough to make me feel as though I'd been turned inside out and hung on a line.

"You there?"

"I'm here."

"This damn cat's scratching at the door again. I need to let her in."

"Yes, you should. She's freezing."

"You worried about the papers? We'll find them. You remember what I told you like a good girl. I'll go now to the damn thing."

We say goodbye, and I take small steps to my apartment. I should be walking in the opposite direction, back to my class, where I'd left in such a hurry my notes are still at my place. I shouldn't miss the rest of the lecture, which the professor had mentioned would be on the final exam. I should scurry back for my thin coat, the money I'd earned from my last translation folded squarely into the inside pocket. But my room waited with its privacy and semi-working radio that Simona had left behind, live company often spoken in too-fast Hebrew, I could hear but didn't have to understand.

Chapter Twenty-Four

THERE IS A KNOCK ON MY BEDROOM DOOR, so faint at first, I believe it is one of the pigeons that seem part of the campus architecture. Then a thick Russian-accented Hebrew, "Miss Gil? Message for you." It's Boaz, the dormitory security guard who sits adjacent to the foyer.

I was perched at my desk, my chin resting in one palm and doodling Guy's name in Hebrew and English down the side of one page. In front of me is a photograph of my parents on their honeymoon, my mother in an imitation Jacqueline Kennedy double-breasted CHANEL suit in strawberry pink, descending the main lobby stairs in an unnamed New York hotel. My father waits at the bottom in a charcoal gray jacket and a crisp white button-down, arm outstretched toward her, their eyes locked. As far as I know it was their last trip together to New York, but now I consider it might not have been their first — or at least not my father's first. Maybe he'd been there with Leah. The thought revolts me. It's too hard to imagine two brothers and one wife.

"Coming? I must return to the entrance." The security guard's voice is impatient and what he's really saying is that he's not a messenger boy.

My chair scrapes the floor as I edge it backward, cross the small room in four steps and open the door. My hand trembles. My brain's saturated with surprises, exhausting me. The guard hands me a folded note, nods, and leaves. It is a message to phone my uncle. He is sorry it is impossible for him to speak in person, but please phone right away. I read between the lines. To me his note reads: *Phone before I lose my nerve.*

I gather my running shoes and socks, my phone card, put my hair in a ponytail, and head for the foyer, feeling lighter with each step. Maybe Leah has solved the problem. Maybe it's over before the administration has gotten wind of it, and my new passport and bursary check are on the way. I'd settle for the passport. So many years in the Interior Ministry must count for something, and she is my aunt.

The number my uncle has given me is unfamiliar. It must be his work number at the museum. After thirty minutes of waiting for my turn, I pick up the receiver, slide in my phone card, and dial. Uncle Moshe answers on the first ring, as though he had been hovering above the phone waiting for my call. There is so much buzzing around me, I have to cover one ear.

"Uncle Moshe? It's me."

"Miriam. It's good you phoned. I have something to tell you, but I don't have a lot of time. Do you have a pen and paper?"

"No."

I tap the student next to me on the shoulder and point to the pen in his hand. He is deep in conversation and devouring a chocolate bar. He tosses the pen at me without missing a beat of his conversation and I roll up my sleeve. I'll have to wash the ink off of my arm later.

"I have something to write on, now."

"You asked about the Interior Ministry."

"Yes?" I don't dare ask if Leah found it in her heart to help me.

"Leah is a good wife, she tried her best as a mother, but nobody is perfect."

"What are you talking about? I'm sure it's not Leah's fault Yakira left. It must have been a complicated situation."

"It means that I cannot help my own daughter, but I could do my best for you."

My heart rises in my throat.

"I have to live with knowing I didn't do my best when it came to your grandmother. Deserting you is not what she would have wanted me to do, and for once I should try to honor what she would have wanted," he says.

"You shouldn't say that about Yakira. You might be just the person to help her one day," I answer. It's way easier for me to talk about Yakira than to address what my uncle said about deserting me.

"God willing," he says. "When Leah and your father were young there was a big drive for Israelis to have children."

"Weren't most people poor?" I ask.

"True, but so many had been lost in the Holocaust, wars, pogroms, big families were a comfort. Leah thought she was smart, going to Canada, but it didn't solve anything. You know this already maybe?"

"I think so," I answer. I suck in a deep breath. Worry grips me. I'm not sure how many more of these family secrets I can take.

"So you know Hanan and Leah are divorced?"

"Yes."

"I figured. I want you to see a bigger picture. She dreamt about your father and a baby day and night, and he was suffocating under it all, he wanted out, it was clear to everyone, but her. But an obsessed woman hears only her desire. Keep that in mind when you go tomorrow," he says.

"Where am I going?" I ask. I rub my eyes.

My uncle speaks to me in riddles. There's a nervous energy in his voice, and I'm sure he's mixing languages. His babble about obsession and desire doesn't make sense to me.

"I don't have much privacy here, so quickly. There's someone at the ministry I want you to talk with, but, Miriam, this is important, don't phone. Go at exactly eight a.m. before he has a chance to get busy, and tell him who you are, bring whatever papers you have," he says.

A prickle runs down my spine. Why would a total stranger help me? If he doesn't, the minute I hand over my Canadian passport at the airport, there will be a red flag. I won't get on the flight with my identity listed as Syrian Christian. I don't know where they'll take me, but wherever it is, I don't want to go.

"Tell him I sent you, and tell him your father's name. This is very important. He liked him. Smile, act like a tourist without a map. You writing?"

"Yes."

My uncle's voice drops and he whispers into the receiver, "Shimon Harpaz."

"But who is he?"

"Do. Don't think. Eight a.m. on the dot because Leah has a meeting with him at nine, and she has her own agenda. Get to him before she does. Good luck."

My uncle hangs up. I return the pen.

I don't need to write down the name. I've already committed it to memory. I consider phoning my father. He told me not to trust my uncle, but Moshe sounds as though he was going out on a limb, he sounds genuine.

***

The second time I visit the Ministry of the Interior, I am alone. It is worlds apart from the time I went with Valerie, our eyes on the lookout mostly for hot guys — or at least mine were.

I'm wearing more hand-me-downs from Simona, bright orange winter tights, a faded jean miniskirt, and a long-sleeved, earth-colored sweater with a turtleneck. She's taken me on as a charity case, leaving random pieces of clothing on my bed with short notes: *from Simona*, and I'm grateful. She can be thoughtful when she wants to be. I've splurged on knee-length brown boots and an orange scarf with light green trim that matches the tights. I skipped any makeup besides black mascara. The less sophisticated I appear the better. I'm the picture of a Canadian autumn in Israel's light winter, desperate to play up the empty-headed tourist.

It is 7:50 a.m. and already a line snakes to the end of the closed reception area and back. It won't open for another ten minutes. I keep an eye out for Yaron. I don't want him to see me here.

People sip takeout coffees, check their watches in the hopes that they'll do whatever paperwork they need, but still make it for a full workday.

A warm chocolate croissant scent fills the air around me. I couldn't eat this morning.

I don't want to take my chances waiting in this line for an hour, so I approach the security guard and ask him if he knows how I can reach Shimon Harpaz. Without looking up or raising an eyebrow, he points to a corridor and holds up three fingers.

"He's in office number three?"

The guard nods, not moving his eyes from his newspaper.

Staying on the edge of the crowd, I head down the corridor and knock on the door marked three. To the right of the door is a small bronze-colored plaque that reads *Shimon Harpaz*, but there is no additional description.

"Come in."

I put my hand on the knob, steady myself, and open the door, put my head in first.

"Yes, come in. Close the door please."

I close the door behind me, and the man motions for me to sit down. He has a receiver to his ear, and he puts his thumb and fingers together: *wait*. The office is bare, there's nothing on the walls at all, not even a photograph, calendar, or a diploma of any kind. The desk is piled with stacks of papers, and there are more piles on the floor, in overflowing open drawers, and on both sides of the filing cabinets. Whoever he is, he's busy.

Shimon speaks in Hebrew in clipped sentences on the phone. He is a short, stocky man with white hair, dark skin, and a clean-shaven face. I observe his short-sleeved button-down shirt and khaki slacks. He's dressed for summer in winter. I can't see his shoes behind his desk, but I could imagine him in sandals with thick black straps. He hangs up the phone with a bang.

"*Ken*? What can I do for you?"

"My name is Miriam Gil."

"You are a tourist?"

"Yes."

He switches to English.

"You've made a mistake. Tourists wait in the outside area. There are numbers for you to take by the guard. Shalom."

Shimon turns back to his papers, a pen in one hand.

"Mr. Harpaz, my uncle Moshe Damari sent me to you." He glances up, an absent look on his face.

"You are still here."

"Moshe Damari," I repeat.

He doesn't respond, but chews on the end of his pen.

"Yemenite man?"

"Yes. And my father is Hanan Gil."

"Hanan Gil or Hanan Damari?"

"Both. He changed his last name to Gil. I'm not sure when exactly, but a long time ago."

I don't know why I'm so nervous. Shimon has big strong hands, thick fingers, and clean nails. I keep my eyes on his hands until he moves them from his desk to his lap. He doesn't say anything for a few minutes, and he keeps his eyes on me; his bushy eyebrows meet on the bridge of his nose.

"Miriam you say?"

"Yes." I sense he wants me to stop looking down, to face him head on, so I take a breath and meet his gaze. I don't know what it is about bureaucracy that scares me. I haven't done anything wrong.

"You look like your mother, Miriam. She was a lovely woman. Classy. I liked her very much. I heard about what happened to her, and I'm sorry for your loss."

I'm stunned into silence.

"Thank you." I'm blown away. This man knew my mother. I'm still clutching my backpack with my passport inside, and I hold it closer.

"You seem like a nice girl. Shy maybe, but that's okay. A year or two in Israel and you will learn some chutzpah to survive. Tell me what are you doing here first thing in the morning, and why doesn't that uncle of yours call to tell me? I would be happy to take you to breakfast, the daughter of my old friend. Is Moshe still living in your father's big shadow?"

His smile turns into a laugh, and his shoulders move up and down. I smile close-lipped. I'm not sure if he's laughing at my uncle's expense or my father's.

"You look hungry. Come. Your father fixed my car enough times, I owe you breakfast. A couple of urgent calls. Wait for me outside. You are free, no? If not, you are free now." He waves me outside, and I stand as he grabs the receiver.

In the hallway I trip over Yaron.

"Excuse me," he says. He's wearing a baby blue button-down the exact shade as his eyes and a thin black tie. "Do I know you?"

I don't want him to hear my accent. I've already learned that Israelis peg me as Israeli until I open my mouth, so if I can just stay quiet, he won't recall the Syrian-Canadian girl masquerading as a Jew in the Holy Land. I shake my head, and I am overcome with a coughing fit, slapping my chest with one hand. He shrugs and picks up the papers he's dropped. My gaze falls over his slim hips and wide shoulders as he walks away.

"All the girls like Yaron," Shimon says. "He knows how to play them. A bit like your father was in his day." Shimon is close enough for me to smell his morning toothpaste. I flush. I can't believe I've been caught gawking at Yaron's behind.

"There's a nice little café on the corner. I have maybe twenty minutes, but we go to the front of the line." Shimon touches my shoulder and motions me toward the elevator. We walk to the café after we exit on the third floor. "Shortcut," Shimon says, winking at me.

We pass through an emergency exit, and there is a café right in front of us.

As we walk through the entrance, a bell hanging above the door rings. Shimon calls out "Two number two's" and heads toward a private corner table. The harmonious smell of inviting bitter coffee mixed with sweet frothy milk and yeasty hot bread wraps around me. I wish I could relax.

"Right away." A voice answers from somewhere I can't see. There are at least two dozen people in this restaurant, but Shimon operates here like the owner or a privileged client.

By the time I'm seated, two steaming café au laits are on the table and two glasses of freshly squeezed orange juice with crushed ice and two sprigs of mint.

Shimon sips his juice without speaking. He purses his lips, which seem small for his broad face, and gulps.

"So," he begins, rubbing his large hands together. "Hanan Damari's quiet, hazel- eyed daughter. What are you doing at the Interior Ministry? Moshe must have told you I moved here from foreign affairs."

My uncle hadn't said a word about Shimon other than that I had to speak to him, but I say nothing. I sip my juice, but I'm nervous, and half of it spills down my chin and into my lap. I wipe it up with the cloth napkin on the table, and Shimon pretends not to notice.

"So how, besides taking you for breakfast, can I help you? You didn't come for a free coffee."

"I'm at Haifa University on the overseas program," I begin. "I heard there was a bursary for children of Israelis, and I applied. Yaron encouraged me to apply for an Israeli passport, too. He said it would be problematic for me to leave on my Canadian one, that I'd need army permission."

"A *p'tor*," Shimon interrupts.

"Yes, a *p'tor* and a citizen departure tax to pay and a general hassle flying out."

I stumble over my words and pray I make sense. I can't read Shimon's expression.

"My passport application was rejected." My voice lowers now. I've run out of breath.

A light of understanding comes into Shimon's eyes. He rubs his hands together again. Maybe he's planning to march me off to some official place where they will lock me up. I squirm in my seat when he doesn't respond.

"It was not an ordinary rejection, I don't think." I lean in closer to him. "I'm the daughter of an Israeli citizen. I'm entitled to a passport."

All of the pent-up tension of the last few weeks releases, flows into his kind, dark brown eyes, not unlike Guy's, and Shimon's expression transforms to one of concern.

"Yaron told me my mother was a Syrian Christian and my father unknown, some sort of alien status. The university will soon kick me out. I don't know how I will get home," I say. I steady myself with my hands on the table. I don't want to whine. I keep my visions of armed airport security carting me off to jail to myself. I don't want Shimon to think I'm some hysterical girl.

"My father's not good at paperwork. My uncle said you could help me. Can you?"

If I thought I was tired before, now I'm depleted. I twist my napkin around and around in my hands, strangling it.

At this moment the waitress arrives. She sets down plates heaped with food, two enormous diced cucumber and tomato salads with scoops of tuna on the side, a basket of fresh brown and white rolls, a plate of crispy toast, a small square plate of yellow butter, a jar of spiced olive oil and another of lemon juice.

"Hey, Aliza. Good morning to the best waitress in all of Israel," Shimon says. The waitress beams. "She is truly number one, Miriam."

"Thank you," Aliza says. She places two slabs of chocolate next to our coffees.

He picks up his fork and digs into his salad. Then he meticulously spreads tuna on his toast with his knife, patting it down with his fork. I take small bites, not interested in food, but not wanting to insult his generosity.

After eating half of his salad in silence, Shimon puts down his fork and knife with a loud clang. He wipes his face with his napkin.

"What we have here, Miriam, sweet young girl, is a classic case of the chicken coming home to roost. You know this expression? I learned it in America. Unfortunately, you are the egg the greedy chicken is sitting on." He sighs. An agonized look passes over his eyes.

I have no idea what he is talking about.

"Have you ever been in love?" he asks.

"I'm sorry?"

"In love, have you ever been in love? I am sorry to ask you such a private question. You don't have to answer. I'm thinking out loud."

It's just as well he doesn't require a response. I used Neil to fill my own gaps. I know that now, and I am reminded of what my father said about Leah: *"We were very young when we married…but I needed to get out of my house.*" At least I hadn't gone that far. Was I in love with Guy? Drawn to him? Yes. Admire his ambitions to feed peace by feeding the world? Yes. Is he sexy and sensitive? Yes.

"I can see you are in love with someone, maybe. You have your mother's eyes, you know," he says. "A pity."

He returns to his meal, and it's obvious he is using his breakfast as an excuse to stall, buy time to think. I feel his mind working. Occasionally he gazes at me.

"You're not eating?" Shimon snaps me out of my daydream. "This is a story for a full stomach."

"What story?"

"I ask you about love because I thought you might be able to relate to Leah as she once was, exactly your age when she was obsessed with your father. You're what, twenty-one?"

"Almost."

"You don't look surprised about Leah and your father."

I push my plate away. "My father mentioned Leah was his ex-wife."

The words are hard to say. The only woman I've ever associated with my father was my mother. I refuse to count Jacquie.

He finishes his salad. I wait, unwilling to break the spell.

"Your popular father could fix anything, and I didn't know how to run a car in that freezer you call a country. And don't think because he is such a bear, he wasn't homesick. He talked about Jerusalem all the time, his Harley-Davidson, his best friend Dudu who taught him everything he knew about mechanics, and especially your grandmother, *miskena*, all alone."

The extra skin on Shimon's neck wobbles as he talks. My coffee grows cold as I imagine Shimon in an ill-fitting navy-blue suit, stocky and young, greeting the newly arrived couple to Canada's capital. My father's muscles burst through his security guard uniform, and Leah sports a short white linen dress that's wrinkled in the humidity, still playing the bride.

"You can fill in the rest." Shimon glances at his watch, heavy on his wrist. His twenty-minute breakfast has already spilled into his morning, and Leah is on her way. Maybe he is thinking he should plug up the leak my appearance has created in his workday, do some damage control.

I look at Shimon slack-jawed.

He reddens, embarrassed.

"You still have your problem, don't you?"

My smile is weak. He hasn't told me a thing my father hasn't already confessed. And so far, my father was right, it isn't any of my business in as much as it's not a daughter's business to know the crevices and crannies of her father's past.

Shimon spoons the foam of his coffee into his mouth. He raises one finger, and in another minute our orange juice glasses are refilled, fresh coffee is on the way, the small square table is whisked clean, and warm *rugelach* and cinnamon rolls appear in a basket.

He tears off a piece of cinnamon roll, crumbles it between his thumb and forefinger, and stares into space.

It is only after the coffee is delivered and the waitress is out of earshot that he speaks again.

"Your parents wanted to marry. He might as well have put it in the papers. Your mother was fresh, not bitter as Leah had become, with no wars attached." Shimon snaps his fingers. "Bang. Leah cut their contract, had them hightailing it back to Tel Aviv in June just in time for the '67 war. I think your father was in Judea and Samaria that time. Tanks."

"She couldn't convince him to adopt?"

"Your father wouldn't hear of it. 'I don't want anybody else's mumbo jumbo,' he told her. I remember because it was such an odd expression I looked it up."

But I wouldn't have had to look it up. It sounds exactly like my father.

Across the table Shimon's cinnamon roll is shredded to bits. I'm supposed to be the nervous one, not him. He's holding back, and all I can do is wait. I sense my worries are about to grow.

The restaurant has emptied, the breakfast rush is over, and the staff clears tables to the beat of the amped up music. It's the first time I've heard jazz in Israel and the first time since I landed that I'm tempted to pretend I'm somewhere else, anywhere out of the country.

Shimon leans forward, his fingers touching in a bridge in front of his mouth. "People could get hurt."

I'm guessing one of those people is me. Shimon rubs his eyes with both hands, and it is at this point the story weighs heaviest on him, his shoulder sag. I try to steel myself for what's coming, but I see nothing, not even a blur. I don't know when to duck.

"After the war, your father left Israel. Gone. He wanted to go back to Canada and your mother. To hear Leah tell it he didn't even take socks. Then Leah's in the hospital unconscious. She never forgave him for not being there. It was so public. Everyone talked."

I'm back with Leah and Vered in the drugstore. My heart sinks.

"But she'd been way ahead of him. She had heightened senses when it came to him and was certain he wouldn't give up on your mother." He leans forward now, his deep voice low. "She made a deal with the ambassador, Miriam. I was second to him, and there wasn't anything I didn't know. That's what you're eating now. That deal."

My eyes widen and I study my salad, still in the dark.

"Deal?"

"I don't know how. A bribe? A favor? Sex? Pity?" He shakes his head, and his face takes on a mournful look. "She got access to all of your father's files. Permanently. Had him marked as a criminal, so he'd never be allowed back into Canada."

"What?" My mouth drops. My fork clatters to the floor.

"Persona non grata it's called. If the computer comes up with a line like that at passport control, you are immediately deported to the nearest port, no questions asked. Your father was turned away in Montreal and waited for your mother in New York. He refused to go back to Israel until your mother came to him, and somehow they got around it."

261

"How can you get around a marked passport?" I ask. I'd like to know myself.

"I don't know how: paid someone to smuggle him down the river in a barrel with cigarette cartons or in the back of a pick-up. There are ways. Once they were married no one could touch him. To this day, I bet he thinks it was an error. If he thought she'd done something he would have made noise."

I sit stunned, digesting this revelation. My father told me he'd studied massage in New York as a poor student. He didn't mention he was there because he couldn't reach my mother and refused to give up on her.

He must have strolled through the low-class neighborhoods near Broadway, cursing his bad luck. He used to muse out loud about living in an eight-floor building while he studied massage surrounded by Israelis on the run. Some were fleeing military service, he said, mumbling about cowards. He had no sympathy for those fleeing crimes and debts either, but his face changed expression when he mentioned how many were hiding from wives. All of them were cutting ties— including my father.

Now I understand he wasn't fleeing, he thought he was waiting to get into Canada because of some mistake.

I could imagine his desperation. If he didn't find something legitimate to do and fast, he'd be forced to say goodbye to my mother, maybe forever. Israelis needed visas to be in the United States. There must have been his pull to my mother and a pull in the opposite direction: to my grandmother. Maybe he thought it was divine retribution for abandoning her in Jerusalem.

That's when he must have asked around. Get a student visa, they told him. He must have ended up at the massage institute that way.

Maybe for the briefest of moments, out of the corner of his eye, he saw the truth, but then it disappeared, as though it had never been. Leah had a fancy title, but she was no more than a clerk, and diplomats don't risk their positions for nobodies. Those guys didn't get to be where they were because they were stupid. It was preposterous. It was all some mistake. What do you expect from a country barely two decades old? My father must have drawn his usual conclusions: They were all idiots.

No, my father wouldn't entertain the thought that Leah might be perched in her official swivel chair in Jerusalem, resting her slender back against the cool mahogany-colored leather. Likely her legs were crossed at the ankles, while she took dictation from the high official, but it was what she did not write that had passed between them: Hell has no fury like a woman scorned.

"You weren't expecting this?"

"I don't know what I was expecting. Why didn't Moshe tell me?"

"He might be second fiddle, but he loves Leah and he's good for her. And they've suffered, the two of them. Yakira's not coming back. Last I heard she'd gotten in touch with her birth mother, who was happy she called."

"How do you know?"

"It's a small world, and the higher up you travel, the smaller the circles are. And besides, most people love to talk. I have to say until now Leah's plan has worked."

263

He narrows his eyes. "You could get Leah into a lot of trouble."

"Me?"

"Put two and two together. It's one thing that somehow your father got himself back over the border and another that he was rewarded with a daughter. No one gives up access once they have it. See it yet?"

"No." I whisper.

"Leah's tagged you since the day you were born. She's been waiting for you to open a file."

The realization of what Shimon tells me begins in my toes and travels upward. My body tingles. Soon the knowledge lodges itself in my throat, and I grab for my juice and drain it. It doesn't reduce the lump.

"Leah changed my identity so that I'd be thrown out of school, out of the country?"

Shimon's nod is deep and slow.

"I'm sorry, Miriam."

I nod. There's nothing I can say. This meeting is over. I rise to leave.

"Please, let me call you a cab."

"I'm happy on the bus."

"No, I insist. I'll have one here in a minute, and take this." Shimon puts his business card on the table. Only his name and phone number are printed on it.

"It's my personal number."

Shimon motions to the waitress and twists his wrist back and forth. "She's calling a cab. It's on me. You're in no condition to wander around. Go to your apartment and have a quiet day with a friend and—" he pauses, drops his voice an octave, "be careful who you speak to."

These last words are a warning, and I shift from one foot to the other as I internalize them.

"Just one thing, Shimon."

"Yes."

"Why did you tell me? You must have promised Leah you'd keep quiet. All these years."

Shimon meets my gaze. He shifts his body in the chair, and from one minute to the next, he looks grayer.

Finally, he speaks in a voice that comes from another part of him, not the assertive, all-knowing part he plays all day, commanding whatever he commands, but a world-weary part, the voice of someone who has seen too much.

"This country needs young, energetic people like you."

He locks eyes with me, and I blink first, look away.

There's a honk outside, and Shimon glances at his watch. It's 9:00 a.m. He gestures toward the door and waves.

"No thank-yous," he says, as I open my mouth to speak. "Just expect a present soon. Be patient and keep your mouth shut."

He gives me a paternal pat on the shoulder and strides over to the coffee counter. I see the waiter pass him the phone.

I push the glass door open with my hip and step into the fresh air, but I'm on the alert for Leah. I have to say something. I don't know what yet, but someone has to tell her off, put her in her place. She should fix my passport immediately, not Shimon. Indignation bubbles inside of me.

"*Giveret*, are you coming? Mr. Harpaz is running the meter, but this isn't a parking space."

"There's no need." I wave off the taxi.

"But Mr. Harpaz insisted."

"No need. Thank you," I repeat. I'm walking in the direction of the main entrance to the Interior Ministry. Good chance Leah knows the shortcut out the third floor to the café.

But when I spot a woman with dark hair pinned at the sides, my hands go clammy, and I breathe out when I realize she's not limping. It's not Leah. All at once every dark-haired woman has her small mouth and narrow shoulders. I harden my resolve. Someone should put her in her place.

I think I've walked farther than I realize or taken a turn that wasn't there before when I spot her across the street, looking straight ahead. That's Leah. I feel my father's burning humiliation all those years ago, turned away like a rabid dog. It sinks in, a sharp nail imprint in my skin, my connection to my father. It's not that cold, but I shiver.

When the light turns green, everything is all at once in motion, dozens of pedestrians, cars, taxis, bicycles. Leah steps out into the middle of the intersection across from me. I scurry as though a rain cloud has burst above me and hide in the nearest store, not breathing until she's passed me.

I feel dizzy, sick. I want to vomit all of the tuna and cucumber and tomato salad I've eaten this morning. The orange juice rises in my throat. I force myself to swallow and taste stomach acid. I clasp my hands together, so no one will see them shake.

There is louder honking from the taxi.

The next thing I know the driver stands over me. He's followed me here. I should have known. Shimon Harpaz is a powerful man.

"Either get in or I'll park and wait for you. Strict orders," he hisses.

Fatigued, I push open the shop's door.

"I'm coming," I answer.

I dig around in my purse for a tissue and wiping my eyes and nose. This morning keeps getting worse. All the signs of impending disaster are present. I can feel it. I see the driver shake his head and turn up the music on his radio, adding to the pile of street noise.

I collapse in the back of the taxi. If anyone's about to split open, it's me, not Leah. If I had any audacity it leaked onto the sidewalk the minute I saw the first brunette. I need time to consider what's happened, and right now the wound is too fresh.

The driver slams his open palm on the horn and the car lurches forward.

"*Giveret*, I'll get fired next time you pull a stunt like that. When Mr. Harpaz gives an order, you don't ignore it."

Chapter Twenty-Five

A LOOSE-LEAF PAPER IS TAPED ON MY DOOR when I return. The university has given me fourteen days to "correct my papers." Until then I've been asked to leave. Arab Canadians are not allowed on the overseas students program. I'll have to reapply as a regular Israeli citizen if that's what I am. If I'm Syrian, I'm not permitted to study at the university at all, certainly not without a much more thorough background check. Syria is officially at war with Israel. Syria is officially the enemy.

All of this a red-faced administrator explains to me as I stand speechless, deflated in his office. An image of a twenty-something Leah, a fire in her eyes, no limp in her walk, her skin flaky and dry from its first exposure to Canada's winter all at once aglow, comes to me. She scratches through my father's documents the way sand scratches the naked eye, permanent damage.

I've gone back and forth on the issue of confronting Leah, but Shimon's words echo in my mind each time I imagine reaching for the phone—*be careful who you speak to*—and I mentally yank my hand back with a heavy wrist, an ache in my fingers. Besides, some issues are not resolvable. I see that now. What Leah's done, she's done, and she's impulsive and unpredictable. Confronting her will neither erase the ink on my documents nor her fingerprints that must be all over them.

My father has so far spared me the temptation of blurting things. He hasn't called me or written to me about finding his marriage certificate or any other proof of identity. If he uncovers anything it will be a miracle and no less a marvel if I hear from my uncle. He's holed up in the cave of his own guilt, shrinking under Leah's gaze like a guttering candle.

I need to focus on my immediate problem. I have to leave my apartment. The only one I yearn to stay with is Guy, but after he'd expressed his Zionism to me, he might reject me too, believe these rumors and lies. And it would be a struggle not to make admissions and then what? He'd be the boy next door living with someone else's sin in his heart and its effects. No. I couldn't do that. If he makes his life on the kibbutz, he has to see Leah for what would seem now like forever.

Outside on campus I run. I gulp thick mid-morning air, not yet scented with Turkish coffee and Marlboros that will be served up with lunch. I zoom past the white sand-colored academic buildings with their rectangular green-tinged glass, up past the overflowing parking lots under the blue and white Israeli flags that stick out among the green foliage. I trip over a loose brick in the sidewalk and fall skinning my knee on the gravel Israelis call *hatzaz*. I run into the science building to use the bathroom, thrilled that there is both toilet paper and soap, both not to be taken for granted in this country, and I am back outside, knees up high. I can see the first hole forming in the toe of my left running shoe, my blue sock showing through the fabric, but I keep on running.

I used to run a lot as a teenager and come back sweaty and exhilarated. I want to feel that now. Freedom.

I hear a faraway voice, "Miriam! Watch out! Bus! *Miriam! Stop!*"

I turn toward the voice, and a screech punctuates the silence in my mind and then a loud honk. Oh no! My neck jerks backward and my knees buckle. I've run into the road and forced a bus to come to a grinding halt.

"*Metumtemet!* Idiot! I almost killed you, girl!" The bus driver screams out the window and I am certain everyone on campus can hear him. My heart beats fast and sweat pours down my back. "Watch where you're going!" He screams as he whizzes past me. He has one hand wrapped around a paper coffee cup, and one hand hanging outside the window.

I hear my name again, hoarse and winded. I turn my head. It is Dalit. She may have been a soldier, but she can't run for her life. She's flapping her arms, red-faced, chicken style, panting. Her shoelace is untied, and a strand of her hair is caught in her hoop earring.

"Are you crazy or what?" She is angry. "You are beyond stupid. You weren't looking at all." Her voice is full of concern. She is still at a distance. I do not go back to her, but allow her to catch up to me. I gulp air, shaken.

"Thanks. Sorry I scared you." My voice is breathy. I can feel the sweat trickling down my back.

"Scared me! You ran in front of a bus." She pants. Now that she sees I'm all right, her tone has changed to scolding. "Need to catch my breath." She has both of her hands on her knees, and she's bent over. "I know you can't relate to being out of breath. Hey, you're bleeding. Did you get hurt?"

"It's nothing." I press my knee into the cuff of my sweatshirt, and a few drops of blood absorb into the fabric, but I don't care. I'm leaving this shirt here anyway, it's washed out. There's no reason to allocate room in my suitcase for it.

"Haven't spoken to you in a while. Is Arslan coming back?"

Dalit looks at the ground and shakes her head. Her hair falls forward, covering her ears.

"I've been avoiding you about it. Sorry. It's hard for me to live there with Simona gloating over me morning, noon, and night."

"It's not what you intended."

"But it's what happened. Right now, Arslan's lost her first year of studies and the Arab girl is happier than before, with all of her friends. Who understands God's ways? I wanted to protect us. I look for fairness in the world, balance, and this is what I get."

I stopped buying cigarettes a week ago, but I wish for one now. I still feel the force of the bus.

"Now I have to live with it, Miriam. But maybe I can help you."

"Help me?"

"We had a big argument, me and my administration friend. You saw her in the apartment that morning."

I nod.

"But she's a close friend of the family, she wouldn't desert me forever and she told me about you. The school was..."

271

The muscles in my shoulders tense.

"…contacted," she continues. "I see you got the letter. But I want you to know I don't believe them. I know a Jewish girl when I see one. I told them there's no way you're an Arab, even a Christian one. I've been looking for you, to ask what I can do to help."

"What exactly did the administration say?"

"They want you out, Miriam. They say you lied on your application. What's taking so long on your papers? Is your father asleep? You're about to lose the year, too."

A jolt goes through me. While I'm taking in the sunshine, getting some exercise, counting on Shimon and his magic to correct a wrong from before I was born, some university clerk has decided the note on my door is a mere formality.

Is this what Israel is all about? Underneath the effusive welcome, it's been who you *really* are, whose side are you on, acquire a side of the line and stay put. In between thick pockets of celestial warmth and a land that calls out to your heart, there's this vein trying to poke out your identity through your genes, your blood and loyalties. It's sticking in me now, right between the ribs.

Another bus zooms by us, blocking out sound for a minute. I shade my eyes from the wind.

"It's some crazy mistake, Dalit."

Dalit steps back and looks me right in the eyes.

"I stood up for you, Miriam, but if the best you can do is *I don't know* then maybe I don't either. Pretending to be someone you're not is a dangerous idea over here."

"Pretending? No one put a gun to my head to apply for an Israeli passport. Why would I have applied?"

"Because you'd had enough warnings about getting out maybe, or just because you slipped up, believed for a few dazed minutes that you really are who you were pretending to be. Liars tend to tell one lie too many."

I suck in my cheeks and stare hard at Dalit. She breaks.

"So someone messed up somewhere. But now it's on your head to fix it, and you're out of the university until you do, and it has to be airtight. I'm sorry, Miriam."

Now it is my turn to back away.

"I won't let anyone take your place." She shakes her head as if convincing herself and continues to babble. "Arslan's not even speaking to me, but hey." Dalit's voice softens, and she puts a hand on my shoulder. "I'd be happy to mail that card. Put it on my desk or slide it under my door if it's locked."

"Thanks. You think she'll write me back?"

Dalit shrugs and opens both palms. "She doesn't see her part in it, said she trusted me the whole way, as if I took over her brain. Dalit the Hypnotist. But you need to think of yourself right now. Have you got somewhere to go?"

Chapter Twenty-Six

HAIFA'S SHUK is not as big as the Mahane Yehuda shuk in Jerusalem that I visited last week. But today it's crammed, there is little room to maneuver through the rows and rows of fresh fruit and vegetable stands, and I'm sweating underneath my turtleneck. It's been unseasonably warm or so I'm told. My claustrophobia makes me dizzy. I need a break. Here the warmth and the yeasty smell of soft pretzels envelop me.

I had to get off campus for the rest of the day. I pop into a corner store to escape the crowd and look around. Alongside the newspapers, there are four shelves of snacks and sundries with magazines and soft drinks in refrigerators at the back.

I stand still surveying the place and then walk to the back of the store and pretend to check out the fashion magazines. I have never been enticed by one, but flip through the pages of *Elle* and *Vogue*, taking my time as if I cared. Slowly the fog in my head lifts and I sip from the water bottle I have learned to take with me wherever I go in Israel.

Not even ten minutes passes before the cashier starts sending me weighted glances. During a lull, when no one is at the till, the woman aims herself in my direction and stares pointedly, her mouth pursed in displeasure, her eyebrows pulled together.

I pretend not to notice but distance myself from the reading racks as my gaze moves over the rows of Kit Kats, Pesek Zmans, Adashim and Elite chocolates to land on the Bamba and potato chip stands. I'm not hungry and wouldn't dare waste money on anything from a convenience store, now that my bursary's been rejected and there are no more translation jobs as an ex-student. I hover over the racks for a moment, eager to appear the paying customer, not an overwhelmed tourist.

The sky darkens further and it's only 4:30 in the afternoon. I touch the key in my pocket. We'd forced the administration to fix the hinge on our front door and buy new locks for all of the doors only two days ago when the tension between Dalit and Simona reached new heights, each accusing the other of stealing from each other's room. Although Simona's obvious wealth made the accusations seem absurd, Dalit was not without a side. Nothing is misplaced or missing on the days Simona sleeps in Tel Aviv with her boyfriend. I don't throw my ring into it. I keep my knowledge of Simona's snooping through my letters to myself. These wrinkles seem laughable, petty now that I've been asked to leave.

The cashier clears her throat. I pretend not to hear as I pivot to the front door and let myself out. I slip off the curb and land on top of a guy in his twenties, who had turned to enter the store.

"Oh. *Slichah*. I'm sorry." My face reddens.

"Were you trying to fly?" He's on the pavement, searching for his sunglasses with his back toward me. It is only when he turns that I see it's Guy, and in one instant all of my troubles evaporate. I am elated. My skin immediately warms. By his feet there is a small envelope. Already passersby have left their footprints on the white paper.

I bend down, pick up his sunglasses, and hand them to him. He brushes his lips across mine, and my whole body tingles.

"What are you doing here? I'm really sorry. I was nervous about the clerk."

He shoots me a puzzled look

"I didn't buy anything and—" I stop there. Am I a dunce around him or what?

"I tried to surprise you, and you surprised me. Surprise!" We both laugh.

"You wanted to surprise me?"

"I got a ride to the dormitories and when you didn't answer at your apartment, I asked around. Your roommate said you'd gone to the shuk. I took a taxi."

He bends down and scrapes the envelope off the ground. "For you."

"What is it?"

"Open it and see. But wait until you're alone. Let's move from the entrance." He puts his hand on my elbow and steers me to the side. "We can share a taxi back. I'll drop you at the dormitory."

"Sounds good. How's your arm? I didn't break it again, did I?"

"No. It's better. I plan to be driving again soon. Until then, we'll wait for the weekend, yes?"

I can't help but throw my arms around him and kiss him deeply on the mouth. I've been so distraught, so upset, just the sight of someone looking at me as though he's thrilled to see me breaks me down, and I tear through my natural borders, his body a rope.

"Hey. I missed you, too." He hugs me closer, and I wish I could slip inside of him, disappear.

I want to tell him, spill my guts on the pavement. Make him understand that even if Shimon can reverse time, who knows what they'll be saying about me on campus when it's over. That girl who went on about her Israeli father was thrown out for pretending to be a Jew. She's back now, but where there's smoke, there's fire.

He'll scoff at my fears. Take me in his strong energetic arms and let me know there's plenty of room at his place until this silly bureaucratic error is resolved. Paperwork lies all the time. It's nothing, house dust. But fear grips me. He's just completed three years in a combat unit defending his beliefs, and he won't want to make a mistake twice with his heart.

"I wish I had more time to be with you." He showers my face with gentle kisses and takes my hand, leads me to the car. "Mmm. You smell good. Where have you been, anyway?"

"I'm trying to get very high grades so I can get another scholarship to come back." Not exactly a lie, more like a fairy tale. "I missed you, too." I can't tell him Leah uninvited me from the kibbutz for starters. Besides, I can't talk. My whole body is on fire. We have maybe a half an hour together, then no doubt my uncle will run into him in the dining hall or on a bicycle path and let him know my troubles. My father said his younger brother's like an airport runway, a mouth full of nonsense words that never stop taking off.

A seed plants itself like a virus in my mind, forcing the words that could have slipped so easily off of my tongue back into my gut. I search his dark brown eyes. Yes, Guy will make it clear he can't afford to give his heart to another girl with her fingers tied behind her back as she speaks. I learned my lesson from Neil. It's better if I say nothing at all.

Chapter Twenty-Seven

THE NOTE FROM GUY burns a hole in my front pocket.

Shalom, Birthday Girl,

This weekend, we are visiting family in Jerusalem, but come to me next Shabbat. I have space for both of us.

If it stays warm like this, you won't need a bathing suit.

L'hitraot.

Guy

That's ten days away. Guy dropped me off at the dormitory with a promise from me that I'd read his note only when he drove off.

It rained last night from about 7:00 p.m. the sun shone all morning, and now the winter weather is on its way back, the wind can't be ignored, swirling the brown and rust-colored leaves up from the ground and forcing me to zip up my worn jacket on my way back from the makolet on campus with my lone pita, one tomato, and one cucumber that I plan to eat with a slice of yellow cheese.

Maybe I should book a flight, take a chance that I can duck out on my Canadian passport.

"Hey, girlfriend." Valerie is waiting for me in my apartment. "You look hot."

"It's windy and cold and somehow boiling outside at the same time."

"No, I mean hot. Your lipstick's smudged all over your face." She raises her eyebrows and I laugh.

"I just ran into Guy at the shuk."

"Things are on a roll with him, huh?"

"Yes."

She wiggles her eyebrows and we both laugh. It feels good, but she knows something, I can tell by the way she eyes me with her head tilted to the side.

"Listen. Dalit the Bulldozer's now more of a faucet where you're concerned. She came for a chat, well actually for a narc."

I stumble.

"You all right? Yes, she told on you. I understand you're having some messed up paperwork snags."

"Yes, I am."

I want to be back in Guy's arms, not packing my bags until I can prove to some faceless Israeli bureaucrat my mother wasn't a Syrian Christian. I want to apologize to Arslan, although nothing can make up for a whole year lost. I want to ask my uncle how he could marry his brother's ex-wife. I need to go home, dig through every paper in the house and fix this.

My mouth, which has so recently tasted like Guy's soft, sweet, urgent kisses, tastes like tin. I resist the urge to sip the coffee Valerie holds out to me, a luxurious looking take-out cappuccino from the cafeteria. Her expression has changed from impatient to edgy.

"Drink it on our way out of here," she says. "You have to focus, Miriam."

She opens the door for me, then reaches into her pocket and pulls out a piece of gum. She unwraps it and tosses the pack at me. She bites down hard on hers. We've reached the dormitory entrance, but we both turn to the right toward a comfortable, popular walking path, the one that leads down to the nature reserve.

My feet itch. I should just run. The dormitory is only four feet away. Whatever it is she has to say won't help. She's broke and heartbroken over her ex, Tracy, she'd confessed only last week. She can offer a shoulder to lean on, but not much more. And I don't want to hear any more surprises. I'm too ground down for anymore revelations.

"We need to map out your options. Stop helicoptering around me. Would you rather sit? There are thousands of students here, it's not as though they're draining their resources on you, the big security risk."

Her attempt at humor doesn't get off the ground. She links my arm, and we keep walking.

"Also..."

"What?"

"I'm packing."

I stop to face her. We're alone on the path. The wind is high now, making my eyes tear.

"You're leaving?"

"My mother can't sleep. She thinks we're dodging bullets. She says since Rabin's peace train left the station there are too many dead bodies. Maybe if something is really signed, but right now, she's terrified."

"I can't believe it."

"Believe it. She sent me a ticket for the last day of the semester and it's one way, not just for the break."

My head rings. Nothing is going as planned. I turn my face away from hers and we don't speak as we make our way to the dormitory, hunkering against the wind. We climb the steps and head to my room. We rub our hands and stamp our feet.

I stare out the bedroom window. The clouds are button-gray with a matching sky. I blow my nose and dig my hands into my pockets. I want to filter out Valerie's words. There can't be much time left with her. Maybe two or three weeks.

"Want me at your uncle's with you?" She breaks the silence.

"Not there, Valerie."

"Why not? Guy is there."

"Exactly. I don't want Guy to know anything. He just met me. What if he doesn't believe me or if it creates doubt in his mind, you know?"

"Why are you so sure?"

"I know how he feels about Israel. He's fierce about it."

"And you're a threat to that?"

"No. But he might wonder if he hears about this, and if I'm right there on the kibbutz, he'll ask why I'm not in school. And my uncle might talk, my aunt."

I don't finish my thought: that my aunt is more like an avalanche to me now, prepared to bury me under her own pain and loss.

"Fine. Fine. Kibbutz is out."

She lies down on Simona's bed. She's plump now, no longer heavyset. Israel's been good to her, she looks less burdened, lighter in more ways than weight, and the streaks in her hair are no longer so sharp and brilliant, they're softer, mellower, allow her brown eyes to shine.

"But there's no one left. I don't know anyone else. I'll have to beg the administration for mercy."

"Forget it. If they didn't let Arslan back in after that terrorist attack, they sure won't look at you twice. You signed a contract, and as far as they're concerned it's out of order."

"There's no other option." I sit in the desk chair with my head in my hands. "I'm really screwed." I can't see her face well. It's in a shadow. It's past dinnertime, but for once, neither of us mentions food.

"Listen, I know your bursary was rejected but mine wasn't. Valerie the Pauper is a thing of the past."

"Really?"

"I meant to tell you. I have more money than I need now that I'm only here another three weeks. I'm staying over Hanukkah and then that last week of exams. I want the credits for the work I've done."

She takes out two cigarettes, opens the window a crack, and lights them both, slipping one into my mouth. I don't tell her I quit again ten days ago. She wants to give me something.

"There's a hostel I heard about. Well, actually I spent a night there, or half of it." Valerie's color reddens and she clears her throat. "With that cute girl, remember? Re'em. That's where we went after the club closed. There's no buzz, but it's clean and cheap. I still have the biz card."

"I can't take money from you."

"You're not taking money. I'm lending it to you. You'll pay me back. In a month's time when you are back at school and picking up translation jobs. This mess will be sorted out, Miriam."

Valerie reaches into her purse and digs around. After a few minutes of frustration, she dumps the contents on my bed. An envelope folded in half spills out.

"I was at the money changer." She counts out ten $100 bills. A small fortune. More than I could ever imagine receiving from my father. "This will take care of you and change."

My mouth hangs open.

"Valerie, I—"

"You'd be surprised what I'd do for one kiss from Miriam Gil." She raises her eyebrows and elbows me in the ribs. "Just kidding." But there is an ache in her face. "Listen, you know the old saying, 'If you can't help your friends, who can you help?'"

"It's so much money."

"You should have received the same amount anyway." Valerie holds out the money. "And when they clear this up, they'll give you the same bursary and you'll return what you don't spend and pay me back. Come on. You think I can sit back and let you go postal on your own here?"

"I am going a bit crazy." I swallow. Valerie doesn't know the half of it though I'm bursting to tell her. The name Shimon Harpaz is on the end of my lips. I bite them.

"Girlfriend, this nightmare's going to end soon. Trust my senses. I'm very intuitive. I'll find the hostel card, and we'll go together. Settle in. Let's bounce."

I don't know what to say. No one's ever been this generous to me.

"Just say 'thank you,' Miriam. That's all. You'd do the same for me."

I'm not so sure, but I look Valerie square in the eyes before I plant a long kiss on her mouth. "Thank you, Valerie."

Valerie's eyes glitter.

"You're welcome."

Chapter Twenty-Eight

I RISE EARLY in the hostel. It's December, the peak of winter holiday time, and the hostel bustles with guests. It's an ideal place to blend in, at least that much grace I've achieved. No one gives me a second glance. The hostel offers a choice of a dormitory or private room with en suite bathroom and a shared kitchen with a stove and fridge. That's all I need.

Valerie insisted I take a private room, beaming as she'd paid for two weeks up front with crisp, sharp bills. Ever since her bursary has landed in her lap, Valerie smells of money, and she wants to spread it around; in her eyes nothing this fortunate has ever happened to her.

"You don't need to make any new connections, Miriam," she'd said gently. "Let's untangle some of the ones you've already made. Privacy's your game right now."

My new accommodation is next door to Haifa's central port, one of the largest in the eastern Mediterranean, the bald clerk with the bad breath who checked me in had proudly told me in his heavy Hebrew accent. He'd also pointed out the nearby Baha'i Gardens, holding up a large colored photograph of its glorious staircase of nineteen terraces all the way up Mount Carmel. He'd circled his finger around the golden-domed Shrine of the Bab, the resting place of the Baha'i prophet that overlooks the bay toward Akko.

I'd felt a pang in my heart then. I wanted to be the keen, wide-eyed tourist he thought I was, not the subdued victim of a three-decade-old obsession, waiting for the next blow to fall. I tried to inject as much responsiveness and fervor into my chit chat with him as I waited for him to pass me the key, a roll of toilet paper, and a spare light bulb.

Lately, my mind has been leading me down dark paths, lodging jittery ideas in the display windows of my thoughts: Maybe Leah would work her old magic with Shimon and he'd double-cross me. Maybe he'd let her know the jig was up in the upscale café and she'd pulled out some dirt on him, dangled it under his nose. Anything might pop up reading through old files.

I force my mind toward Guy whenever these imaginings spill over so hard that I start to believe they've already taken place. His warm kisses and strong, secure arms envelope me, and I'm soothed.

I wish I knew more about his past. The only problem is I'd have to reciprocate, which is enough of a reason for me to keep my distance, phoning him only once to thank him for his note and pretending there was far too much static on the line for me to continue. I'd made up something about another school excursion so he wouldn't phone the dormitories. This weekend he's in Jerusalem, and I've got this wild fantasy that Shimon will come through for me next week, and in a few days I'll be back in my dormitory apartment, this nightmare behind me, planning a shopping day with Valerie before she leaves. I need a new birthday outfit if I'm going to spend the following weekend with Guy, something bought for me, not one of Simona's hand-me-downs.

I sip my coffee on the edge of the single bed and watch the sunrise streaking the sky with a range of pinks from hot to champagne. There are mental airplanes I can step into with a bit of extra effort, a few hard pushes, and a shove, and I am far away, transformed, no longer moving under anyone else's shadow or misdeeds. There is a feeling of tranquility, and I know my intense feelings for Guy are inseparable from my love for Israel that has not diminished, in spite of Leah's best efforts. I won't give her that.

I stir my coffee with a thin, white plastic spoon and finish the plain glass mug in one mouthful, then sitting up straight, startled, my tongue thick. I could have sworn I'd placed a square of milk chocolate at the bottom of the mug as I boiled the water in the kettle in the shared kitchen, in my half sleep, in Valerie's forgotten flip-flops that I'd found in my shower stall yesterday. Instead, what hit me and flooded my senses was a mouthful of bitter coffee grounds that stuck in my throat, not an auspicious sign in the infancy of morning. I reach for my water bottle and gulp, but the harsh taste remains, it has seeped in between my teeth.

I flick on the small transistor radio I found in the drawer next to the bed.

I listen to the international headlines: Former U.S. President George Bush pardons six in the Iran Contra Affair, fending off a Weinberger trial; prosecutor blasts cover-up; pain and prayer at Christmas season in

Sarajevo, newly elected U.S. President Bill Clinton's new cabinet; U.S. Department of State issues travel alert for all U.S. citizens in Israel because of possible crisis after Prime Minister Rabin's deportation to Lebanon of 416 Hamas suspects. Suspects are now in the Lebanese Army controlled buffer zone.

My clothes land on the floor as I grab a towel and head for the shower. I've been here a couple of days, and I still can't figure out the water faucets. I burn myself or freeze my naked calf or shoulder while I turn left and then right, seeking a comfortable temperature. Today is another failure, and I leave the shower with a film of soap in my hair rather than suffer more discomfort. I take my empty mug, rinse it out, fill it with tap water, and stick my upside-down head into the sink, pouring the water from the base of my neck. The sink I can handle.

By the time I'm dressed, I hear the murmurings and occasional stark shouts of the other visitors at the hostel. It's nothing like the steady drone at the university dormitory. The young people here are on holiday and overwhelmingly European. The languages that seep through the walls are French, German, Swedish, and British English. The whole atmosphere is one of detached gaiety, not daily grind.

It's the fourth day of Hanukkah and Christmas Eve, nearly everybody has something to celebrate. Even the local Muslims cannot be impervious to the rows of fresh soft *sufganiyot*, hole-less doughnuts bursting with every flavor from red jam to butterscotch to halva, filling the display windows of every café and bakery, and the brightly lit menorahs balanced on windowsill after windowsill, commercial or residential. I haven't run into a Christmas tree or a Santa Claus—though I'm so preoccupied with my troubles I'm not a reliable source. I'd read that 10 percent of the local population is Christian; no doubt their festivities have permeated the holiday atmosphere, too.

One of the remarkable things about Israel on December 24 is everything functions normally, schools, businesses, public transportation. It's another weekday, and Valerie and I are heading to Jerusalem. She's counting the days until her flight at the end of next week. The moment her flight was booked and paid for, her schedule ballooned. Her mother sent lists of gifts, tchotchkes, and must-haves for every relative. It's as if all of her religious items disintegrated at once with the printing out of her daughter's return ticket home.

She needs a new mezuzah with a real *klaf* inside, a Passover Seder plate from the Holy Land, candlesticks, mud from the Dead Sea and a rock from the fortress of Masada for her collection, not to mention crucifixes and holy water for her non-Jewish friends at work. Valerie has lost more weight running up and down the country for a yarmulke for this or that uncle and tefillin for this or that bar mitzvah than she ever lost working out with me in her shared bedroom.

Today it's the Kotel. She has a fax with a hand-written prayer her mother has written out that she insists become part of the very stones, one of the thousands of prayer notes stuck into the Wailing Wall every year by tourists, locals of every stripe, famous politicians, and celebrities.

I told Valerie it was crazy to travel to Jerusalem on Christmas Eve, but she'd insisted the Jewish Quarter would function as usual. We weren't about to enter the Christian or Armenian Quarters and, sure, there might be more of a crowd at the Kotel for Hanukkah, but it's spread out over eight days. As I organize my backpack for our day trip, the news comes on again, and this time my ears perk up about the U.S. travel alert.

"The *New York Times* quoted Prime Minister Yitzhak Rabin defending the expulsions that led to the travel ban as a necessary blow against Islamic fundamentalists who in recent days have killed four Israeli soldiers and a border policeman and who, he said, would destroy Middle East peace negotiations unless stopped."

For all I know Valerie's heard the news on the bus on the way over and she's already rescheduled our day. She's been so jittery about security since she landed, I can't imagine she'll want to take a chance.

On the other hand, the warning said Israel and we're already here. Uneasiness washes over me. We should stay local. The way my luck has gone the last month, I wouldn't label myself a charm.

An increase in police and security guards is not what I want. Anyone with access to a government computer is on my avoid list, until Shimon contacts me. I haven't spoken to him since our breakfast meeting, yet I sense he's well acquainted with where I am and how to reach me. This has me throwing backward glances when I turn corners and cross intersections, but I've never seen anything but ordinary people in ordinary circumstances.

There's a knock at my door.

"It's me."

I let Valerie in.

"How's the new digs?"

"Great."

Valerie wears new Parasuco jeans, the latest fashion with stripes from waist to ankle, and her hair is tied up in a red bandana. A mood ring is a deep blue on her wedding finger.

"Pull on a sweater over that T-shirt and let's move. It's drizzling on and off, but the clouds don't look heavy."

"Did you hear the news?"

"You know part of my policy of staying cool in Israel is no news."

I pat the seat beside me, and she slides next to me on the edge of the bed.

"I heard it, and the U.S. State Department's issued a travel warning. I don't know if the Old City is where we want to be."

"*You* are insecure? The offspring of the war-weary soldier."

I busy myself with mascara and lip gloss. I'm upset that my father hasn't phoned. Valerie takes a plastic box of *sufganiyot* out of her bag.

"Can't get enough of these," she says, holding the box open. I use my shower towel as a napkin, holding the pastry on the edges and bite down hard. My mouth fills with halvah, drowning out the remains of the bitter coffee taste.

"Heaven or what?" Valerie has already finished hers. She has sesame filling on her nose and chin and doughnut powder all over her face. With her hair streaked blonde, flopping out of her wide red bandana for a moment, she looks foolish rather than stylish, a clown. I giggle and wipe at her face with the clean end of my towel.

"Shoes. Sweater," she says.

I lick the last sweetness from my fingers.

"Why don't we do the Kotel next week or after the Sabbath when it's darker and I'm not so noticeable?"

Valerie puts her hands on her hips.

"So this is what it's about—as if. You expect me to buy that you're trippin' over some news report? What's a good news report in this country? You heard one yet?"

I can't argue. I want to stay in town. The Old City on Christmas Eve sounds like an ideal spot to take revenge for deporting hundreds of Palestinians or for random passport checks.

"My mom's going to blow if I don't put her wish list in the Kotel. She hasn't been here since 1969, and she's got no plans to come until she sees the Arabs and the Jews singing "Kumbaya" together on Dizengoff. And will you stop playing the part of some fugitive in an action movie!"

She picks up my backpack, swings it over her shoulder, and heads for the door.

Chapter Twenty-Nine

I DISTRACT MYSELF ON THE BUS with the view while Valerie thumbs through her tourist book.

"Want to hear about the history of the Jewish Quarter?" Valerie asks. It's a rhetorical question. She'll tell me no matter what. "Turns out Jews have lived there since the eighth century B.C.E."

"And in 1948 the two thousand or so Jews were forced out by Arabs," I offer.

"How did you know?"

"My grandparents were thrown out," I answered. "My father told me. Everything was destroyed, even the ancient synagogues and Jordan controlled it all until the Six-Day War in 1967 when we figured out how to access the Kotel again."

"Was your father one of the paratroopers who captured it?"

"Too old. He was a tank driver by then."

"Your old man must be something else."

I nod and swing my leg forward, accidentally kicking the back of the seat in front of us. One of the guys with the body odor gives me an icy stare before he faces forward.

I can see Valerie wants to explode with laughter, but she's too polite. She clears her throat and reads on.

"The section of the Jewish Quarter destroyed prior to 1967 has since been rebuilt and settled. Many educational institutions have taken up residence." Valerie stops reading.

"Educational institutions, huh?" she says. She's added a matching red baseball cap over her bandana, giving her a boyish look. "Imagine studying all day in the heart of the Old City?"

"They're not just anywhere in the Old City. They're even in the Arab Quarter," I respond.

Valerie makes a face. "I'll take Haifa any day," she says.

"These boys who study in the Old City aren't afraid to walk around. Guy told me he had a few of them in his combat unit, and they were the least afraid of confrontation with Arabs anywhere. As far as they are concerned, this place is ours, not theirs. I think he really admired their convictions, even if he himself is more interested in peace through economic prosperity than through ideological principles."

"Guy sounds perfect for you," Valerie says as they get off the bus. "The heavy, analytical type."

Finally, we are only minutes from the Kotel. Already I can see we are in for a genuine tourist experience. The roads are jammed with cars and pedestrians. There are at least twenty other people waiting with us for the light to change, so that we can cross over to Jaffa Gate and the weather can't make up its mind. The sun shines for a few minutes only to be swallowed by a cluster of clouds; patches of blue are infrequent, and the sky is mostly a dull gray, the air opaque with fog.

At Jaffa Gate the scene is dizzying. There are hordes of people outside of the main entrance wall, as well as on the inside. There are money-changers; kiosk vendors hawking soft drinks, soft pretzels, newspapers, cigarettes, and snacks; and endless lines of people dressed in every manner. Women in wigs covered from their necks to their toes in long sleeves and thick stockings walk unruffled alongside tourists in tight, ripped jeans and halter tops. It would be difficult to discern the season from a snapshot of the scene before us. American tourists huddle in long, black winter coats, and French tourists pass in cut-off shorts, long button-downs draped over their shoulders.

We stand for a while, taking in the scene. I smell gasoline, cigarettes, fried food, and *sufganiyot*, as well as an underlying scent of sewage and some sort of incense or flavored tobacco, but it's not a carnival feel, in spite of the crowd and bustle. The path toward the Kotel is at most two or three abreast down slippery cobblestone, and cars honk as they amble along at different speeds among the crowd in both directions, in and out of the imposing gates. People have to watch where they're going or risk being knocked down. If we were expecting traffic and crowd control at one of Israel's main tourist attractions, we were wrong.

"Well, here's the Jewish entrance," Valerie says. "I've figured out that much from the map." She looks pleased with herself. "Ahead of us is the Arab shuk, and there's the Tower of David Museum on the right. I think there's a police station after that, or that's what I gather from this map." Valerie still holds the book.

"Thanks. I can tell that much," I snap at her.

"Just trying to be the helpful tour guide," she says. She jabs me with her elbow.

I don't answer.

"I meant, do you prefer we go the other way? Would that make you more comfortable, lighten up? The book says it's shorter through the Arab shuk. There's a huge crowd here. Nothing can happen." She reads from her book again. "We can go to the Kotel this way, and then the book suggests we come back up through the Jewish and Armenian Quarters."

I'm a heel. Valerie's just trying to be a good daughter, fulfill her mother's wish list.

"Well, yeah. Maybe heading right in the direction of the police station is not so necessary," I answer. I should apologize. She didn't drag me here. I could have stayed in Haifa. Last time I came here with my class there was no time to place a note in the Kotel. I could use some divine intervention to prod Shimon along.

Behind us the crowd swells. I see people who look like tourists holding short white candles and realize there must be some sort of Christian march happening for the holiday. This is a popular meet-up point. We are increasingly jostled forward before we've chosen a direction.

"I'd light a smoke, but I think it's a hazard. I'd burn someone's eye out." Valerie's attempt at humor is weak, but I force a laugh anyway. "I'll just inhale everybody else's," she adds.

I tell her to make sure her backpack is zipped in case of pickpockets. When I glance behind me I see hundreds of Christians, most of them sporting silver or gold crucifixes around their necks. We arrived with the celebration, but I'm not worried. I doubt they're on their way to the Kotel. The crowd will ease as we continue in that direction.

Valerie grabs my hand, and we head in the direction of the signs that read *Western Wall*. We tread down the wide, slippery steps with our eyes and ears on the shopkeepers inviting us in and tossing out prices for any item they think might have caught our attention. Valerie leads me into one of the shops near the top.

"Hey, check out these bracelets. Cool! How much?" she asks the store owner.

"Fifty shekels," he responds. "Beautiful. You like also necklaces? I have necklaces, rings, earrings. Come." He beckons us farther into the store, and we follow.

Valerie whispers in my ear that we should bargain or at least play good cop, bad cop. I should pretend to leave if he doesn't give her the right price, see what happens. From what she's read about the Old City it is expected, unless you are a really dumb tourist.

I shrug. I want to get out of here. My breathing is uneasy. I've never liked crowds. They make me want to run. The smell of hookah smoke is overpowering. There must be someone burning flavored tobacco right in the back of this shop. But heading in the opposite direction toward the entrance is no more comforting; I'd only be jostled and dragged along with the momentum.

"You think Tracy would go for this?" she asks me, holding up a silver wire Star of David necklace with a turquoise stone in the center. To me it's a cheap souvenir, this whole store a trap for naive tourists.

Before I can respond, she asks how much, and the owner tells her 100 shekels, but for her, ninety. Valerie winks at me. I shake my head exaggeratedly and turn to leave. I slip through the crowd that seems red and sweaty in spite of the winter month and into the almost identical jewelry and souvenir shop next door. The Arab owner puffs on his pipe, sips tea from a small glass cup with no handles. I have to steady myself from the force of the crowd. In a moment Valerie arrives, laughing.

"It worked!" she announces, triumphant. "He went down to fifty as soon as he saw you disappear."

"Great."

"I think we should pick up a few more souvenirs here before we go. What do you think of these cool scarves?"

"Where would you wear them?"

"Good point," she says. "Wall hanging?"

I shrug, but I'm catching the shopping bug myself. Maybe a cigarette lighter or a necklace for Guy. I've never seen him with any jewelry. What could he want from the shuk?

Most of the light is blocked from outside, and my eyes are slowly adjusting to the dimness. I can hear tarboukas playing in the background and fast Arabic between the store owner and his friend or assistant. Clothing and curtains hang from the doorways of all of the shop entrances, and the narrow pathway is crammed with people, men with long beards and black hats, tourists, babies and small children in strollers. Every so often, two or three — never one — security guards with rifles slung across their fronts, tall antennas protruding from behind one shoulder and the handle of a club from the other, pass by us. I don't know if they're here because of the warning on the news or if this is normal.

Maybe if I buy one or two things the crowd will die down by the time I'm done and I'll focus on something else besides the sweat building under the damn sweater Valerie insisted I put on. The air is much cooler in the shade of the shuk, but I'm hot.

"I liked the stuff better in the first store. I'm going to go back and get one of those little leather purses."

"I doubt it's real leather, Valerie."

"Still the buzz-kill? Come on. We're here now. Can we enjoy it? Next week you'll be here. I'll be on a plane before next weekend." Valerie keeps her voice low. She doesn't want us to scream "tourists" everywhere we go, although it's obvious from the large backpacks, our accents, and the tourist guide book she has stuffed under her armpit.

"Okay. Get me one, too. We should have matching souvenirs. We can wear them together." Her face softens. I hit the right note.

"Maybe there's more stuff for men across the way. I'll be right there."

Concentrating on Guy lifts my mood. I have no idea if he is the tchotchke type, maybe just a T-shirt. I hold my breath, put out my elbows, and jostle my way across the narrow path and into the T-shirt store or what I thought was a T-shirt store. There is everything from intricately carved pipes to key chains to silk and wool shawl-like pashminas in here. So many colors hang from the ceiling, it's dazzling.

In no time the store is more cramped as a few shoppers outside step in. Outside of the small shop, there is the sound of a drum, but louder this time, as though announcing something official. I make my way from the back of the store where the owner shadows my every move to the front. The parade has begun.

"The patriarchal procession," the Arab store owner says to me, sticking out his chest. He is proud of his English. "Every year, for the Christmas." I have no idea what a patriarchal procession is, but I doubt he does either. He has memorized it from working here so long, and it works well with Christian tourists, his knowledge and interest.

I hear tambourines, even flutes, and now the space between Valerie and me is thick with people, all smiling, all marching and waving. There's no way I'll get across this human river. I'll wait it out. I caress a grass green frock hanging from the ceiling. It's no wonder they call this place "Little Istanbul." There isn't one unused space. I could not imagine working in these narrow alleyways day after day. I dig my nails into the palm of one hand. I won't panic or hyperventilate. It's a small space, nothing more. The parade will pass and make its way to the Christian Quarter in a few more minutes.

There are three other tourists in the small shop with shocked looks on their faces. They're not leaving either, not unless they want to risk getting trampled in such a constricted space. They are Germans, and they light cigarettes to pass the time. Perfect. Now it's not just a tiny space, it's also airless and smoky.

I'm grateful to them with their wide, white legs and pink necks, their cameras dangling over their chests. They've bought one-third of the store and kept the owner so occupied and happy, he's not only stopped shadowing me, he hasn't given me so much as a glance. I can't imagine why I thought Guy would want something from here. For him this isn't classic artistry, it's commonplace. I'll get him something from a mall.

My patience is over. The longer I wait, the more tourists arrive. I sip from my water bottle and splash water on my face and neck, make sure my shoes are tied so no one trips me in the stampede, and double-check the zippers on my backpack. I dive into the crowd moving as one wave and zig-zag through it, knees and elbows first.

But when I reach the shop across from the path, feeling as though I deserve an Olympic medal, Valerie, who should be easy to spot, even in this crowd with her fiery red bandana and matching baseball cap, is nowhere in sight. Reaching the store beside me is easy. I have to go with the flow of the marchers, not against the tide.

There again is the same German trio, but no Valerie. I haven't gone beyond five-meters the entire time we've been here. Where can she have gone? I brace myself and retrace my path to what I thought was the T-shirt store. It's empty. I panic. I push my way to the open space at the entrance to the shuk and look all the way down, but I don't spot her.

She must have lost sight of me and continued to the Kotel. It will be much easier to find her there. I plead with my heart to stop beating so fast, pray I won't take a wrong turn and end up so deep in the Arab Quarter that I'll be targeted by pickpockets or worse. I didn't even glance at the map Valerie grabbed from the bus station and getting lost is one of the things I do well, that and panic in crowds. I dig my hands into my thighs. Damn. I never wanted to come here, and now I've lost Valerie. I search for the soldiers and the few posted wall signs.

Stop whining! I tell myself as I stare up at the stone walls. The signs indicate that to get to the Kotel I should go right and then make a left. It seems as though an hour has passed since I lost Valerie, but I don't know. It can't possibly be that long. She's probably already there, smoking a cigarette and chatting up some hot girl from the United States who happens to be on her flight home. *Concentrate on that*, I tell myself as I put one heavy leg in front of the other.

Chapter Thirty

IT'S RAINING. I hear the pattering outside, but the roof is high and narrow, and little water seeps through. Well, I guess that's the closest to snow Jerusalem can get on Christmas Eve. I peer at the map for the fourth time in as many minutes. It looks as though it's been drawn by a third grader, and I still can't make heads or tails out of it. Valerie must know the old kindergarten rule: If you get lost return to your original spot.

I have to give it one more shot before I plunge into this forest of people. The thought is terrifying. It has to be worth another quarter of an hour to try and avoid it. Besides, Valerie must be here!

I take a deep breath and dive into the crowd, elbows and knees first. If I can only find her, we can suck in our guts and skim this parade somehow. I can't believe we've been separated for so long. What is she doing? I glance for the tenth time at my bare wrist. My watch broke a month ago, and I haven't had time to fix it. I should pick up a cheap plastic one and fix my good one at home. It costs double to fix here.

"Come on, Valerie. Where are you?" I place a hand over my mouth. I hadn't realized I'd spoken out loud.

"Here! Miriam, here!" I look up and the bright red baseball cap is there. I can't believe it. Valerie is right in front of me. We hug in the middle of this ocean of people and get knocked down the slippery steps together, like two bowling pins. Valerie links elbows with me and drags me back into the first shop we'd entered.

"Where the hell have you been?" I try to keep my voice controlled, but I'm angry. "You scared me to death! I told you I didn't want to come and then you traipse off to who knows where."

"I'm sorry. It's my fault," Valerie says. She holds her hands together as though praying. "Forgive me. I must have scared you out of your skin. I'm so sorry, I couldn't say no to the shop owner's invitation." She indicates toward the owner with her elbow. He is busy in conversation with someone who might be his son, but could be a nephew or cousin. "He asked me if I'd enjoy stepping into the back of his shop and viewing what he called his 'special collection.'" Valerie points to a barely noticeable, smaller room at the back of the shop.

"And you went? Are you crazy or what?" I whisper.

"I knew you'd say that."

"I can't believe you went. You were invisible. Anything could have happened back there and it must reek of hookah because that's what you smell like." I sniff the air around Valerie and wave my hand in front of my nose.

"That it does. I won't say it was the smartest thing to do, but it was a small price to pay because you know what happened?" Valerie asks. She lets her bag slide off of her back and sets it on a black stool in the corner, unzipping the top. She yanks out a plastic bag, holds up the first item, and puts on a game show host voice.

"I bought these dazzling Bedouin tapestries, passed on the hand-painted ceramics, but they're worth a look. Check out this shell-covered chess set, a separate backgammon set, and two pastel-colored sparkly scarves — feast your eyes, they have the most spectacular gold trim. And for us, my best girlfriend — " Valerie holds up two charming identical leather purses, waves them like flags. "Mmm. Smell that genuine leather."

"I can't believe you. That bursary has gone to your head. Were you thinking we'd cab it back to Haifa? You want to schlep all this around all day?"

"You've got it wrong. I covered almost my mother's whole list. This has been the biggest time saver, and you won't believe the price. Now we need to do the fax in the Kotel thing, throw in a Seder plate, and we're done. Home free."

I moan. I don't feel home free. I feel like crawling into my bed.

"Let me help you repack." I approach Valerie's bag.

"Stay back," she says. "Miss neat and organized is not invited. I like the way I pack."

"You don't pack Valerie, you cram and shove."

"It's been working for me until now."

"Your new gifts will get broken before you have time to give them away."

"I said stay back." Valerie whisks her bag out of my reach. I'm surprised she still has the strength after our long bus ride and hour of hide-and-seek.

"All right." I hold up both hands in the air. "I give up."

"You know what you can do for me?"

"Anything if it will get us moving."

"I wrote my own prayer to put in the Kotel, and here's my mom's. I'm afraid if I reopen this bag I'll never get it closed again, and it's so tight, I can't even get in the side pockets. Take them for me, will you? Did you get a chance to write your own? You don't get a chance every day."

I fold Valerie's prayers neatly and slip them into the side of my bag where they won't get wet if it's still raining.

"I'll compose a prayer as we walk, okay? Let's get out of here and this time, we're linking arms, holding hands, I don't care what. It's the Kotel and then a restaurant. You're not getting away from me again."

"Words I've longed to hear." Valerie winks and blows me a kiss. I notice the store owner watching us and giggle.

"Merry Christmas and Happy Hanukkah," the shop owner says, as we link arms and step toward the front. I can smell Valerie's perfume from this close, which has gone from gourmand to powdery in these cramped quarters for so long. "Wait one moment, please."

Valerie nods. There is a tremble in her throat and a flicker in the corner of her eye. All of her recent bluster's infused by her bursary, not her newfound security in Israel. She hasn't lived with Arabs in the dormitories the way I did, and she didn't grow up hearing the language in her home. I watch as she turns her head, and I imagine she's hoping to spot a soldier or police officer, but there's only this never-ending parade. Some of the candles from the marchers have fallen to the ground, burnt out by the rain, turned to stubs.

"Where you going?" the shop owner asks. His tone is friendly, and he speaks through coffee-stained teeth. "Let me guess, the Kotel?"

Valerie nods. She still hasn't said a word. Only moments ago, she was speaking with this same person in a hidden back room, fishing around in her wallet for change, dropping it into his outstretched palm. What is her problem? She trusted him alone then. It must be the lack of fresh air.

I smile and he nods toward me.

"Crowd is by the church. You must go around," he says, in a heavy Arabic accent.

"Muhammad?" He calls and out of nowhere a teenaged boy materializes. I am amazed. They must be in every nook and cranny. I imagine them somehow stuck to the ceiling along with the frocks and shawls, maybe resting in between them on work breaks. I understand by watching his hand gestures that the shopkeeper tells the boy to take us to the Kotel.

"Come. He will show you a shortcut. Don't worry. He is my son." The shopkeeper smiles and beckons with long arms toward his son. Should we tell him we're staying put or politely refuse? But there doesn't seem much point in losing any more of our day, and he's right, it will be a struggle to make it to the Kotel through this bottleneck with our heavy backpacks. I can't believe how weighty Valerie's is now with her mound of gifts.

Our eyes meet, and we nod at the boy at the same time. I tail behind Valerie, a tight grip on her hand. She follows him slowly at first but relaxes as she sees that he is, indeed, correct: Up ahead there's a mass of people wall to wall. It's suffocating just to watch them from afar. There's no way to jam through that. I groan. At least the rain has let up and the hammering overhead has stopped, but now the cobblestones are even more slippery than before, as well as muddy.

We continue left down a side alley, off the main path, and in an instant, it is obvious even to a tourist that there are only Arabs on these narrow cobblestone streets. Here they sell mostly food, not touristy trinkets and souvenirs, but foodstuffs and fresh produce I can't even identify. There is the odor of raw meat, and flies buzz around the slabs hanging from the ceiling. I struggle not to make a face. I don't want to insult anyone.

At least the large bowls of spices are familiar. Valerie points out cumin, coriander and saffron and lets me know how much her mother enjoys spice stores, as an amateur gourmet foodie. I spot zaatar, that's where my expertise ends, but Valerie babbles in a low voice about her mother's favorite recipes, and she's stopped walking.

She's not even dreaming about stopping here, is she? I'll kill her.

The shopkeeper notices her staring.

"Moroccan harissa," he says, pointing to one spice, the brilliant color of roasted red peppers. "Tunisian harissa," he says, pointing to another similar looking seasoning. "Iraqi baharat." He continues his mini spice tour, sticking his chin out at a third bowl overflowing with what seems to be a blend of dried mint and hot red chili pepper.

After a half pause, Valerie shrugs and points forward and my shoulders relax. She holds out both hands, palms open, and then taps one finger on her wrist, as if to say, "What can I do? I want to buy, but a friend is waiting." The owner says something to the boy, and I guess he tells him to convince her to buy something. She shakes her head and points again at her imaginary watch, hoping her smile is soothing or at least easygoing, hiding the tension I know she feels. I can see the tightness around her mouth. She's had enough excitement for one day. I see it in her eyes now. She was worried about me, too.

"I don't know if my mother would take spices from here," she whispers. "And I doubt I'd get through passport control smelling like a Middle Eastern shuk." I nod at her, but I need to keep my eyes down, so that I don't slip. The mud is even worse in this section. There's a knot in my side from the weight of the backpack and no doubt I've acquired some bruises on my shins and shoulders, and we still have three buses to get back to the hostel, where Valerie's staying with me tonight. I'd insisted the bed was big enough, without mentioning that she's paying for it.

We've been in the gloom of the covered shuk so long, I've lost track of time. It must be approaching sundown. Valerie slips, and I struggle to hold my balance while she regains hers. While I'm staring at my shoes, she's concentrating on the route the teenager takes.

"He's squaring around the crowd," she murmurs. "I want to make sure he's not leading us off course. My instinct is to go right, not left. I don't know if it's worth stopping to take out my map again."

"No stopping. What if he gets fed up and leaves us here in the middle of the real Arab shuk? No way."

She shrugs. "I think he's taking us out to the bottom entrance, near the restaurant or those yeshivas, not the regular Kotel entrance."

I don't care which entrance he chooses, as long as it's away from the crowd and fast, although there's only so fast we can go on this damp, slick floor. All I know is that we made a left, weaved left and then right, and we've been on a downward trajectory ever since.

"You come again to my father's shop," the Arab teenager says in broken Hebrew.

"Of course," she says. "He has nice things."

The teenager beams.

In contrast to Valerie, I'm less interested in chitchat and keener on getting to the Kotel, moving this weight off of my shoulders, and sitting down to a hot meal.

"Are we almost there?" I ask.

"Excuse me?" The teenager stops, eyes me.

"Are we almost there? We'll be there soon? At the Kotel." I put on the best smile I can muster under the circumstances.

"Yes, yes. This way. The Kotel."

He beckons for us to continue following him. He's misunderstood. I was hoping he'd tell us how much longer it will be. Five minutes? Ten? I don't have the energy to ask again, and each time one of us speaks, his ears perk up and he slows down and slowing down is the opposite of what I want right now. We continue stepping onward. Valerie clutches my wrist. Our hands are too sweaty for holding.

Lost in concentration, the last thing I need is to slip and end up limping all the way back to Haifa. I don't see the three Jewish boys sizing up the Arab and the two Jewish girls coming toward them until they are on top of us.

They have soup-bowl sized white knitted yarmulkes, extra-long payot, and extra-large tsisit worn over their white T-shirts, flowing downward, spilling over their jeans, the threads swinging over their hips as they glide along, all three of them in wide-strapped leather sandals.

"Hey!" one of them calls out in Hebrew. "Hey, you Abdul! What are you doing with Jewish girls? Where do you think you're taking them?"

"I don't need your permission to move around," the teenager says, switching into a rough, guttural Hebrew and speaking in a low voice. His back straightens to his full height. I'd never noticed how tall he is until now, maybe he's not such a young teenager.

"Who do you think you're talking to?" one of the yeshiva boys responds. Something clicks in my mind. These must be the boys from one of the local Arab Quarter yeshivas, the ones Guy told me about. I remember him telling me they don't take shit from anybody and they are very protective of what they consider to be their turf. They look about our age, standing in a solid row, blocking our path with their arms crossed on their broad chests. As usual, I freeze in a confrontation. Anything intelligent I might say leaks before it reaches my mouth. I look panicked at Valerie.

"I think there is a misunderstanding," Valerie says in Hebrew, as her backpack bounces down her arm, banging against her leg to the ground. I can see small drops of blood where something she's stuffed into one of the outside pockets has scraped her arm. Before I can ask her if she's all right, she confronts the yeshiva boys.

"This is all a misunderstanding," she repeats, ignoring the small trail of blood pooling at her wrist. "This boy's helping us. There's a big Christian parade today and it was packed. Hey, are you guys listening?"

No one's looks at Valerie, let alone listens to her. I sense a fight. The yeshiva guys have their eyes trained on our Arab guide. I need to act.

"Listen, guys. We want to get to the Kotel, do the touristy thing." I turn to the Arab teenager. "Thank you so much for your help. I think from here we follow the path down, no?"

The Arab teenager digs his heels into the ground. He's not going anywhere. It's a matter of respect. Pride.

The tension is palpable, and I'm not thinking clearly anymore. Valerie is half crouched to one side, rubbing her wrist.

The teenager, who had been walking abreast of Valerie, stiffens and stares hard, and a stream of curses flows out of his mouth in Arabic as he comes nose to nose with the tallest yeshiva boy. In one instant he transforms from the quiet tour guide to a hostile, angry combatant. His curses are getting louder.

313

"Listen," I try again, inching away from him as his knuckles clench, his face reddens. "Let's just all go on to wherever we were all going." I sound like an idiot and I'm ashamed, swirling in a pool of my own emotions. This is all our fault. We should give him some money for his troubles and ask the Jewish guys to take us to the Kotel. He doesn't mean any harm. My diplomacy's no more effective than Valerie's. I take a breath and open my mouth to explain again when one of the yeshiva guys grabs the Arab's shirtsleeve. The Arab responds with an angry shove, loosening himself from his opponent's grasp and yelling,

"We were on our way somewhere. Move!"

As the Arab teenager bends to pick up Valerie's backpack, the tallest Jewish boy says, "You're not taking Jewish girls anywhere!" and pushes the Arab shopkeeper on his bent shoulder, causing him to stumble over Valerie's bag and land on his buttocks and hands. His screams alert some other neighborhood boys in the alleys, and before I can get a word out, I hear the sounds of feet pounding on pavement behind me.

Whirling around, I see two Arab teenagers running at top speed, followed by a young boy panting behind them who doesn't look more than ten. All of them appear to be screaming at one time. There's so much noise at once, my hands cover my ears. They're all wearing T-shirts, sneakers, and jeans, a look of fury on their faces, and I see only one unified force heading toward us.

"Run, Valerie!" I run in the direction of the Kotel, fall forward, and land face- down on the wet pavement.

"Miriam!" Valerie screams, moving toward me.

I raise my head, wiping the dirt from my eyes with my fingers.

"Here!" I call out, terror in my voice.

But she doesn't take more than one step before the hand of the front runner reaches out toward her chest to punch her, and she is pushed backward against the wall behind her. The same Arab throws his fist into the shoulder of the yeshiva boy to her left. He yells, grabs his shoulder as his fingers start to turn red and the blue of his T-shirt darkens and stains.

I scream and try to stand up, but someone's hand on the back of my head forces me down. I can feel warm blood dripping into my mouth. My nose is bleeding or my mouth is bleeding or both. My lip burns. Valerie! In an instant the chaos dissipates. There's no sound at all, except the beating of my heart flapping in my ears.

Chapter Thirty-One

A QUARTER OF AN HOUR AGO, I was convinced I'd throw up. A wave of nausea overcame me. I haven't eaten since Valerie offered me that plastic container of Israeli doughnuts hours ago. This morning? Yesterday?

Valerie. When will they let me see her? They told me to stay put. I can't remember now if it was a police officer, nurse, or social worker. My mind's a blur. I can still hear the ambulance siren in between my ears, still taste the warm blood in my mouth mixed with dirt, and of course, my swollen lip hurts.

"You're lucky you didn't choke on a tooth." For some reason this ridiculous sentence bounces back and forth across my mind. Maybe the paramedic said it in the ambulance or the nurse in the packed emergency room. Either way it's stuck, and like an elastic it keeps pulling me back. "You're lucky..."

Once the doctors were done examining me, I was put in a room with the two other yeshiva boys, the ones other than their friend in surgery with Valerie. That much I know. One had a bandage over his right eye, the other a fat lip larger than mine. Both of them had fingers taped together.

They had sat, their heads touching, and I heard the words *stabbed, lower back, 15- cm blade,* and *sensitive* from across the small room in soft voices. I am ashamed to say

I dozed on and off in the chair. Even when they explained to me they were giving me a sedative, I didn't believe anything could make me sleep. Now, I've missed vital information I can't get back.

At one point, the shorter blonder boy asked me if I wanted a cup of coffee. They were going to morning prayers and could bring me something from the cafeteria.

"We're in Shaare Zedek Hospital, you know?" His eyes were wet with pity, gazing down on this tourist, this foreigner who'd become hysterical for a moment, blabbering in an incomprehensible mixture of Hebrew and English when someone in uniform asked her for ID. That much I remember.

Now I can't recall if I nodded or stared at the boy's offer. Man really. He must have been at least my age. They haven't returned and I don't know how long it's been or how long it takes to pray, and I imagine however long it usually takes, today it will take longer. They are surely praying for their friend and Valerie. I saw the concern in their eyes.

For the second time, I rifle through my backpack in search of a morsel, a crumb. But I am a meticulous packer. I know there's nothing but a squashed pack of gum in the side pocket with one out-of-shape pink square left. I pop it into my inflated mouth and chew slowly, savoring the burst of sugar in spite of the raw pain.

For some reason Valerie's backpack is here, too. It looks pristine, as though it hadn't been on Valerie's back when she fell, hadn't absorbed a drop of rain or fell in the muck. Could someone have cleaned it up?

But now that I consider the circumstances, I inflate the backpack's importance beyond all proportion. My memory is on overdrive. It had slipped off Valerie's shoulder; something jutting out had scraped her arm. At any rate, it hadn't been on her body when she fell or when she was stabbed. Oh, God. Please be okay, Valerie, I whisper. Please let someone come soon.

My stomach rumbles. There's a stash of pastries inside Valerie's bag, but I won't touch it. It's hers. There are her gifts inside, her things. I tell myself I don't want to violate her privacy, but I know I wish to avoid the smell of her familiar gourmand scent, the combination chocolate-berry smell she wears on every article of clothing. And I don't want the odor of brand-new matching leather purses to leave a tang in my mouth, especially those.

I shiver, and I'm grateful for the sweater and silently bless Valerie for mothering me into taking it. I slip it off my waist and slowly ease it over my face, over the bruise on my chin. My hands sting. They'd been rubbed rusty red with anti-septic along with my knees.

The door opens and a short woman walks in. She is plump and blonder than the yeshiva boy; her hair is almost white.

"I'm Suzanne," she says in perfect English. I look up.

"I understand you're Canadian, and you're lucky I'm on today so we can speak in English. You'll be more comfortable."

You're lucky you didn't choke on a tooth. He distracts me in the ambulance, so I don't look at...

"I brought you a breakfast. Nothing to write home about. Hospital food."

She places a tray on the table in front of me. I smell the white cheese, the blob of artificial strawberry jam. The wave of nausea returns, and I clutch my stomach.

"Shall I take you to the bathroom?"

I shake my head. After a few breaths it passes. She opens the small container of water and nudges it into my hand. I sip. It feels cool on my sore tongue. I drink until the container is empty, and I am rewarded with a smile from the nurse.

"Valerie. How is she? When can I see her?" The water has jolted me awake. I can feel it sliding down my throat, into my stomach. We'll be here for a day or two, even a week, and then I'll take Valerie home, wherever that is. I wonder if anyone's phoned her mother.

"Miriam, I'm a social worker, not a nurse."

I nod, but nothing registers. She looks disappointed, but I'm not interested in her feelings.

"Could you take me to Valerie?"

"Your friend, you know her from the States?"

"No. We met here at Haifa University in the dormitories. Is she okay? Could I just see her for a minute?"

Why won't this social worker answer me? Her face tells me nothing.

"She's not okay, Miriam." Suzanne puts an open palm on my forearm. "Your friend passed away. She died in the ambulance. I'm sorry it's taken so long to get

319

to you. I need you to come with me, to identify the body." She speaks in an undertone.

"What do you mean? We were together an hour ago. What are you saying?"

"I'm sorry. This isn't easy for you, but I need you to come with me. Her family's been contacted, and she'll be on a flight home once all of the paperwork is done." She applies pressure to my forearm. "This is your chance to say goodbye."

Chapter Thirty-Two

THE SOCIAL WORKER HELPS ME STAND because I am unsure if my legs will hold my weight and leads me out the door, her arm under my elbow.

Outside the world looks ordinary, how a hospital should look. Busy people in white squishing down the corridors in soft sneakers or flats. The rattle of breakfast trays on a steel trolley. The ding of elevators, the whoosh of their heavy doors opening and closing.

Valerie's dead.

Someone holding important-looking papers nods at Suzanne and she nods back. A broom moves back and forth in the hands of a cleaner at the end of the hall.

Valerie's dead.

Suzanne switches into matter-of-fact Hebrew when a police officer stops her with a raised hand, pulls her to the side, and speaks into her ear. An elderly man pushes his elderly wife inch by inch down the corridor. They pass me by, the man's shoes squeak against the white linoleum.

I can't believe this woman is taking me to identify Valerie's body. The social worker has my elbow in her palm again. She keeps up a quiet patter of talk.

"Apparently, they thought she was a boy with that baseball cap on and, of course, it was dark, the rain brought the fog with it."

I cry and whimper. Hot tears gush down my cheeks. Suzanne stops and hugs me softly. She hands me a pile of tissues from her large pocket and leans me against the wall.

"Did she suffer?"

"She suffered difficulty breathing, but not for long. There were large crowds to get through on Christmas Eve from what I understand. There's another boy just coming out of surgery. I'm not a nurse, of course. Luckily, the attackers ran away before anyone else was hurt."

You're lucky you didn't choke on a tooth. He distracts me in the ambulance, so I don't look at Valerie's dead body.

Less than an hour later, two sour-faced police officers ask me the same questions again, this time in different order. One is taller and leaner than the other. Both have dark complexions and matching buzz cuts. Their faces are clean-shaven, and one has a scar across his left eyebrow. The skin is lighter there. Studying their similar faces, I wonder if partners begin to look alike after working together for a while or if it's just the same haircut and uniform that plays tricks with my tired eyes.

The larger one looks down at me with narrowed eyes.

"How do you know Valerie Ruben? How long have you known her? Where did you say you were staying again? What are you doing in Israel? What were you doing in the Arab Quarter? Where is your Israeli passport?"

This time I snort.

"You've got my Canadian passport. That's all I have."

I can smell my own sweat mixed with stale deodorant and old tobacco. I can feel the open wound in my heart. It might as well be on the table in front of us. Valerie. She'd looked asleep when I saw her for the briefest of moments with Suzanne's hand on my back the entire time, a pressure in the numbness.

And in the ambulance. How did Valerie look then? He didn't want me to look at her. I see that now. If we'd arrived five minutes sooner, would she be recovering from surgery now, the way the other victim was? They'd told me his name, but I'd forgotten. Avraham maybe. He was going to make it, not like Valerie.

"Unusual for a young woman to be alone in a hostel, no?"

"I told you I've been in the dormitory at Haifa University. There was a mix-up with my papers. I've only been at the hostel a few nights. Is that illegal?"

The officer sighs.

"Let's go over it one more time, just to make sure we didn't miss anything. I know you're exhausted and upset about your friend, too, I suppose."

I'd like to punch him in the mouth. He doesn't believe I'm upset about Valerie. He thinks my puffy eyes and red nose are an act, like I'm trying to fool them.

"Would you like to use the bathroom first? Coffee? Yonatan here will call for three coffees." He nudges his friend who picks up the phone.

His words drip with disbelief. I don't blame him. A suspected Syrian Christian is involved in the fatal

323

stabbing of a Jewish American female tourist studying at Haifa University. The incident takes place in the Old City, one of Israel's most famous tourist sites on one of its most crowded evenings. There is a second injury of a Jewish Israeli man and it all happens on Christmas Eve at dusk, mere days after hundreds of Palestinians are deported to Lebanon in a controversial government move that's made international headlines. Her father is unknown, according to initial computer checks at the Interior Ministry. He might be a relative or sympathizer of the deportees.

Maybe I'm the linchpin in a set-up, betraying my false friendship for money or more likely Valerie Ruben's U.S. passport that had been found at the bottom of her bag on top of her airplane ticket home scheduled for one week's time.

I rub my eyes with one hand, the other on the back of my neck. The bruise on my shoulder feels more like a cramp. I don't know if it's from the weight of my backpack, or a shove I received in yesterday's crowd or during the *incident*, as the police are calling it. Well, that's the first word they used. In the last hour, they'd changed their tune to *attack* or *stabbing*; the word itself jolts me, and it's obvious they know it.

The horror of what Leah has done keeps growing— now its tentacles had wrapped tighter around me. They think I have something to do with Valerie's death and this passport mess backs up their theory. A sob escapes me. This is my fault. Had I been using my head, allowing that Arab teenager to take us through a shortcut? Why didn't I insist those guys let us pass? There are tissues in front of me, and I cry into a handful.

"Would you like a minute to yourself? I know you said all the telephone lines you tried were busy a while ago. Would you like to try again now? Then we'll go over the passport issue one more time."

We'll go over the passport issue one more time. My own story is unbelievable to me. Why should they believe me? So far, I haven't said a word about Leah, which would really draw raised eyebrows. I told them I'd been notified of a computer error and it was in the process of being resolved. If I can just get hold of Shimon, this nightmare will be over. At least for me. For Valerie it is all over. I can't believe it.

The police officer encourages me to phone again, sliding the office style telephone toward my chest. Their heavy footsteps echo across the tiles, sticky and streaked from muddy shoes, as they leave the room that is no bigger than three-bathroom cubicles put together. Even a bathroom has more ornaments than this room I've been in for I don't know how long. The walls are bare and spotty with gray smudges and a color I can only aptly call hospital green. There's one window that looks as though it never really opened, and I can't tell the weather outside, the glass is opaque.

The room is empty except for three white plastic chairs, a long rectangular table that is as stained as the walls, and a telephone. Outside I hear the continuous noise of a place in motion: many phone lines ringing at once and raised voices, mostly in Hebrew, but also in Russian and Arabic. When the policemen had opened the door to leave, the smell of burnt coffee and antiseptic wafted through.

I dial Shimon Harpaz again, removing his business card from the inside pocket of my backpack with fingers that move from numb to cold when I rub them. Last time all I got was an answering machine that didn't even confirm his name or number. I bang my fist on the table as the answering machine comes on again.

"Thank you for calling. Beep."

This time I leave a shriller message. Last time I'd tried to retain control, but that's over. I'm a wreck. I need to get out of here, but I won't leave without my Canadian passport, and so far, they've refused to return it to me. They'd let me know that I was free to leave, but they'd have to hold on to it until further notice. Screw that. Leah might have temporarily trapped my father over a border, but hell if she's going to trap me.

"Shimon, it's me, Miriam Gil. Hanan's daughter. I need your help. I'm desperate. I see that problem we discussed is not fixed yet. I need it fixed now. It's really important. I'm at Shaare Zedek Hospital in Jerusalem. I don't even know where to tell you to call."

The machine cuts me off before I can say anymore, and I pray I made sense. My mind's scrambled.

My hand trembles as I replace his card. I phone Guy. His line was busy last time I tried. At least I knew he was home or was. I'd nearly fallen on my knees with gratitude when I realized it was Friday, and Guy was on his way to Jerusalem for the weekend, on his way to me whether he knew it or not, to take me wherever I wanted to go, which was anywhere and nowhere without Valerie.

My heart soars as I hear Guy's voice on the line.

"Guy, it's me, Miriam."

"Miriam. Hello there. I can't wait to see you next Shabbat. Maybe I can pick you up this time."

"Listen, I'm in trouble. Can you come and get me?"

"Trouble? Where are you?"

"Shaare Zedek Hospital. Do you know where that is?"

"I know it's in Jerusalem. What are you doing in a hospital? Are you hurt?"

"I'm fine." I twist the cord around one finger until the blood drains out of it, throttled.

"I'll explain later. I need you to come now, can you?"

"I'll see what car is available. Mine's only booked for 3:00 p.m., but someone will switch with me. You sure you're not hurt? My God, Miriam, what's going on?"

"I'm fine. I need you to come and get me."

"Should I bring your uncle?"

"No, he'll call my father. I'll speak to him when I get out of here. When we're together." The thought of speaking to my uncle on my own makes my head spin. It's too much. And my father. Forget it. He'll curse Leah, curse the day he allowed me to buy a ticket. Not that I asked his permission. I can't handle any more waves of emotion right now.

"Tell your father what? Are you sure you're okay?"

"Just come. I don't even know what floor I'm on."

"I'll find you."

The door opens the second I hang up the phone with Guy, as though the policemen were eavesdropping outside. I don't care anymore. They think I'm an Arab involved in betraying and murdering my friend. Valerie is dead. Let them eavesdrop. Shimon has to hear his messages eventually.

The phone rings on the desk, and the policeman, carrying three steaming coffees and a plate of sandwiches, places them on the desk before he answers. He nods and motions for his friend to sit down, allowing the ringing to continue.

"Eat," he says, pointing at the sandwiches and then at me.

I'm starving, ravenous, but I don't want to eat with them. It's a trick, a real friend in mourning wouldn't be able to eat at a time like this, but a fake, she'd eat with gusto. I ignore the smell of fresh rolls and tuna fish. The aroma of melted cheese on toast.

Finally, he picks up the receiver. For a long time, he doesn't speak. His partner polishes off one sandwich and begins another. I sit listening to the sound of him chewing and swallowing, feeling as though I might hit him if he smacks his lips together one more time. I keep my eyes and my hands on my knees.

There is a click. The long conversation's over and I brace myself, for what I don't know.

"Well, Miriam Gil, you're fortunate to have friends, how do they say it in English? In high places," the policeman says, as he sits on the table. He peers down at me, into my eyes, and I stare straight back at his light blue ones and it comes to me, all of it.

Shimon the Prophet. He'd seen back in time in the café over breakfast, hadn't he? Put two and two together. He hadn't lost his touch. Shimon Harpaz is a man of his word. He didn't fall under Leah Damari's spell twice.

A measure of politeness injects itself into the officer's tone, the one on the desk, who dislikes me the most, who is the most disappointed. The other, tuna mayonnaise smeared on his chin, offers me a small smile. It's no prize after Valerie's brutal death, a cruel comfort, one of them believed me all along.

A form is pushed under my nose, but I refuse to sign anything Suzanne doesn't read to me first. The social worker is called.

"It's only a form that says you've received all of your belongings. Valerie's possessions belong to her mother. I'll take them now."

"Could I just?" I gulp for air, ignoring the eyes and ears of the two police officers across the table. "We'd bought souvenirs together. Matching purses. Could I have mine?"

Suzanne's eyes soften. "It's against procedure. Her mother will receive a list of her possessions."

"Please. Open it. You'll see there are two of them."

I know the bag had already been searched, every item catalogued.

"Please." My eyes beg.

"All right." Her voice is a caress. "Let me do it."

Suzanne unzips Valerie's backpack and produces the purse as if she knew where it had been packed and in which pocket. I close my eyes and turn my head away. My heart is being squeezed.

When I open them, my Canadian passport is in my lap, and Suzanne is zipping up my own bag.

"It's there for you for when you're ready to look at it."

Chapter Thirty-Three

ONCE I HAD MY CANADIAN PASSPORT in my hand, I couldn't breathe in the hospital any longer. Already there was a ghost I couldn't face in the bowels of the building.

I decline Suzanne's offer to wait with me in the parking lot and make my way to the elevator alone. I press *knisah* once the doors open and step inside, not looking left or right. *Knisah* means entrance, but my mind translates "ground floor." I gasp sharply, pressure on a nerve: ground.

It rained again this morning. I'd seen the water slashing at the windows in the hospital corridor, smearing over the view. It's freshening, the air. Until now every drop of air I'd breathed since the news of Valerie's death seemed recycled, already traveled through someone else's windpipe and gut and somehow purged back out into the atmosphere. Just as abruptly, the downpour stops. If the ground wasn't dark and wet, someone might not believe it had rained at all.

The cleaner air is refreshing and I breathe deeply, rotating my shoulders backward and forward. I'd taken to dragging my backpack around with me, alternating hands, allowing my shoulder muscles a break. They are raw to the touch.

My water bottle was drained long ago, but I'd refilled it at the water fountain adjacent to the women's bathroom, though I have yet to sip. I don't know if it's safe to drink from the water fountain at a hospital. I laugh at this thought, almost a grunt. The emergency already happened.

I slump down on a wooden bench at the entrance that is mercifully empty. It could take Guy easily three hours to get here, four in Friday traffic, and that's if he had no trouble exchanging his kibbutz car for one that was free earlier. I no longer know when I spoke with him. It might have been one hour ago or three.

I'll bum a cigarette instead of the trouble it takes to find a food counter, purchase an item, wait for change, chew and swallow. To hell with quitting. To hell with everything. It's easy to find a smoker in Israel. It takes more time for a light to change or a blade to draw blood.

In a minute, I'm thanking a short Israeli man in an Egged bus driver uniform, returning his lighter. No doubt if Valerie were here she'd be hitting on him, at least chatting him up, or else reciting passages from her guide book, telling me who put the foundation stones in this hospital where and who ruled over them when.

There is a honk and I raise my eyes. Guy is the most welcome sight I've ever seen. He parks illegally at the curb and I collapse into his arms, knotted hair, filthy, smelling of murder and death and betrayal.

"Miriam, Miriam," he murmurs into my hair. "What happened to you? Your lip? Your arms are covered in bruises. Where have you been? Thank God you're all

332

right." He holds me close. "Come. They'll arrest me for stopping here."

He guides me into the passenger seat, as though I am a flower and, indeed, my head wobbles on my neck, a broken blossom on its stalk. A policeman screams at Guy to move or he'll get a ticket, but I no longer fear policemen.

Guy zooms off, and in a minute, we are away from the hospital, heading I don't know where, not for the first time.

"Where do you want to go?"

"I don't care," I answer, my eyes close and flutter open. I feel Guy trying not to stare at my face. I haven't seen a mirror since yesterday. I must look like a monster, confirming Leah's true description of me.

We exit the hospital with a short left, turn right on Herzl Boulevard, taking the main road before turning right again.

"Didn't they give you anything to eat at the hospital? Why didn't you buy something? You look as though you need some food and a shower."

I don't respond. I just want to be near him without speaking for a few minutes.

"I hope I didn't offend you."

"No."

"Why don't we check into a hotel for the weekend? I've been sent here once or twice by the kibbutz for agricultural seminars, fish farming workshops."

"Hmm."

"So, they know me there. I could put the bill on the kibbutz for now and then back-pay at the next seminar.

There's usually one or two a year, though I've missed a few because of the army."

"Sounds good."

"I have a map. We'll go right to Shazar Boulevard and down to Rambam, I think. I don't come to Jerusalem so often."

I feel the car turning left, picking up speed, and I'm back in the ambulance with Valerie, the yeshiva boy, and I don't know who else, or maybe he was in a different ambulance with his friends. I feel us zooming, flying through the Old City gates. Maybe it was the Damascus Gate. That's where the paramedic crew waited. They dived in through the heavy back doors, and like lightning we sped down Jaffa Street at full speed, yielding for red lights but stopping at none. Was Valerie already dead by then? Guilt pulses through me. If I'd have responded faster or said no to the shopkeeper in the first place. Hadn't I just given it to her about shopping in that back room? Then I go and do the same thing.

"Do you mind slowing down?" I ask. My voice sounds as though it's coming from far away. Besides dozing on and off in that hospital chair, I can't recall the last time I slept. I don't want to travel back in my mind to the ambulance, not now. Better to leave my memories ships at sea, at least for the moment.

"No problem. That lip must hurt. You get in a fight or an accident?"

"Yes." I don't specify which question I'm answering. Guy's knuckles grip the wheel.

"There's a chocolate bar in my bag. I think some Bissli, too, a cola. Take. For me."

The "for me" strikes a chord. Isn't that what I'd done to Valerie just yesterday? "Get me one, too. We should have matching souvenirs. We can wear them together." Guy's never met Valerie. How will I begin to explain to him how she saved my behind? How much I liked her, adored her.

I twist toward the backseat and haul up his bag, a quarter of the size of my own and soft cotton. It smells of laundry detergent. In the side pocket there's a cold can of Coke, a bag of Bissli and a chocolate bar I've never heard of. I tear open the Bissli and eat it piece by piece, the sharpness of its spicy texture overpowering, but Guy's right. I feel better. Without pausing I polish off the chocolate bar and the coke, crumple the wrappers in my hands.

By now, we're driving toward the center of town, crossing King George. I pray he doesn't drive by the municipal building. I'm not sure I can spend the night in Jerusalem, even with Guy.

All at once my brain shifts gears and I know where I want to go. Where we must go.

Guy interrupts my thoughts. "I don't want to pry, Miriam, but you look the way I used to when I came back from a military excursion. Do you want to tell me what happened? No pushing. When you're ready."

I do want to tell him what happened. I just need time, and there's something I need to do first.

"The Kotel," I say. My voice is energized. "We need to go to the Kotel."

"The Kotel? Now? I really think you need a shower and a nap. Then we can take a stroll down there after a nice dinner. The hotel I'm thinking of isn't far at all. If you're feeling up to it or tomorrow after a solid sleep or—"

"Please, Guy. I'll explain later. I need to go to the Kotel now for a friend. She tried so hard to get there yesterday, but she didn't make it."

I'm crying now.

"I don't understand." He passes me tissues from the glove compartment, steering with one hand. His right hand looks thinner than the left, since they've taken the cast off. It's only bandaged now. I hadn't even noticed.

"You will understand soon. Please."

"Only if you promise to let me take care of you afterward. My way. A shower, sleep and I think you should see a doctor again on Sunday morning."

"I promise."

We hold hands as we pass through Jaffa Gate, and I am flooded with emotion and grief, like so many who've come to the Kotel before me. I know I'm at the right place, and I seem to be above the crowds somehow. I pull Guy the long way down through the Jewish Quarter. I'm not taking any chances on Christmas Day, and I'm way too raw for the Arab Quarter.

My heavy heart lifts as we approach the Kotel plaza, which today is effortless, no more difficult than crossing the street. Surely, Valerie leads me here, waiting for me, ready with a wisecrack, a pastry from her never-ending supply, and a hug. But that was a lifetime ago: yesterday.

Today is blue and sunny. There is no trace of yesterday's rain and fog. Before I part with Guy for the women's section, I stick my hand into my backpack and remove Valerie's prayers. Hers and her mother's. I imagine her mother's is very different today. Borrowing a prayer book from a group of seminary girls, I shoulder my way to the front of the line of women worshippers.

I couldn't have anticipated acting so forward only six months ago, but today is a different reality and my whole body burns to touch the stones. On my class trip here, I was too intimidated to squeeze my way through and had satisfied myself with praying from a vantage point as close as I could politely get.

But I had no mission then. I do now. I slip the prayer notes in between the stones of the wall, hot tears pouring down my face, and I hear a door close somewhere, a creak. I stare at my hand and bring it to my lips, the feeling of Valerie's hand yesterday, holding my own as we made our way down the narrow, wet path still upon it, still warming my skin. I press my forehead to the holy stones and wait for my own prayer to come.

Chapter Thirty-Four

Ottawa, Canada, June 1993

ON A WARM DAY IN JUNE I haul my suitcase onto the trolley, but the long strap catches on something and I need to yank hard, so it's balanced enough across the base for me to push it forward. I'm surrounded by small groups of people, mostly in business suits and ties or in casual summer wear. Some gather around the carousel studying each suitcase and others speak in low voices, waiting for their near-by carousels to roll.

There are plasma screens of arrival and departure times hanging from the ceilings, but my eyes pass over them. Unlike Tel Aviv there are no cascading fountains or eye-catching works of art decorating the walls, and there's little noise. Colorful tourist posters are absent as well, confirming that I've left the hustle and bustle behind in the Middle East. Here there's conformity, order and quiet, gleaming chrome and faux wood paneling with a lot of clear glass thrown in.

Door to door, I've traveled for eighteen hours in one taxi and two airplanes, all of them filled to capacity. My eyes are worn out in spite of the fresh black eyeliner I'd applied before we landed. It's 5:00 p.m., the borderline hour that can pass as dinnertime. I still have the hummus packets and challah roll that I'd slipped into my carry-

338

on, along with the miniature water I hadn't bothered to drink. I stop trying to inch my trolley forward, remove the take-out water from my handbag, push back the foil with my thumb, and drink it greedily now. In a few hours the Mey Eden symbol on the bottle has gone from an everyday object to a powerful reminder. It's a souvenir that brings back the smile of a love out of reach and a second smile of a good friend, who I'm determined to keep alive in my memory. I'd already sent the check for the money Valerie had lent me to stay in the hostel to her mother and asked her to donate it to a cause Valerie believed in. It was a small token, but it was a start.

My shoulder hurts from fighting the weight of the trolley. I'd stretched too much bringing my carry-on down from the overhead compartment on the flight to Toronto, so now it is sensitive to the slightest tug. My whole life my father has bent down to shoulder weighty objects, something he takes obvious pride in. I'd had less than a year of practice.

I'd refused the offers of the men who asked if I needed help. I plan to continue carrying my own belongings from now on, even if I can't do it as effortlessly as my father. I position myself in the small crowd to snap up my second case from the conveyor belt and balance it on top of the first one, until everything I own in the world is on one cart, the carry-on handle scraping my chin and my two passports in a pouch under my shirt.

Moving around Ottawa's international airport feels like negotiating a large department store compared to the craziness of Tel Aviv's Ben Gurion, but that is about all I can handle right now. I'm wearing the Eilat stone necklace from my uncle and a matching bracelet Guy bought me last week as a going-away present. Both pieces flatter my sea-green shirt dress. The Roman-style Israeli sandals that buckle two inches above my ankle are the identical pair Valerie bought in Jerusalem a lifetime ago. I've had my long, dark, crimped hair cut in a short, inverted bob style, lobbing off all of the ends that had been lightened by the Middle Eastern sun. My hair never looked so black.

I'd told my father in a postcard my flight details that I'd find my way without mentioning where I was headed. I couldn't bear to ask him about Jacquie, and there is no way I would sleep under the same roof as her. She'd ask questions about my trip I'm not ready to answer.

I search for him tuning into the classical music filtering through the speakers in an attempt to put on a relaxed face. My eyes weave through the small groups of people in the waiting area. Most of them have their necks stretched seeking their loved ones, friends, or colleagues, and some are untying the cardigans they have tied across their waists and slipping them on. The air conditioning is on full blast.

My father would never be one of those locals straining his eyes and neck to find someone in an airport. On the rare occasions I'd been here with him, he had grabbed a Hebrew newspaper from the stack on a corner of the kitchen table that he refreshed once a month at the Israeli embassy and jammed it next to his leg in the car. On arrival he sought out a lounge chair on the end of a row and settled in, feet planted wider than his shoulders. There he'd wait, eyes scanning the pages until he was tapped on the back or beckoned from afar.

How I envision him from the past is how I find him ten minutes later, his broad back to me, his head turning left and right as he thumbs the Hebrew newspaper, filling a chair in the arrival lounge. I turn my neck in all directions, whirl around, but there is no sign of Jacquie's buckle wedge sandals or knockoff Yves Saint Laurent tuxedo jackets. There are enough French accents at the airport that hers wouldn't stand out.

I park my loaded trolley at the end of the row of attached chairs where he sits whistling under his breath and pad toward my father until I sit a chair away him.

"Shalom, Abba," I say.

My father stops reading and looks at me, and in his eyes and the set of his jaw I read, "I told you so," and guilt for Valerie's death washes over me, but this time from the pit of my stomach downward. I might be reading my own feelings in his eyes. I've never breathed a word to him about Valerie. Does he blame me somehow for befriending a girl who was murdered only feet from me? Is he thinking a daughter of his should have been smart enough and strong enough to save her, or to have never been in such danger in the first place? He jumped out of airplanes into enemy fire without scratching a toe, and fought in a tank division, and I can't walk through a major international tourist attraction without someone getting killed.

Resentment creeps up my throat. He's the one who forced me to rip open the locked door to Israel I'd never so much as sniffed before last spring, or that's what I thought then. He never forced me anywhere. I see that now, even though it's clear he wanted me out of the house.

But in reality, my father hasn't said a word. My greeting is met with silence. I place the small purse I'd removed from Valerie's backpack on the chair between us and sink down. My shoulders droop and the discomfort between us grows. I could just walk away. For a moment I see myself hopping a cab to Neil's.

Jacquie was right about one thing, it wouldn't take long to arrange the transcripts and it would only be for ten months. Then I'd be only a year away from an English literature degree. Even that victory pales next to Guy's achievements and ambitions. No hungry child would have a fuller plate because of my efforts, and we wouldn't be any closer to world peace. It's what I had, and I'd make it count for something.

With any luck Guy will be waiting for me on the other side of the world next summer. We'll make a plan. Focusing on Guy gives me courage.

"You're thinking I ignored your advice," I blurt. I have no idea why I'm apologizing. The roles seem to have reversed in my mind since Valerie's death or at least my priorities. "It was hard for me, Abba. When you asked me to leave the apartment. Can you see that?"

My father still holds up his newspaper, shielding himself from public view. Now he folds it neatly and places it on his lap. He takes his time, licks his lips, smooths down the folds.

"It's so bad that I wanted company after I lost your

342

mother, after so many years alone? You judged me without thinking what it's been like for me with no mother for you. What do I know about teenage girls? Canadian ones. *Kloom.*"

"Jacquie and I weren't exactly buddies," I answer.

"Why? So, she dreams she's from Paris or Montreal, so what? She's got exactly nothing in life. She's not fooling anybody."

"You threw me out of the house." I stop there. I've never been so forthcoming with my father and it feels unnatural, but I'm not sorry, only startled.

My father curses in Arabic.

"Did you find your clothes outside and new locks on the front door? What the hell are you talking about, Miriam? You were studying day and night or out with that dummy. So what's the difference if you live with a few girls your age? Like who knows what. You had the whole summer for the papers you needed to find a good place. No one made you bust your tachat on two, three jobs."

"You didn't give me a choice. Maybe I wanted to finish school at home."

"You think there's always a choice in life you're going to like? Your mother didn't give me a choice either. I told her not to drive, that those migraine medicines were too strong and she drove. Jacquie wanted to come in for a laugh, to joke around, but it was uncomfortable." My father throws up his hands and his newspaper falls on the ground, his careful folds unraveling at his feet. He bends to pick it up. "No use talking to you. No use talking to kids." My father shrugs

343

his shoulders and turns his head, looking off into the distance.

A woman's voice over the loudspeaker tells us the next flight to Edmonton will be delayed by thirty minutes and she's sorry for the inconvenience. She welcomes us once again to Ottawa International Airport. The message is repeated in French, so it stretches out the time and I can pretend we'd be speaking if it wasn't such a strain over these intrusive announcements.

Upstairs there's a Harvey's hamburger place, a Starbucks, a lounge bar, and a Grab & Go, but down here in the arrivals section there's only a Tim Hortons. The doughnuts, muffins, and doughnut holes lined in neat rows contrast starkly with the heaps of self-serve potato, cheese, and spinach *bourekas*; white and whole-wheat pitas; braided challahs; and cinnamon and chocolate *rugelachs* in Israeli bakeries. It's been a long time since I've smelled maple dip, and the aroma distracts me. My stomach aches, but I'm not hungry.

"It was a lot to ask, Abba," I offer.

"Yes, you showed me that. You ran off to Israel straight into Leah's jaws. She must have danced when she saw your letter. God should burn her up. She is so bad."

My father's eyes sparkle with anger. "I'll get back there one day, and then she should watch out. I haven't planned it all yet, but I will. Now I got you back and that came first, but give me some time to think what I can do to her."

I am so used to my father's threats it's hard for me to take them seriously, even this one. He hasn't been to

Israel in years.

"She loved you," I answer. I regret this the moment it tumbles out of my mouth and my father's look lets me know I should. He glares sharply at me, a fire in his eyes and I understand I've crossed forbidden territory. I inch away until I'm on the edge of the seat. There is still one empty seat between us. I stare at my knees, pull my tube skirt down as low as it can go, to mid-calf, and my bracelet jangles.

"She loved herself. You have books up to the sky, but you're a dummy sometimes. You think you know everything. A girl is dead now, no? Christ, what a waste."

My eyes well with tears.

Leah. Moshe. Shimon Harpaz. Or just those stacks of newspapers my father studies. I don't know how he knows about Valerie or what he knows.

"Everything that Leah touches dies. Babies. Jobs. Everything. Even other people's kids. Yes, I heard about Yakira, too. Coward. The worst kind. And Leah's been dying to get her hands on you from day one, screwing up her own wasn't enough." My father's curses are in a mixture of Hebrew and Arabic now. I gaze around, but the arrival hall has emptied out. The closest group of people sits two rows behind us.

"So why did you marry her?"

My father stares at me as though he doesn't recognize me for a moment.

"Why did I marry her?" he says finally. "Weren't you listening on the phone? I was young, a soldier. I had to get out of that house."

I know how that feels now. Maybe that's something I have in common with my father. We both wanted to get away so badly, we didn't stop to think about where we were headed.

"My parents had finally divorced, but the screaming continued, he didn't work so far away from the house. He wanted Moshe to come with him to a new house and my mother, God rest her soul, Moshe was her baby, even if he didn't take after her."

My father speaks in a low, deep voice that is so filled with emotion a stranger might think these events happened yesterday.

"Of course, my brother laughed at them both. He'd been living on the kibbutz for who knows how long already, so they were fighting over nothing as usual. The point was the fighting."

Silence. Some of his emotion has worn off on me and I need to collect myself. It was a long flight.

"That sucks," I answer.

"Damn right. The way the neighbors looked at me all the time with pity in their eyes. Everywhere I went, the street, the shuk, more pity. Leah's mother, the gorilla, she should have worked for the Mossad. She never left her alone, watched her day and night. Leah wanted to get out, too. So, we married. That's it."

"And?" I ask.

"And what? I told you," he says.

"Why did you leave her?"

My father looks at me, bewildered. He throws up his hands.

"I talk, but you don't hear," he says. "Leah hated her

mother on her all the time, so she was on me all the time." My father puts on an anguished female voice. "Where are you going? What are you doing?"

The people immediately around us stare, but I ignore them. I am finally having a real conversation with my father.

"Like a scarf tight on the neck," he continues. "If she had a baby that wouldn't have happened to her, but without one, that's how she became. She had nothing to watch but me."

I have no words to respond to this. I try to catch my father's eye, but he's not looking at me. His body quakes enough for me to notice, and it dawns on me what he never says: He loves me. It's me doing this to him, the thought that it could have been me instead of Valerie, or more likely the opportunity for revenge that landed on Leah's doorstep like a wish come true. Maybe he could taste her desire to trap me in a country behind bars. Either way I'd presented her with an easy route to assuming control, power over the one part of my father's life that was connected to his soul and threaded to his real love, my mother.

It's been over six years since I've seen my father emotional. Not since my mother's death, and even then, he fled from me as soon as he felt my eyes on him. I study the side of his face, it hasn't aged one bit in the last year. I don't know what he sees when he looks at me now.

"You met a boy there. He's strong? Smart?" he asks.

"He was a soldier," I answer.

"What kind?"

"Combat. Now he's a biology student. He wants to feed the world. He believes in peace," I answer.

"Peace?" My father considers this. "You can't clap with one hand. Everybody wants peace. As long as he knows how to fight in case it doesn't come," he says.

I won't tell my father now that Guy and I have plans to go scuba diving off the coast of Eilat on May 1 next year, the day after final exams—not while I'm still at the airport.

"I came here to take you home." My father stands. "My friend's not giving us the free parking forever."

He aims himself at my trolley, leaving the newspaper behind on the lounge seat. He's done with it. I walk behind him as he maneuvers my trolley toward the exit. He's wearing a light green button-down, wide open at the chest. It's almost the identical color as my own tunic. His blue shorts appear closer to swimming trunks. I'm not sure if he can tell the difference or if he'd care, as long as the price was right. His keys jangle in his right hand and clink against the trolley bar.

"I met a Druze girl in Israel, Arslan," I offer. He'd told me so much. I want to share, too.

"*Druzim* are fighters. Good people," he says.

"She invited me to her village near Karmiel. I want to go next summer with Guy," I say.

"You're already worrying about the summer," he says.

"You want to see the card she sent me?" I ask my father.

"Who?"

"Arslan. It has a photograph of her village inside and her sisters." Arslan had received my card and had wasted no time writing me back—from two floors up. She'd worked things out with the university with help from her father and Dalit.

"Sure. At home. Jacquie had to help her *tembel* of a son with his little boy," he says, his head half turned backward toward me. I quicken my pace to catch up to him. "The mother, a drunk, took off to who knows where, and there's no one to watch him in the afternoon."

This is my father's way of telling me that my bedroom is made-up with fresh sheets and a laundered towel and waiting for me at home. For now, my father takes my cold hand in his large warm one, and it is enough.

END

Acknowledgements

THIS BOOK HAS LIVED MANY LIVES. It began as a twelve-page story in a classroom that would not have been if Shaindy Rudoff had not created a writing program at Bar Ilan University. This book is part of the legacy that she left behind.

The reaction was so strongly negative (it really got under some skin), that I knew I'd have to turn it into an entire novel. To double check I sent it to a literary magazine. I still remember the response, "Err, we're not going to publish this." Then I *really* knew I had to turn it into a novel.

The first three chapters of the very first draft were read by Anna Levine, Sari Friedman, and Rachel Biale. My thanks to all of you. Later, Margo Dill read a little more and I thank her for every minute. Then it passed over to Haskell Nussbaum who shared his thoughts. *Todah rabah.*

As more time passed, it was read and commented on by my virtual companion in so much that I write, Pearl Luke and then back to Anna Levine and our frantic virtual workshops (Email me something in thirty minutes. Go.)

A lot of time passed until the warm, generous, and professional Jackie Mitchard emailed me that she loved it along with a whole flood of comments. Thanks, Jackie.

What more can I say? Your vote of confidence was like literary oxygen. More rolling and shaping happened. I'll spare you the details (hint, it was still really getting under some people's skin).

But *Passport Control* would neither stand still nor settle down until it fell into the capable hands of editor and publisher, Dixiane Hallaj. I would like to thank Dixiane and her editor, Lenora Rain-Lee Good, for their tremendous support and insight, for sharing their experience and for their wisdom and patience.

Of course, my husband was with *Passport Control* from the first short story until the novel it is now. And I thank him and our five children for being exactly as they are. Always.

About the Author

CANADIAN GILA GREEN is a writer, editor, and EFL teacher. As the daughter of a Yemenite-Israeli father and an Ashkenazi- Canadian mother, she often writes about the immigrant experience including dislocation, alienation, and racism. She spent a year living in South Africa before she settled in Israel between Tel Aviv and Jerusalem.

She is the author of *White Zion* (Cervena Barva Press, 2019) and *King of the Class* (NON Publishing, 2013). Her stories have appeared in dozens of literary magazines in five countries including: The Fiddlehead, Fiction, Akashic Books Mondays are Murder Series, Many Mountains Moving, and Jewish Fiction.

www.ingramcontent.com/pod-product-compliance
Lightning Source LLC
Chambersburg PA
CBHW050031030726
47506CB00001B/216